Blood Spiral

Book 1 of the Mitch King Mysteries

Sam Waas

Deja Vu Imprint of TT

About the Author

S.D. Skye is a former FBI Russian Counterintelligence Program Intelligence Analyst and supported cases during her 12-year tenure at the Bureau. She has personally witnessed the blowback the Intelligence Community suffered due to the most significant compromises in U.S. history, including the arrests of former CIA Case Officer Aldrich Ames and two of the Bureau's own—FBI Agents Earl Pitts and Robert Hansen. She has spent 20 years in the U.S. Intelligence Community.

Skye is a member of the Maryland Writer's Association, Romance Writers of America, and International Thriller Writers. She's addicted to writing and chocolate—not necessarily in that order—and currently lives in the Washington D.C. area with her son. Skye is hard at work on several projects, including the next installment of the series.

Dedication

To those icons of mystery fiction, Dashiell Hammett and Raymond Chandler, who started it all for American private detective writers.

To the present day greats who continue the tradition: Robert B. Parker with his literate and sarcastic Spenser, Bill Pronzini with his dedicated, moral Nameless, and Robert Crais with his ever-petulant Elvis Cole.

And to the steady support, companionship and affection given me by the beloved woman and dearest partner in my life.

Praise for Blood Spiral

This is a smart book. And Mitch King is real.
- Tom Wade, Boulder, Colorado

Blood Spiral is a top notch P.I./police procedural that matches Robert B. Parker's "Spenser" in its modish sensitivity; Raymond Chandler, in its cracking imagery; and Mickey Spillane, in its moments of unflinchingly graphic violence.
--James Blakley, Amazon

Excellent first entry for a new author. With a style reminiscent of the old "detective noir" novel but set in wholly modern times, the story charges ahead with developments and twists that you think you saw coming, but wind up affecting the main character, Mitch King, in ways he himself probably doesn't even realize.
Martin Visser, Amazon

Chapter 1

Police Headquarters in Houston is a seven-story concrete monstrosity that squats on a downtown cul-de-sac named Riesner Street. Since city jail is on the top two floors of the building, Houstonians refer to the jail as the Hotel Riesner. I was on my way there to meet a client, currently a guest of the hotel.

It was a bright June morning, humid as always and though it was only ten, the thermometer had already zoomed past eighty. Spring lasts about four days in Houston, yet even that short season was a memory distant as teenage love. Now the weather was firmly locked into the lengthy sweatbox we laughingly call summer, which is okay by me. The MG's top is down and I intend to keep it that way, because I like warm weather. Steamy summers are part of the equation here, so you adapt and live with it. Or move.

I tooled east along Allen Parkway, doing about forty. Rush hour was over and traffic was light. Exhaust burbling pleasantly, my vintage and slightly rusty MGB swooped along the gently curving roadway.

To my left lay the rolling greensward of Eleanor Tinsley Park, dotted with sculpture, fountains and picnic tables. Grim-faced runners pressed along a jogging track near the road. Just past the parkland was Memorial Drive, parallel to me. And between the two expressways, the little stream of Buffalo Bayou gerrymandered the land, forming a tidy valley where the city held outdoor festivals and concerts. It delighted me how this cozy park nestled hard against the skyscrapers, thumbing its nose at the gleaming Philip Johnson architecture juxtaposed before it.

Steely Dan was on the classic rock station, playing *Do It Again.*

I turned up the volume and helped Donald Fagen sing a few bars. We went on about how the wild one brings me sorrow and my wheel kept turning round and round. I didn't get all the words right, but it was only a song, no moral to learn, no object lesson to teach. And real life is never about rock lyrics anyway.

I dropped off Allen Parkway, cut over to Riesner and turned into the HPD visitor lot. The squat dented machine at the gate buzzed angrily and stuck out its paper tongue at me. I took the ticket. The box quit complaining and lifted its splintery wooden arm in a tentative, jerky arc. I drove in, parked, exited, zipped the tonneau cover and sauntered across to the cop shop.

Clusters of people were hanging out around the building. Some solitary sullen folk sat on the broad concrete steps that led up to the front door, angrily puffing cigarettes and ignoring each other. They didn't want to be there and they made sure everyone else knew it.

Nearby, the mood was different. Whole families lounged on blankets spread over the tiny lawn in front of HPD, creating an impromptu picnic ground. Boom boxes competed with their anthems of rock, rap and salsa. Children darted between the camouflage of their mothers' cheap print frocks. The women chatted, the children squealed, handfuls of chips and packages of Twinkies were gobbled, sodas guzzled.

Some Hispanic guys dressed in work togs stood by their pickups in the parking lot. They talked quietly among themselves, sipping beer from cans wrapped in little brown paper bags. They held the beers down by their sides in a failed effort to conceal this slightly illegal act, though you'd have to be stone blind not to instantly spot what they were doing.

This practice of sucking down beer so early is ironic because most of these people were waiting for Jim or Carlos or Maryann to get bailed out of jail for drunk driving the night before.

The story is always the same. Your phone rings at an ungodly hour, a sheepish and slurry voice in your ear. "This is Bill. I'm down at the Hotel Riesner—yeah, jail. Can you come get me?"

"Sure. Glad to help," you mumble. Which is a barefaced lie, because bailing someone out of jail is a tedious and lengthy process, requiring Job-like patience.

First you drag yourself out of a perfectly good bed, snag a couple of beers for the road and head downtown at three am, when the only other drivers are either cops or people trying to avoid cops.

Next, you choose a bail bond office. These are easy to find because they're brightly lit storefronts hawking their goods along the dark streets like whores during a salesman's convention. And just like the whores, the bondsmen each promise to give the best service but in truth are all alike, only going through the motions. So you emulate that tired salesman on his last night away from home and pick the closest one.

You go in, fill out lots of forms and give them lots of money. You wait a long time, then drive over to the jail and wait a while longer. It takes forever. All this time, your friend sits inside nursing a hangover while you sit outside nursing a cold one. Finally your pal emerges, ready and eager to get right back to doing what landed him in jail in the first place.

I've always suspected the delay is intentional. The cops have your ass and they simply don't want to let it go. Whatever the reason, though, the wait is exasperating. You rush downtown only to sit around for hours.

Today was different. I was in no hurry this morning because my client was going nowhere. The charge against her was not drunk driving.

It was murder.

Chapter 2

This had already been a long day for me. I was up at four and an hour later, sitting with my friend Antonio Villarreal in his Eldorado, drinking acidic convenience store coffee and waiting for Tony's mark to show.

We were parked at a condo development in Seabrook, a bedroom community on Galveston Bay. The condos are large and luxurious and acquired by people who believe they have saltwater in their veins. A row of docks runs along the back of the property, where you can keep your half-million dollar cabin cruiser named *Jimbo Two*, brag about it to your friends and sit on the deck every Saturday afternoon, drinking margaritas. You might even start the engine now and then, just to prove it worked.

The Caddy's windows were cranked down and in the pre-dawn quiet, I heard the slap of waves under the docks and sniffed a tang the bay wafted to us on a cool sea-breeze. Across the water I caught the distant running lights of tugboats and cargo vessels, grinding along to their diverse destinies, some as near as the next tie-up, and some across the world.

This seafaring panorama elicited a strange nostalgia in me, a desire to be back on the water and sailing off to my next port of call. The emotion was strange because I'd never been at sea before. Yet somehow the attraction was there.

We all yearn for the water. Maybe it's genetic, the cells in our bodies struggling to reunite with our great Mother Ocean from whom we all emerged. More likely, it's the image of freedom the open sea imparts, the idea that one fine afternoon you could forego all your appointments, leave the office, drive down to the docks, sign onto a freighter and never look back. And some people actually do just that.

Problem is, you take your head with you when you ship out, and that's where your grief truly resides. Not in the world around but in your mind, and in your heart. And that baggage you carry with you always.

* * *

I sipped my coffee and looked at Tony. He returned the glance, grunted and shifted uneasily in the driver's seat, peering across the sloping hood of the Caddy toward the condo. "I dunno, Mitch. Think he's there?"

"How the hell should I know?" I looked at the building. Number eight and all its cloned companions were dark and silent. The flames from a few flickering gas yard lamps were all that moved. "You're the one who dragged me down here, said this was a done deal. Now you're playing Doubting Thomas?"

"He's there," Tony reassured me, and himself. "I got this neighbor watching. She called me late last night." He squirmed again and tugged for the umpteenth time at the queue in his salt-and-pepper hair. "Makes me look like Steven Seagal," he always said. Which is a crock. Tony bears no resemblance to Seagal at all. He is in fact an economy-size Caddy-driving Wookie.

Tony Vee is a very big guy. When he played guard for the Oilers, the roster listed him at six-five and two-sixty. Never one to pass up a meal, Tony would now clock in at three hundred plus, assuming you could talk him onto a scale. Good luck with that.

Of Salvadoran and Samoan descent, he has a broad face with intense black eyes and a flattened, crooked nose, hair long and matched with a full shaggy beard. He normally wears all black and presents an imposing figure coming at you in a dark alley. Or in broad daylight, for that matter. To say he's large is to say that Derek Jeter played an okay game of ball.

The extra bulk serves Tony well, though. He does favors. He's a process server, bodyguard, securities courier and all-round muscle provider. Not that he's a thug, exactly. It's more like he skirts the law and its restrictions. Say your ex made off with your prized Beatles LPs? Tony will retrieve them, unscratched. Say your sister's old flame just got out of prison and is phoning her all hours? Tony will make the calls cease. And Tony will do other things, too, favors far less trivial. That will cost you more.

Tony and I first crossed paths some years ago. An insurance company hired me to track some missing jewelry and Tony was recommended as backup. I found where the thief was hiding, kicked in his apartment door and had the man cuffed in twenty seconds, but I missed his pal behind me in the stairwell. Tony grabbed the guy by the neck, lifted him off the ground and shook him like a dog shakes a rat, making him forget the knife in his hand and most of the last week. Since then, Tony and I had covered each other's tails in some close situations and were now friends.

* * *

This morning we were waiting for a man named Lou Masters to leave his girlfriend's townhouse. Masters had run up a heavy gambling tab with Danny Angel, then balked at paying his note, telling Angel that since gambling was illegal, the money was not collectable.

Little did he know that holding out on Dante Angelino was like ignoring the IRS. You could try it for a while, but in the long term, it was a rash decision. If Tony could persuade Masters to change his mind, the vig would be five percent. Tony offered me a couple of bills to watch his back, but I suspected it was mostly to sit and listen to him gripe.

Tony sipped from the foam cup, grimaced. "Jesus, Mitch. This is one shitty cup of coffee. Remind me not to—" Abruptly, he stiffened. "They're up."

A glimmer from the upstairs bathroom window. Presently more lights, then more, tracing a path to the ground floor.

"Time," Tony said.

"What about me?" I slid my new Smith and Wesson 9mm from its Alessi hip holster. "Need help?"

Tony took one glance and sneered. "Haw! With that little popgun?" He reached into the backseat and groped beneath a blanket. "Here." He handed me a 12-gauge Winchester Defender pump. It had pistol grips front and back, a barrel shroud and extended magazine tube. The whole affair was just over two feet long, a small but deadly package.

"Loaded?" I asked.

"Six in the mag tube. Chamber's empty."

On the left of the receiver plate was a sidemount carrier holding several more double-ought shells, perched in a lethal bright green row. I pointed to the extra shells. "What's this? Figure I'll need more than six shots to take 'em out?"

"Naw. Just makes it look scary."

I thought how much more scary it could be, having a 12-gauge leveled at you. "Okay."

The porch light of the townhouse blinked on. "Gotta go. Only be a sec." Tony heaved himself from the Caddy and ambled toward the target. The front door opened just as Tony got there and Lou Masters was framed in the light. What light managed to get past him, that is. Masters was even bigger than Tony.

"The fuck?" Masters' voice boomed. In a flash, he jumped for Tony and the pair sprawled on the grass. They flailed away but neither could get in a good punch. Divots were kicked up from the sculpted lawn, Godzilla and Mothra in an MMA heavyweight title match.

The big men rolled around a while, grunting and puffing and cursing, then Tony came up on top, sitting astride Masters' chest. Tony had Masters by the hair and pointed at him like an angry parent. "You owe, Lou, and you gotta pay!"

By now, lights had come on all around, several anxious neighbors peeking at the freeform combat through their windows. This had to end quickly, before the cops showed.

Movement at Masters' townhouse door. A tall rangy blonde wearing a filmy nightgown and nothing else rushed out. She carried a big iron skillet and before Tony could react, she swung full on and whanged him on the head. I heard the *clang* from where I sat.

Tony went over on his side. He tried to get up, but Masters seized the moment and began whacking on Tony with renewed vigor. The woman circled the melee, looking for a good opening so she could let loose with another skillet shot.

My turn.

I got out of the Caddy and strode to the action, swinging the shotgun casually in one hand, as if I did this every day. I reached the scene and raised the gun port arms across my chest, jacked the slide, *thwack-thwack*.

The sound was clear as a trumpet call and brought an immediate halt to the fight. Everyone, Tony included, stared at me and the shotgun. I held it so the extra shells in the side carrier were nicely visible and scary.

I tried to look scary, too.

Tony pushed up from the grass and brushed himself off with exaggerated daintiness. "Don't shoot 'em, Tiger," he told me.

He looked down at Masters. "I tried to warn you, Lou. You gotta pay. Next time, Danny Angel will send Tiger here, and I won't be along to stop him. Got that?"

"Yeah. I got it," Masters replied, resignation in his voice. "Tell Angel tomorrow." He got up and took his girlfriend by the hand. "Come on, Hon." He led her to the condo. "Tomorrow, I promise," he said, closing the door.

His eyes never left the shotgun.

Chapter 3

Tony Vee and I were having breakfast at Katz' Deli on lower Westheimer and chatting about the early morning fun. The restaurant is open round the clock—Katz Never Kloses—and serves reliable, hearty fare.

Tony sat across from me. There was a big welt on his forehead but the injury hadn't blunted his appetite. He'd already put down two stacks of pancakes and now was polishing off a half dozen fried eggs and a thick slice of ham. He also kept the waitress busy delivering glasses of orange juice, five so far. People at nearby tables watched Tony eat like they'd watch feeding time for crocodiles at the zoo.

"Tiger?" I said. "Where'd you come up with that?"

"I dunno." He shrugged. "Tony the Tiger, Tony and the Tiger. Sounded good at the time." He pulled a thick roll from his pocket, counted off some fifties, handed them over. "By the way, thanks."

I looked at the money. Three hundred. "Too much."

Tony flicked his fingers at the bills in dismissal and scooped more eggs into his mouth. "Figure you earned a bonus," speaking around the eggs. He grinned. "Tiger!"

I put the cash in my pocket. "Just warn me before you call on Tiger again. Give me time to put on my game face."

"You did well. More of Tiger inside than you let on, dude." He sopped the remainder of egg from his plate with a slice of toast, popped that in his mouth, chugged the last of the juice, stood up. "Got to scoot. You get the tab. And tip good." He trundled off, stopping by the cashier to buy a pecan pie on the way. I wondered how long it would last. Two blocks, three? I'd give the pie no more than four at the outside.

I couldn't help smiling. Working with Tony Vee is always an adventure in new and untried situations, some of which I'd prefer remain untried. Still, the money would help.

* * *

I thanked the server for a refill, sipped my coffee and pulled out my new smartphone to play with. My older cell fit nicely in a jeans pocket but this time I'd bought one of the fancier models. It had a camera, e-mail, Web access and probably an app that would scratch my ass at regular intervals. Regardless, no way it could be jammed into my pocket, so it rode yuppie-proud in a little belt holster. I accepted this as a nod to breaking technology, but there are limits, and I would not succumb to wearing a Bluetooth earpiece that resembled a big pet dung beetle. I'd talk on my phone the way God meant, held up to my ear while driving dangerously through heavy traffic.

I set the phone down, gooped strawberry preserves onto my toasted English muffin and some of the preserves dribbled onto the phone. An egregious error. It wouldn't be smart for crooks to catch me like this.

"Hey, Bruno, what's dis on his phone? Blood?"

"Naw. Just some sticky stuff."

"Tiger ain't here. Let's get him."

I plucked a napkin and began to wipe off the phone and in seeming protest it cheeped. Reaching past the smear, I was possessed by a whimsical mood and answered in a growl, "Tiger Malloy, enforcer and jam spreader. Whadda ya want?"

"Hello?" A pleasant female voice, clearly surprised. "I'm trying to reach Mr. Mitchell King, King Investigations. Do I have the correct number?"

So much for the new identity. "This is Mitch King."

"Mr. King, this is Julie at Cohen and Boudreaux. Donna Boudreaux is calling. May I put her through?"

"Sure."

"Please hold." The secretary's cheery voice was replaced with the nasal lament of Patsy Cline. "Craaazy..."

Donna Boudreaux is a criminal attorney for a law firm that kept me on retainer. I hadn't worked with her in a while so I had no idea why she was phoning. As Patsy continued her mournful quest for lost loves and missing pickup trucks, I cradled the phone against my ear and tried to wipe off the jam. Like Patsy, I was mostly unsuccessful.

* * *

The line clicked. "Mitch?" Donna's familiar Cajun twang bubbled from across town. "How's my favorite private eye?"

"Fine. Shot three people today and haven't yet finished breakfast."

"Time to work me in between gunfights?"

"For you, sweetheart, always. What's up?"

"The Trevillian shooting. Know about it?"

"Just what was on the news?"

Donna filled me in. Overnight, police were called to the Memorial area home of one Lawrence Trevillian on the report of shots fired. They arrived to find Trevillian lying by his swimming pool but in no shape to enjoy it. Someone had blown a large hole in his chest. It had the earmarks of a domestic quarrel turned sour. Trevillian's live-in girlfriend, Theresa Bartlett, was taken into custody at the scene and homicide charges were pending.

"You her lawyer?" I asked.

"Yep. Her boyfriend used Jeff Converse for his financial stuff. Terrie called Jeff, Jeff called me. The arraignment is at nine tomorrow. I'm hoping to get Terrie out on a writ. Or reduced bail, at least."

"And?" I prompted.

"And I'm down at the jail, just finished talking with Terrie. The office patched me over to you. Aren't cellphones wonderful? Remember before them, how life was sometimes quiet and sedate?"

"Ah, yes, cellphones. Light of my life. Just got a new one and can scarcely figure out how to dial the thing."

"Tell me about it. Anyway, I'm due in court on another case. Could you see her in the meantime?"

"How can I help?"

"Terrie is freaking out. She says she's innocent, didn't shoot her boyfriend. Maintains it was a pro job."

"A mob hit?"

"Something like that. Weird however you slice it. Seems this total stranger walked into their house, killed her boyfriend Larry, and then went for her. She grabbed Larry's gun and shot back, chased the killer off before the cops came. Now she's next on the list. Or so she says."

"You believe her?"

"Of course I believe her!" Donna replied with mock indignation. "She's my client." Then Donna turned serious. "Something's wrong, Mitch, that much I know. She's scared shitless."

"Want me to find the hit man? If he exists?"

"At least satisfy my doubts."

"Cops working on it?"

"They wrote it all down, but I don't think they're putting much effort into the search. They're pretty sure she did the shooting."

I affected a bad Bogart accent. "So I'm alone on this, sweetheart? Can I wear my trench coat and slink around to zither music?"

"Only if you bring your own zither. And Bogie wasn't in *The Third Man.*"

"Devil's in the details, they say."

One-liners concluded, Donna and I chatted a while as I keyed some of the devil's very details into my phone. Then she formally hired me in my capacity as private investigator and hung up.

Being hired by the attorney of record gives me certain immunities and privileges. It also gives me money. Like anyone else, I need to pay bills. My imaginary tough-guy private eye Bugsy Binton always refuses the extremely generous check from the husband or graciously donates the money to a handy orphanage. The story ends before the light company shuts his power off.

I'll keep the money, thank you. I work hard for what I earn. I stay on retainer for insurance companies and law firms. I also land the occasional security job as bodyguard or nursemaid. And people like Tony Vee sometimes need help. Now that I'm single and the house is paid for, it's enough.

What I do is typical of real world private detectives. We track down bad check artists, embezzlers, insurance scams and other assorted small-time grifters. We locate accident witnesses, search for missing heirs and take videos of people with bad backs who play touch football. The bulk of our work nowadays is done online.

Yes, I carry a gun, but I prefer to leave the hardball to the cops. There are more of them and they're good at what they do. It's so much bull that private eyes regard the police as adversaries. I'd be out of business within two weeks of screwing the cops. We work together. I go where they cannot and ask questions when they cannot. And they move with the force of law and arms when I cannot.

My cell beeped again. Speaking of cops, Homicide Detective David Meierhoff was calling.

Chapter 4

Meierhoff's bright and chipper voice: "Any idea where I might find a good private detective?"

"Check the yellow pages. And try Google. There's this newfangled thing called the Internet."

"I was thinking about you, actually."

"You wanted good. All I can promise is cheap."

"That'll have to do. Got some free time this afternoon?"

"I'm tied up today. Tomorrow okay?"

"Tomorrow's fine."

"So what's up?"

"Know who Tarah Jacoby is?"

"The astronaut, right? Nickname TJ."

"Yeah." Meierhoff chuckled. "You keep up on all the astronauts?"

"Like anybody, I'm a spaceflight fan. But Tarah Jacoby has a special spot in my heart."

"She's a looker, that's for sure."

"Not only that, she's one nifty gal. Last March she was a celebrity guest at the Erin Pub St. Pat's party. Took second place in the Guinness beer-drinking contest. Not bad for a PhD physicist. A woman after my own heart."

"Dream on, brother."

"Hey, a guy's gotta hope."

"So," Meierhoff brought me back to Earth. "I was at this benefit last week, Anti-Defamation League. They had me talk about what it's like to be a Jewish cop."

"Why'd they pick you?"

"Rumor going around that I'm a Jewish cop."

"Funny, you don't look cop-ish."

"Trying to pass."

"Happy for you, Detective Meierhoff. And this is significant because?"

"Tarah Jacoby was at the dinner. She got me aside, wanted some advice."

"And so you called me to get my opinion about the next ISS mission?"

"What do you think? You're being hired as a consultant?"

"I could only hope, figured it was my turn in the box. I pay my taxes on time and everything."

Meierhoff sighed, humor in his voice. "How could you not? You're a totally law abiding citizen, or have you gone astray recently?"

"Not when being coached by the ever-puissant Detective Meierhoff."

"You're lucky I know what *puissant* means. Otherwise I'd have to shoot you for calling me a pissant."

"Had to take a chance those four years at A&M weren't wasted."

"Least I didn't go to a cowboy school."

"I'll share a dirty secret. When we University of Texas Longhorn snobs want cowboys, we rent 'em."

"Long as you don't hire us Aggies, make us wear spurs."

We laughed. Meierhoff and I often ragged each other about our UT and A&M roots. It was a source of recurrent point scoring.

"Now," I said. "Luxuriating in your spare time, or is there some actual purpose to your call?"

"Tarah Jacoby has a problem. I told her you might help."

"Specifically?"

"I'd rather she tell you. Can you meet her at JSC tomorrow? Say two pm?"

"Sure."

"Okay. You know Space Center Drive right off NASA Road One. Go to Gate Four and they'll be expecting you. Drive over to Building Nine. That's the astronaut training facility."

"Okay. Anything else?"

"Yeah," Meierhoff said. "Don't you sometimes pretend to be a realtor as a cover?"

"Want me to show you a little fixer-upper?"

"Not. But sign in with your real estate alias, okay?"

"Low profile, keeping the cards close to the chest, are we?"

"Makes sense."

"So I get to meet Tarah Jacoby, Girl Astronaut?"

"Only if you promise to behave." Meierhoff gave me her phone number.

"What if I ask for her autograph?"

"I can't invite you anywhere, can I?" He clicked off.

The prospect of meeting an astronaut would make my day. And my week, actually, because the dustup this morning was unusual. Most of my work is mundane, boring in fact. We private detectives rarely have an exciting time. And never like the movies or TV.

Nevertheless, I sustain my fantasy. A stunning redhead waltzes into my shabby third-floor walkup, sniffling, dabbing at her watery but deep blue eyes. She offers me a chunk of dough to recover the historic Elsinore diamond brooch without her husband being the wiser. I fight my way through hordes of assorted villains, finally plucking the brooch from the scrabbling hands of Mr. Big just before he's pulled beneath the quicksand. Case solved and the lady's honor restored, I chivalrously turn aside her amorous offer and march bravely into the rainy night like the loner I am.

I looked around. No redhead. The present assignments would just have to do until she came along. I ignored my now cold coffee and muffin, paid the bill, added a generous tip per Tony's admonition and headed for the jail.

Chapter 5

I climbed the steps to the police building, pulled open the big metal and glass door and as I'd left my gun in the car, passed easily through the gauntlet of metal detector and security screeners. There was zero ventilation in the lobby and the humidity glued the shirt to my back in seconds. I'm amazed at the lack of foresight, putting up a building in Houston without adequate air conditioning. I do all right in steamy weather but lots of folks don't. Maybe the designers expected Houston Police to be headquartered on the Alaskan North Slope? But then again, the phrase *urban planning* has always been an oxymoron.

The post-art-deco neo-nothing school of interior design common to all government buildings was here in excess, the surroundings drab, stuffy, depressing, walls a tasteful fifties color scheme of slime green and cat shit brown. All the signs above doorways used lettering stolen from old Republic movie serials. Trash, both paper and human, littered the hallways.

The lobby's original lighting had featured big institutional glass globes. These were torn out and replaced by cheap fluorescent fixtures that mostly didn't work, but nevertheless hummed their transformers threateningly as you walked beneath. The ones still shining at all flickered with a fitful glow, but this was a plus because good lighting would only reveal more of the accumulated grime and crud.

You can't blame the housekeeping staff, though. It's a Herculean task to maintain cleanliness because of all the traffic. Police Headquarters is an unceasing parade of lifestyles and philosophies. Here travel Houston Police, Harris County

Constables, Texas Highway Patrol and that paradigm of Western law, the Texas Ranger. Here go flashers and addicts and parking ticket scofflaws and murderers. Defense lawyers, county prosecutors, city attorneys and similar riffraff join them. Mingled with this legal and illegal traffic are TV news crews, reporters, politicians and all the assorted citizens who have a keen interest in seeing justice done. And preferably, seeing it done to someone else.

* * *

The women's jail was on six, but I wanted to stop by Homicide on two and chat with Joe Duggan, so I took the stairs. The steps were hard marble, yet bore shallow depressions in the middle, treads worn down by millions of police and suspects and visitors who had grooved their weary history deep into these steps and deep into the bowels of the criminal justice system. I added my part.

Hot as the lobby had been, it was positively Arctic compared with the second floor. Flecks of moisture began to form in my hair and eyebrows as rivulets of sweat slid down my back. In the second floor stairwell, an enormous electric fan was propped on a shaky frame, laboring to send what cool air existed down the hall toward Homicide. It roared, but like a politician giving a campaign speech, had little real effect.

A row of vending machines shared the stairwell with the fan and Detective David Meierhoff was there, confronting the candy and chips machine. He poked the Butterfinger button again and again, cursing. "Deadbeat! Gimme that sonofabitch!" Nothing came out.

Meierhoff stood back and kicked the machine square into its coin changer with the flat of his foot. The machine rocked and rattled and dinged the wall, but still no candy. He lunged for the controls again, slamming the buttons and banging on the coin return. Nothing. Meierhoff mumbled further curses and stepped back for another kick, but as he positioned himself for the telling blow, he saw me standing there, serene. He broke off the assault and smiled shyly. "Hey, Mitch. If I knew you were going to be here I'd have saved my cell minutes."

"If I knew you were coming I'd have baked a candy bar?"

"Or opened a beer."

I pointed to the machine. "What's up, Meierhoff? Interrogating a suspect?"

"Bitch took my money and won't put out."

"Sounds like most of the women you run with."

"Huh! Least mine are women." He grinned. "Last time I heard, you were trolling Pacific Avenue with your fly unzipped."

"Funny you should notice that, Detective Meierhoff. You always concentrate on my zipper? Searching for a cheap thrill?"

"Force of habit, King. We police are trained to observe the smallest of details."

We laughed at that and shook hands.

As usual, David Meierhoff was dressed to the max. He wore a keen navy blazer with gold buttons and long lapels, tan slacks pressed to a razor crease and polished loafers. His shirt was yellow broadcloth and his silk tie aswirl with colors, neatly Windsor-knotted and centered.

Meierhoff is tall and wiry, with a head of tight curly brown hair topping a pleasant face, a slight resemblance to a youthful Elliott Gould. Meierhoff is one of the upcoming breed of cops, smart and college educated. He'd made a fair name for himself in Narcotics before moving to Homicide a year ago and loved the new job.

One of those people who had energy for five, always on the go, working late, jogging miles and tearing through the Nautilus regimen in the police gym, Meierhoff somehow found time to earn a brown belt in *Shotokan* karate. I'd gone through a couple of *kumites* with him at Darrell Craig's dojo and he nearly killed me.

"Carrying the new Smith today?" I asked.

He pulled the lapel aside to reveal the Bianchi shoulder rig and his 9mm auto. "Yeah," he answered, letting the lapel fall. "Doesn't spoil the drape." It didn't.

Meierhoff and I made the gun show last month and we both pounced on the new S&W compacts. I bought the blued steel model, while he preferred the flashier version in stainless. Figured.

"Mitch, say we head out to the range Saturday? Fifty bucks?"

I considered the wisdom of shooting against the second best marksman on the force. "And afterwards, we stop by Cue and Cushion for some nine ball. Fifty bucks?"

Meierhoff grinned. "Why bother? You hang on to your fifty, I'll keep mine."

I smiled cordially. Eventually I'd get him into a game and win back that hundred he'd taken from me in baseball bets. So what if he backed the Rangers while I stuck with the Astros? At least I was loyal to the home team.

"Business okay?" I asked.

"Booming, pardon the expression. Five over the weekend and two last night, all shootings. Couple of stabbings, too." He thrust an imaginary knife downward and made a *zzzt* sound. Acting is clearly not his forte. "You here about one of 'em?"

"Yeah. The Trevillian thing."

"Trevillian. Out in Memorial? Girlfriend shot him." Meierhoff cocked his finger and fired. "Pow! Right in the brisket."

I rolled my eyes at the histrionics. "So they say. Duggan in?"

"Just missed him. He walked over to the garage to pick up his car. Water pump went out. Should be back soon. Wanna wait?"

"Think I'll go up and see the girl you're holding. Theresa Bartlett."

"Interviewed her last night, and holding is what I'd like to do." Meierhoff cupped his hands, palms upward like judging cantaloupes. "Great garbanzos."

"Detective Meierhoff, I'm ashamed of you. You exhibit a complete lack of professionalism. I may have to report this to Lieutenant Duggan."

"Save it, Mitch. He'd agree anyway." He cupped his hands again. "Garbanzos."

"Thanks for briefing me on the status of my client." I turned to head for the elevator.

Meierhoff stopped me, a tug on my sleeve. "Got spare change? I'm having a sugar attack and this golem took my last quarter."

"Broke from making payments on that Porsche?" Meierhoff had recently squandered his life savings on a used 911.

"Just short of coins is all. I'm hung up here at the office and haven't time to shake down the school kids for their lunch money."

"Feed your habit. See if I care." I dug in my pocket and handed him some quarters. "Later."

As I walked away, I heard the threats resume. "Bastard! Open up! Last chance!"

Accompanied by Meierhoff's curses and the crashing of metal, I went around the corner and punched the elevator UP button. I didn't have to wait more than a week or so. When the door finally screeched open, everyone inside groaned because they were already sardine-like but I managed to fold myself into the car anyway. The compressed humanity and resultant humid effluvium made breathing oppressive, and the ride to six was slow and in dire need of Right Guard.

Chapter 6

If you visit the Hotel Riesner courtesy of the police, you ride straight up from the basement garage in an express elevator. It opens into a steel cage behind a security wall and surprise, you're in jail! The volunteer route is slower but at least you can change your mind.

The elevator door rattled open on six and about half of us tumbled into a small lobby just outside the lockup itself. The other passengers stayed in the elevator, headed to the men's jail on seven.

The change in climate was immediate. It was far cooler, approaching chilly. The sweat on my back turned into little goose bumps and I could almost see my breath.

Visiting time wasn't for a while, so the elevator passengers ranged themselves along the wall to wait. They looked impatient and nervous, but coming to a jail does that to you, even if you're outside the bars. The fact that most of these folks had at one time played the inmate game didn't allow them to assess the return visit with boundless enthusiasm.

Two uniform cops, one man, and one woman, sat at a raised counter built into a partition that ran across the lobby. They had a phone and a computer. There was a chest-high swing door you had to be buzzed through. Behind the partition was the jail proper, fronted by a steel mesh door set in the rear wall and flanked by bulletproof observation windows.

I walked over to the counter to say hello to the guards. Like all cops, these two had seen everything and took pains to look professionally bored. If an eight-armed Martian were to slither out of the elevator, they'd casually ask it for a valid driver's license and inquire who it was here to see.

I knew one of the cops, John Burlingame, a big thickset fireplug of a guy from motorcycle patrol. He'd been nailed broadside a while back by a drunk running a red and was not yet well enough for street assignments, hence an easy turn with desk duty at the jail. "How's the leg?" I asked.

"Better all the time." Burlingame demonstrated by turning and lifting his right leg for me to see.

It looked like any other cop leg concealed inside any other cop slacks, for all I could tell, so I nodded my approval. "Tell me, John, why'd you leave the refrigerator door open?"

He shook his head. "Can you believe this crap? Some smartass in City Hall read that prison riots happen when it's hot, so last week they screwed with the AC. Now everybody up here is freezing their butts off and all the poor suckers downstairs are roasting. Let 'em cook. They're only cops."

"Least you won't have trouble from the prisoners. They're too busy keeping warm."

"Most likely Popsicles by now." Burlingame shook his head again, then beamed a broad smile. "How come you're here anyway, Mitch? They pick up your girlfriend hooking on South Main again?"

"Yeah. She'll never change but I love her so."

We laughed. "Mitch, this here is Marcie Lawton." He nodded to his partner at the desk. "Marcie, meet Mitch King. An honest to goddamn goodness private eye."

The female cop looked up, raised her eyebrows, and offered her hand. "Hiya, Mitch. Marcie." She was a big woman, solid but not fat, pretty, with bunches of frizzy blonde hair. "What brings you up to the ladies' room?"

"Representing Cohen and Boudreaux. To see Theresa Bartlett." I glanced at my phone. "Case 173-5257. Is an interview room open?"

"Yeah. Hang on. We'll thaw her out and bring her over." Marcie typed into the computer. "Bartlett, you say? Oh my, homicide. Been a naughty girl, hasn't she?" Satisfied with what she saw on the screen, Marcie picked up the phone. "This is Marcie. You have Theresa Bartlett in cell fifteen? Yeah. Can you bring her to interview room two? Mr. King is here to see her. Thanks. I'll need your ID."

This last comment was directed to me. I handed Marcie my driver's license and investigator's folder. She wrote my numbers on a clipboard form and rotated it for me to sign. I did. Marcie smiled at me and I smiled back. Everyone was happy. Filling in blanks does that for people.

"Come on." Burlingame motioned me. He stood up with the help of a cane, buzzed me through the partition and ran a metal detector over me. "The rules," he explained.

I sighed. Rules would be the death of me.

* * *

All that beeped was my phone but he let me keep it. Burlingame gave Marcie the high sign and she pressed a button under the edge of the desk. The lock clicked and Burlingame ushered me through the steel door. "See ya later." The door clanged shut.

One of the most depressing sounds there is, that latching. A tone of finality exists in closure of metal on metal, snap of steel deadbolts, echoes ringing from cell walls. It chilled me even more than the cold air.

Here I was, a free man, visiting on official business, yet still I felt trapped. Because trapped I was. I could knock. I could shout. I

29

could threaten. But no matter how I carried on, if they didn't want to open that door again and let me out, here I would stay.

I stood in a small transfer cell. The outer and inner doors were fitted with an interlock so that only one could be opened at a time, allowing prisoners to be herded easily, like cattle at the railyard. Right now, a herder waited behind the second door, watching me through the heavy mesh.

"Mitchell King, to see Theresa Bartlett," I said.

The guard called over her shoulder. "OK, Judy! Open on four!" A solenoid clacked and the door slid aside.

"Room two," she said, pointing, "It's right between one and three. Number's on the door. It's unlocked. We're bringing Terrie now."

I thanked her and walked thirty feet down a dead-end hall while she watched. Sure enough, there it was, room two, right smack between one and three. Amazing how these things work. The door was solid steel with a small security peephole. I opened the door and went inside.

The room was furnished in Modern Prison Danish, a ratty metal table bolted to the floor, generously offset by three cracked and warped plastic chairs, also mounted into the concrete. A small foil ashtray played centerpiece to the table. The concrete walls, once yellow, now lapsed into a crazed pattern of scrapes and chips that mostly eradicated the original paint. Overhead loomed the ubiquitous humming neon fixture, set in a security recess. Now here was a place you could kick back and meditate, really get in touch with your inner self.

As soon as I sat in the least dirty chair, the door opened. The guard showed me the call button on the wall, told me to press it when we were finished and locked me in the room with Theresa Bartlett.

Blood Spiral

31

Chapter 7

"When am I going to get out of this fucking place? They locked me up and I haven't done a goddamn thing! The prick who killed Larry is out there running around and the cops don't give a shit! Jesus Christ! I was right there when he was shot dead! I could be dead too, not that anybody gives a fuck! Can you believe this shit? Are you that private eye? The lawyer said you were coming. I don't know what you can do unless it's get me out of this fucking jail. You got a cigarette? I need a smoke!"

I sat without interrupting and watched Theresa Bartlett. She rushed about the tiny room, a whirlwind of frustration. One moment she was at the door, next at the table, then around the room and back to the door. All the while, she waved her arms in the air like a frenzied commodities trader on the floor of the stock exchange.

Theresa Bartlett was young—my notes said twenty-four. She was of medium height, about five-four and weighed around one fifteen. She wore a faded plaid work shirt, T-shirt beneath, blue jeans with frayed cuffs and old tennies, stuff the cops let her grab on the way to jail.

She plunked down in the adjacent chair, crossed and uncrossed her legs and arms a couple times, nervous. Then she stood up again and resumed her pacing.

I looked her over. She had long legs, slender hips, and boyish buttocks with a narrow waist offset by broad shoulders. And from what I could tell, large breasts for a woman her size. Meierhoff was right. Garbanzos. A shower of curly brown hair fell in ringlets about her head. Her face was round with high cheekbones and she had great, deep brown eyes that shined with intense feeling and passion.

Then I looked into her eyes and I was lost. Some connection, some vital current in her drove a bolt of desire straight through into my core. I don't know why. I didn't foresee it. But the brilliance of her sexuality struck me head on.

Maybe there's a chemical attractant, a pheromone specific to one or two people. Perhaps time and place generate the energy. Perhaps the forces that drew me to her were set in motion a thousand years before. I did not speculate long nor did I care. I only knew that I was instantly and uncompromisingly in love. Call it lust but I still thought *love*.

Theresa broke off her tirade when I didn't react. She planted herself in front of me, arms akimbo and stared. "Well, are you just gonna sit there all day?" She blew out a puff of air in frustration and it made some curls dance around her face. "What the fuck are you gonna do?"

"Ms. Bartlett—Terrie. Please sit down. Your lawyer Donna Boudreaux is doing everything possible to gain your release. And yes, I'm the private investigator."

"Can you get me bailed out? I've never been in jail before. I've got to get out of this fucking place!"

I couldn't learn anything worthwhile with her so tweaked. "Terrie, I need your cooperation to help you. Please have a seat, okay?"

She dropped back into the chair, leaned forward and slammed both palms flat on the tabletop. The flimsy ashtray spun and rattled. "There! Good enough for you?" She glowered.

I looked into her eyes and again I was caught. My breath ran shallow and my stomach knotted in that old familiar throb of desire. To stay busy, I paged through my smartphone notes. "I'm

Mitchell King. Call me Mitch." I took a business card from my folder, flipped it over and wrote *173-5257* on the back. "This is your case number. You might need to refer to it later. Call me any time, day or night. My phone numbers are on the card, email when you get out." Terrie took the card without reading and laid it on the table, drummed her fingertips on the cracked Formica and glared at me.

I ignored the stare. "Donna Boudreaux is an excellent criminal attorney. You have a hearing at nine tomorrow morning. Donna will ask for bail. Try to be patient. You'll be out soon."

The first positive reaction from Terrie. "When? Tomorrow?" A brief smile.

"Tomorrow or the next day at the very latest." At this, she slumped in the chair and pouted. I raised my hands in a placating gesture. "This is a serious charge, Ms. Bartlett."

"I didn't shoot him! I didn't shoot Larry!"

"I understand. But it doesn't prevent the county attorney from filing charges. It takes a certain amount of time for the paperwork to move through the system. Did Donna Boudreaux explain this?"

"Yeah. Sort of. I wasn't paying much attention at the time."

"Donna and I have discussed your case." I scrolled my notes. "She's already spoken to Mr. Trevillian's civil attorney, Jeff Converse. Your boyfriend had considerable funds in his personal account and stipulated the money to be used however the attorney wished in an emergency. Which means it'll be posted for bond. You'll be out soon. Still, it takes a day or two because of the severity of the charges. Okay?"

She nodded.

"Meanwhile, I've been asked to help locate the man who shot your boyfriend. And sorry, I don't smoke. I'll get you some cigarettes later. Be a bit thankful—they're banning smoking in the jail August first. What brand?"

"Anything." She hesitated. "Well, not really. I hate filter cigarettes. I like those imported ones, English Ovals. You know?" I nodded. "But right now I'd smoke a dog turd."

I typed *Terrie-Cigs-Eng Oval*, resisting the temptation to write *Terrie-Cigs-dog turds*. I browsed through my notes again in an attempt to convey competence, because I was uneasy in her presence.

"Now. Tell me," I said. "And take your time. About last night?"

Some of the sharpness left her eyes. She stared blankly, as though I'd asked her the atomic weight of Cesium. "I don't remember much." She shook her head and cascades of brown curls followed the movement. "It happened so fast. All I can think about is Larry lying there." Terrie fell silent. Her head sank slowly and she seemed ready to cry.

I reached out to touch her then, and stopped myself. Behold this woman. She is in jail with me hired to find who shot her lover scant hours before. She may be lying and have shot him herself. She's outrageous and rude. She's years younger than I. So what am I thinking? How to solve the case, locate the killer? No, God help me, I was thinking how to hold her in my arms, hold her and not let go.

I dug in, continued the interview. "Terrie, take a deep breath, okay?" I took one, too. I needed it. "We have to talk. Tell me."

She looked up. "Larry went for a swim." Her voice was subdued and I strained to hear her. "He'd been back inside, oh, five minutes."

"What time was this?"

"About nine."

"And?"

"The back door, the sliding glass door to the pool, it opened and this guy walked in. I don't have any idea who he is—never saw him before. He had a gun."

"What sort of gun? Could you identify it?"

"It was, you know, a revolver. That's the kind Larry has. He took me shooting a couple times. But I don't know much else about guns."

"Okay. Did the man say anything?"

"No." She swallowed. "Then Larry said, 'Who the hell are you?' but the guy didn't answer." Terrie's head sank again. "God. That was the last thing Larry said before..." She sobbed and her breasts rose and fell. The chill of the room had stiffened the nipples beneath her shirt and this stoked my desire despite my efforts to remain steady.

I cleared my throat and tried to clear my head. "Terrie, you're doing fine. I know this is difficult, and I know the cops have asked you the same questions. But the quicker I get the details, the faster I can start looking for the shooter."

This gave her some incentive. "Sorry." She glanced at my card. "Mitch." She sniffed and went on. "I must have screamed or something. The guy came over and grabbed me by the arm. Larry shoved him into the wall and ran to our bedroom. He came out with his gun, and the guy saw it and ran back out the door."

"Out to the pool?" I asked.

She nodded. "Larry went after him. I tried to stop him but he went anyway. I heard this *bang*. I went out and Larry was there." She gestured toward the floor. "The blood was..." Terrie looked at me plaintively. Despite the weariness in her eyes, I was carried away by her beauty and felt ashamed. Under the circumstances, it was like peering down the neck of a lady's dress in church. But it made no difference. I wanted her.

"What did you do then?"

"The guy was just standing over by the whirlpool." Terrie pointed, showing it was some distance. "I saw Larry's gun. I picked it up and shot at the guy. I missed, I guess. He ran out the back gate. The cops came but they fucking arrested me!"

"What can you tell me about the man? Was he white, black, Hispanic, short, tall? How old?"

"He was a white guy, oh, six feet tall. No, shorter. Maybe."

I stood up. "Okay. I'm five ten. Was he taller than I am?"

"About the same, I guess. Bigger than you are, though." She spread her hands, pantomiming wide shoulders.

"What did he look like, facial features?"

"He was—" She crisscrossed her hands rapidly in refusal. "I'm no good at this!"

I sat back down. "Terrie, here's a trick. It helps if you describe someone in terms of a famous person. Did the man resemble any celebrity from TV or the movies? Even a little?"

She pondered this. "I know it sounds stupid, but he looked like Mel Gibson, younger though."

"Okay, that helps. So the guy is athletic, mid-thirties, five-ten, one-eighty, rugged good looks. Clean shaven?" She nodded. "What was he wearing?"

"He had on jeans, I think. Yeah. And a T-shirt."

"Regular blue jeans? And what color T-shirt? Plain white?"

"Yeah, regular jeans. But the shirt was black. And it had this, this eagle on it."

"Like the American eagle? USA?"

"No, it was, you know, a Harley shirt."

Great. Harley-Davidson. So far, I'd narrowed the search down to a couple million Harley riders and sixty million wannabes. "Anything else?"

She frowned, thinking. "He had this tattoo, here." Terrie pointed to her right forearm.

"What was it? Could you tell?"

"It was red and blue, and had these wings." She flapped her fingertips. "The Harley thing, like bikers have."

Better. Few men would get a Harley tattoo and not actually ride. "And he didn't say anything?"

"No. He just walked in and he... he..." She began to sob again.

"All right, Terrie. Enough for now. Get some rest. Donna will meet you in court tomorrow morning. And I'll keep in touch with her."

Terrie lifted her head and smiled wanly. She reached out, put her hand on my arm and squeezed gently.

It was like an electric shock. I tried not to let it show.

Her smile disappeared and she squeezed harder. I could sense fear beneath her nervousness. "Mitch, I'm scared. He knows who I am. You can find him, can't you?"

"Yes, Terrie. I'll find him." I hadn't the slightest idea how, but right then, had she asked, I would have promised her the presidency. I stood up, patted her on the shoulder, and made all the comforting noises. I buzzed for the guard.

I was escorted through the steel gates while Terrie was led back to her cell. I signed out and rode down to see Joe Duggan in Homicide.

As I stood in the elevator, Terrie Bartlett was foremost in my mind. Not as client, just as Terrie. I wanted her free and I wanted to be with her, to have a chance with her.

But to do that, I had to find the man who killed Larry Trevillian.

Chapter 8

I glanced at the candy machine on my way through the second floor lobby. Its plastic front panel was cracked open and the display Butterfinger was missing. I knew nothing.

The humidity down here seemed even more oppressive, and the cold of the jail only served to accentuate the heat. Sweat soaked my shirt. The monster fan still rumbled and I welcomed the blast of air as it urged me toward Homicide.

Homicide takes up most of the second floor. With several hundred murders in Houston a year, they need all the space they can get. Principally, it's one large open area filled with old metal desks, cheap chairs and filing cabinets jammed with paper. An ancient portable TV with a rolling picture sat unwatched on a high shelf. There were two coffeemakers and a box of donuts on a table in the corner. I checked, just in case. Only half a plain cake remained.

A row of glass-paneled offices for the higher ranks ran along the left wall. Plainclothes cops and uniforms sat at desks, on desks, or just stood around. They were writing and lounging and working and drinking coffee and talking sports and bullshitting like anyone does at any job. Some of them knew me, waved and I waved back.

In a symbolic gesture to modernization, the city installed chin-high partitions with pastel panels in the big room to form cubicles. They don't add much to the décor, but they do lend a modicum of privacy to the detectives and serve to keep the noise a notch lower. Less symbolic and a shade more useful, computers sat on each desk. They give modern cops advantages over their predecessors. Instead of spending hours typing meaningless reports, they now spend hours entering them into the computer. The bureaucracy still demands reports, but for a while a cop could at least pretend that the process is automated.

Every wall and flat surface in Homicide is plastered with stickyback notes, taped messages, charts, diagrams, posters and photos. There's a steady thread of conversation punctuated by ringing phones and beeping pagers. Constant traffic, too. Cops and criminals and ordinary human beings and even lawyers parade around in the unceasing pirouette of those enforcing the law and those dodging it. You've seen the same thing a thousand times on television. And in truth, Houston Homicide looks pretty much like a TV cop show.

Life models art.

* * *

Art wasn't in but Joe Duggan was. He sat in his office, feet propped on the desk. At least it may have once been a desk. Papers were stacked in foot high mounds and foam coffee cups nested in shaky stained columns, leaving none of the original furniture visible. Even the computer on a sidebar table was draped with paperwork. Breeze from Joe's window air conditioner ruffled through the debris like a casual browser at a book sale.

Anthropologists could reconstruct a chronology of Houston crime by carefully excavating each stratum of Joe Duggan's desk. I imagined a grid of tightly stretched strings hanging over the site and a bearded graduate student carefully bagging a moldy half-eaten sandwich, marking the artifact "Sector G-5."

A call-director phone, all lights blinking furiously, sat precariously on one very lopsided pile of papers. I fought the urge to answer one of the lines, but instead I loitered before the alleged desk to watch Homicide Lieutenant Joseph Duggan at work.

Duggan is a ringer for Ned Beatty. Muscular, a bit pudgy, beset with a crooked grin, Joe is often mistaken for the actor. He would bear this with kind amusement until he was asked to squeal like a pig, a request always met with an icy stare.

Those piercing gray eyes of Joe's were a glimpse into his sharp, incisive cop brain. He had a reputation for intelligence and patience, toughness tempered by decency and right-mindedness.

Besides looking like Ned Beatty, Joe Duggan also resembled his desk. Unkempt. His sparse brown hair frizzed in every direction. His slacks were wrinkled, his thick forearms jutted from untidy shirtsleeves. A tie, once red and blue, now patterned with an indefinite brown ripple, hung askew. The knot was so low that Joe could pull it over his head at night instead of untying it, which he probably did. The only stylish accessory to Joe's wardrobe was a composite Shooting Systems shoulder rig and the big Les Baer.45 auto filling it. This was coordinated by his Kevlar vest, which hung across an adjacent chair.

Joe was studying a folder, making notes in the margins. He continued to read, not investing so much as a flicker of acknowledgment in my existence, though I knew he could describe precisely what I was wearing down to the color of my socks and compare that with what I wore six weeks earlier.

I stood there a while longer, then decided I didn't have all day. "Ahem."

Duggan grunted. "People don't say *ahem* except in movies." He made another note and turned the page. He still hadn't looked up.

"In movies, homicide dicks haul the shamus down to the basement of the cop shop in cuffs to work him over. I show up voluntarily and this is all the courtesy I get?"

Duggan peered at me over the top of his half-height wire rims. He wearily dropped his feet to the floor, reached back to his belt and came up with a pair of handcuffs. He tossed them across the desk. "Put 'em on if it'll make you feel better."

"Want to frisk me first? Rough me up? I'm easy."

That brought a laugh. Joe laid the folder on the desk and stood up. "We only abuse private eyes on weekends and never before lunch. You shoulda made an appointment." Joe walked around the desk, grabbed my hand and gave it a shake. I don't think he broke any bones. "How the hell you been, Mitch? When we gonna shoot some more pool?"

"Whenever, Joe. Tonight?"

"Nope. Got to meet Margaret for dinner. You know how it is with us old married folks. Tomorrow?"

I didn't know how long I'd be tied up at NASA. "Thursday might be better."

"Thursday it is. Your place at seven."

I nodded. Joe was no real match for me but he was a careful and solid player. I looked forward to our games.

"Meierhoff said you were here. The Trevillian thing, right?"

"Yeah. I'm working for Donna Boudreaux."

"Nice lady. Have a seat." Joe said this without looking around, then noticed that all the chairs were piled with paperwork. He scooped a pile off the nearest one. "Sit."

I sat.

"Gotta be quick, though," he said. "Meierhoff's bringing in a suspect and they want me to talk to him." Duggan rubbed his stubbly chin and studied his desk. "Lemme see... Trevillian... Here!" He stuck his hand somewhere in the middle of a stack and extracted a manila folder. I couldn't have found it in two days. Joe flipped the folder open for me to read. "You're welcome to it for what it's worth, but it's a slammer. Miz Bartlett got pissed and whacked her boyfriend. Like I always say, *done is done.*"

I skimmed through the police report and interview notes, noticed that Terrie's description of the shooter to the cops was a lot hazier than what I got from her. She didn't mention his Harley shirt or tattoo at all. Probably too upset to remember details so soon after.

"What does the young lady say?" Joe asked.

"Sticking to her story. She told Donna Boudreaux the same. Swears some stranger came in, looking to shoot her boyfriend. Trevillian grabbed his own gun but got plugged anyway. Terrie shot back and the guy took off. She says it's a pro hit."

"Yeah, I know. It's all in the file. But it doesn't wash, old bean."

"Why not?"

"For one thing, contract hits are usually made the gentleman's way. They stroll up when you're getting in your car and pop you in the ear with a twenty-two. Sometimes there's a shotgunning or a strafing with your basic AK-47. This one doesn't fit the pattern."

"What makes it so different?" I was being contrary today.

"Here." Joe took back the folder and opened it to a crime scene photo. It was a color print of what had been a handsome young man, lying on his back. He wore khaki cutoffs and nothing else. There were dark stains around the crotch. The man's forearms were raised slightly, hands apart in the manner of a supplicant. Centered on his left chest was an irregular dark red hole surrounded by dried blood and splats of pinkish lung tissue. His eyes were open and there were trickles of blood in the corners, tracing down his cheeks like crimson tears. His face held the look of surprise shadowed with the grimace of violent death.

Joe poked at the photo with a hairy forefinger. "See that hole? It bust the aorta." He turned to a close-up photo of Trevillian's face. "Blood in the eyes? Hydrostatic shock. Comes from being hit with hot loads. Not what a pro uses. Too much muzzle flash and noise."

I wanted to shake Joe's tree. "You said pros occasionally use heavier stuff."

"Sure. But never a wheelgun. Always shotguns or full autos."

"Still—"

"Not finished," he said. "Pathologist pulled out a slug and ballistics has it now. Wasn't too messed up so we should get a match. Your gal was holding her boyfriend's Ruger, standing over him when the uniforms arrived. A smoking gun, literally."

I felt chagrined. Could my feelings for Terrie have led me to a rash judgment? Then I decided. No, Terrie was not a killer. She couldn't be.

Joe leafed through the folder. "Here you go. Gun we took off her. Ruger GP-100 .357 Magnum, loaded with Hornady hollow points. One powerful fucking piece, just what the average citizen keeps in the sock drawer next to his baggie of weed. One round fired. And straight into her boyfriend."

"Joe, she admits firing the gun, but not at Trevillian. He was already down. She picked up the gun and shot at the hit man to protect herself."

Duggan smiled benevolently and shook his head. "Jesus, Mitch, you been around too long to believe that shit. Nobody, at least no straight citizen acts like that. They either turn asshole to elbows and hightail it halfway to Galveston, or they just stand there and crap their pants. You think this chick is gonna have the *cojones* to reach down next to what used to be her boyfriend, snatch the gun and shoot back? Never happened, Mitch. Never."

I didn't believe him and opened my mouth to tell him about Mel Gibson and the Harley tattoo, but for some reason I didn't. Instead, "Maybe you're right, Joe," came out.

"'Course I'm right. We got complaints from neighbors going back coupla years. Fighting, yelling, smashing dishes. Cops called three, four times, disturbing the peace. Never took him to jail but it was close. This time it got outta hand. This time he slapped her once too often, and she did him."

"You don't think it's possible there was anyone else?"

Duggan shook his head again. "Doesn't make sense, Mitch." To illustrate, Joe employed a tactic he often used to make a point. He stuck one hand up, four fingers wiggling. "Count 'em off," he said. "One," pulling his little finger down and tucking it away. "A mob hit because of shady business? No. Jeff Converse was his lawyer and Converse says Trevillian was clean, far as money goes. Know what that means?"

"He was clean," I said. Converse had a solid reputation, a good attorney.

Joe nodded. "Two." The ring finger down. "Drugs? Nope. I checked in Narco. These folks were strictly small potatoes." This got a rise out of me and Joe noticed. "You think they were virgins? Ha!" Joe chortled. "Terrie and her boyfriend were doing blow just like half of fucking Houston, but recreation only. Not enough coke to waste an arrest warrant."

I shrugged. "Go on."

"Three." The middle finger. "A random kick burglar? Nope. Trevillian's house wasn't the biggest or the fanciest on the block. Pretty ordinary for the neighborhood. And a kick-in when the people are home is only done when the target is drugs or lots of cash, which we already covered."

"And four?"

"Four," Joe said with finality, pulling the forefinger down and making a big fist. "A second boyfriend? Again, no. If there was another guy, he'd zap Trevillian elsewhere or do it when the girl wasn't around. Otherwise, she'd be a suspect. Which she is, 'cause she's guilty."

I shrugged again. I was getting good at shrugging. Maybe I should teach a seminar.

Joe closed the folder and patted its cover. "Take it from Uncle Joe. Little Miss Bartlett will be a guest of the State of Texas for a long time."

I got up to leave, smiled. "And I say she walks. Six pack of Dortmunder?"

"Sure." Duggan reached out to shake on the bet and as he did, his gaze drifted to a point just over my shoulder.

"Hoo, boy!" I heard a familiar voice behind me and felt a tug at my waist. "Lookit what I got here!"

I turned around and my heart sank.

Chapter 9

A uniform cop waved the cell he'd lifted from my belt holster. "Jesus, King, you trade in your gun for this fag toy?"

The cop was Phil Jenks. He hated me and the feeling was mutual. "Give it back, Jenks." I tried to keep my voice steady.

He ignored me. "Got a permit for this fucker?"

Meierhoff, uncharacteristically subdued, was standing with Jenks in the doorway to Joe's office. A pale-faced, chubby teenage boy stood between the cops. His long greasy black hair covered part of a heavy metal theme shirt, a grinning skull. Below, dirty jeans over high-top sneakers. The sneakers were stained with reddish brown paint. The kid looked like any other teenager surfing the mall, if you overlooked the handcuffs.

"Give Mitch the cellphone, Jenks," Meierhoff said. "We don't have time for this bullshit. It's not like you haven't seen one before."

Jenks continued to inspect the phone. "Only people who use these fancy types is fags and dope dealers." He showed it to the teenager. "Your old man got one of these, Jeffie?" The boy didn't answer and just looked down at his feet.

Jenks was milking the most from his fifteen seconds of fame and he needed all he could get. His species of policeman is a thankfully dwindling stereotype known as a *black glover*. Despised by civilians and distrusted by his peers, Phil Jenks is the archetypal nasty cop, essentially a crypto-Nazi who barely slides by on the regs.

Phil Jenks is tall, well-built and handsome, blond hair and a neat blond cop moustache, but his good looks are overshadowed by his permanent sneer and crappy attitude. He'd never be promoted on the normal schedules and never have a clue why.

My patience was at an end. "Look, I have work to do and I'm sure you have some innocent bystanders to harass. Everybody and his dog has a cell these days. Give me the phone, Roscoe."

The smirk vanished. Roscoe Rules was the stupid, brutal cop in Wambaugh's *Choirboys*, and Jenks couldn't abide my reminding him of his well-deserved nickname. He concealed his anger by scrutinizing the phone more carefully, looking for a way to turn the tables. "Jesus, what's all this sticky crap on it?" He handed the phone back. "You take it. I don't want to catch no AIDS."

I put the cell in its pouch. "If you want to avoid disease, Roscoe, you should quit rousting those North Main hookers for free blowjobs."

Duggan and Meierhoff both snickered.

"Fuck you, King!" Jenks jabbed his finger at my chest. "Don't you step outta line. I got your number."

"My number's ten digits long, Roscoe. Better have someone write it down for you."

He started for me.

"Enough!" Duggan intervened. "Both'a you knock it off! Mitch, you got places to go and we've got a witness to interview."

Jenks now seized upon a new target for his meanness. "Witness?" He leaned around and smirked into the teenager's face. "Shit! You call this a witness?" Jenks grinned knowingly at me. "Guess what Jeffie did, King."

"Cool it, Jenks," Meierhoff warned.

"What he did," Jenks continued, "was take this big hunting knife and stab Mommy and Daddy and Sister while they was asleep. Over and over. Cut 'em up real good. Hamburger."

"Damn it, stop!" Duggan ordered.

The boy hadn't reacted all the time we'd been arguing, but now he began to cry. Despite the humidity in the room, I felt a cool wind pass across me as I realized that the red stains on his sneakers were not paint.

"Tell me, Jeffie," Jenks swiveled his face up close to the boy's. "You fuck your sister before you killed her? Or was it after?"

Meierhoff put his hand on Jenks' shoulder and tried to push him back. "No more!"

Jenks knocked the hand away. "Don't screw with me, Jewboy."

There was a flash of movement, almost too quick to perceive and Jenks was suddenly bent over, face first into the doorframe. Meierhoff had first jabbed Jenks with a *nukite* blow into the side of his neck and now had him by the nape, fingers pressed deep into the muscles and tendons, right at the nerve bundle where it joined the shoulder. The grip was so intense that Jenks could scarcely breathe. "Jenks," Meierhoff spoke harshly into the cop's ear, "you are the biggest dickhead on the force. Do you want to get written up again? Do you?" Meierhoff let him go. "Pinhead!"

Jenks straightened up. There was a reddish streak on his forehead where it had been jammed against the metal door. He rubbed his neck. "I'm filing on you, Meierhoff."

"Officer Jenks." Duggan's voice took on a sharp edge. "I think you are mistaken. Seems that you tripped and struck your head."

"Yeah," I added, "just an accident."

"You—" Jenks began.

Duggan interrupted. "Or, if you insist, I will testify that you attempted to interfere with the suspect and Detective Meierhoff restrained you." Duggan skewered Jenks with his patented icy glare. "Your call."

Jenks tried to stare Duggan down. A mistake. "Homicide hangs together, right?"

No one spoke.

Jenks turned to me. "Watch yourself, King!" He spun on his heels and headed out. The tension lessened with each of his jackboot strides.

"And now, Mr. Mitchell King," Duggan said. "Will you please get the hell out of here? Detective Meierhoff and I have a difficult story to hear."

Duggan put his protecting arm around the boy's shoulder, grinned his big friendly Ned Beatty grin.

The boy, crying softly, sagged against Duggan, relieved that he no longer needed to bear the terrible truth alone.

Duggan gently led the boy to a chair. "Sit down, Jeff," he said. "Detective Meierhoff, please remove his handcuffs. And call the police psychologist. Extension forty-three, I think. We'll also need a stenographer and someone from legal aid." Duggan squatted and looked the boy in the eye. "Now Jeff, I'm sure you're eager to tell us what happened, but first I need to inform you of your Constitutional rights. You have the right..."

Meierhoff waved me away. I retreated down the hall, not wanting to share in this horrific confession. I stood for a moment before the big fan, the rush of air in my face and tried to regain the buoyant mood I'd felt earlier. But the close confines, the photos of Trevillian, the encounter with Jenks and the enormity of that sad boy's crime all conspired to fix a grayness to the day.

Instead, I turned my thoughts to Terrie Bartlett. I held the image of her in my mind, and concentrated on the memory of her large brown eyes and the deep smile she graced me with. The more I filled my consciousness with Terrie, the better I felt.

After a time I could move on.

Chapter 10

I slept that night with darting and uneasy dreams, waking more fatigued than previous. I shook off the malaise with a quick run, showered, ate a microwaved bagel that I sinfully splurged with a thick smear of pineapple cream cheese. Then I phoned Tony Vee and told him about the Mel Gibson character.

"I'll check around. You think he's a pro?"

"No. He's a bad guy but likely an amateur, especially when it comes to murder. Probably his first."

"For love or for money?"

That question impinged on my warm feelings for Terrie, newfound as they were. "Joe Duggan says money and I'm inclined to agree. The lover's triangle thing doesn't make a lot of sense."

"Either way, I'll run through my sources, let you know."

I made more calls, put out some feelers, then headed down to NASA for my appointment with Tarah Jacoby.

* * *

The prospect of meeting a genuine astronaut was a boost to my otherwise ennui-laden soul. Like all kids, I'd dreamed of becoming an astronaut, right after cowboy and just ahead of fireman in precedence. And even though the job was actually a lot more science and engineering than gee-whiz Flash Gordon, astronauts are still a rare and intriguing bunch.

I dressed accordingly—navy shirt, rep tie, new slacks, and polished shoes. I also had my Listerine PocketPals at the ready and kept in mind that I'd promised Meierhoff not to make a scene. I took the 4Runner down I-45 South, exited onto NASA Road One toward Johnson Spaceflight Center.

When originally built, JSC was out in the sticks, the host City of Clear Lake being mostly farmland and open fields and cows and rural crap. Now Clear Lake is a busy suburb with JSC solidly hemmed in by housing developments, ratty apartments, cheesy franchise restaurants, strip shopping centers and urban crap. Either way, you get crap.

JSC is a sprawl of buildings mixed with a generous landscape of parklands, ponds and meandering paths. Displayed along the front of the property are historic launch vehicles, including a massive Saturn 5. Working at NASA has always been a peachy gig if you survive the cyclical restructuring and purges. Mundane civil service jobs like clerking are secure as Krugerrands, but highly trained engineers are subject to layoffs. Go figure.

The glory days at NASA are no more. Operations are far less experimental, much of the exploration performed by robots, the Challenger and Columbia disasters casting a somber tone upon the whole spaceflight enterprise. With the Orbiter missions shut down and the new Orion project on eternal hold, there was no way to predict how JSC would fare in the next few years, the human spaceflight part at least, in that piggybacking on a Russian rocket to the ISS is one step up from Galaxy Hitchhiker, as I see it. Still, NASA's a beautiful operation.

Only a few years ago you could tour JSC whenever you wanted, look in on astronaut training and see Mission Control, but increased security after 9/11 and tight budgets put that on hold. Working with a commercial developer, NASA built a new facility adjacent JSC, Space Center Houston, a sort of hyped-up spaceflight museum cum amusement park.

I took my daughter Chrissie there when she was younger. It's a bit too Disneyesque for my taste but otherwise okay. There are historic displays like moon rocks and space capsules, plus a big

IMAX theater where you can watch high definition movies of Moon landings, orbital rendezvous and other spaceflight maneuvers.

There are also interactive exhibits where kids could try their hand at docking a spacecraft, climb inside a mockup spacesuit and otherwise pretend to be an astronaut. Chrissie enjoyed it and I wanted to get in line myself, but I was too tall for that ride.

At the visitor gate, I signed in as boss of *MK Realty*, passed through security and parked at the building where honest-to-goodness astronauts could be found. I left my pistol in the car and went inside. They paged astronaut Jacoby and she soon stood before me, shaking my hand.

Chapter 11

Dr. Tarah Jacoby was tall, slender with a runner's physique, had a thick mane of shining dark hair, rich black eyes, an intelligent and alert countenance and a stunning smile. Because of my mild crush on her, I'd read Jacoby's bio on the NASA Web, followed up with some casual surfing into her area of expertise.

Jacoby is one of the principal astronaut scientists, a physicist drawn into the astronaut corps because of her satellite communications work that took advantage of a bizarre aspect of quantum mechanics. This involves tagging an electron with information via its spin orientation, then either reading that data, or intending to read it, pretending to read it, or not reading it at all, even though you really did read it anyway, in a backhand application of the Schrödinger's Cat paradox. Or it may have been the Two-Slit paradox. Both theories are beyond me anyway.

Regardless of which quantum theory you championed, spin tagging somehow let you encode a message and transmit it instantaneously at any distance without regard to the speed of light. Kind of like a Trek transporter. Or so the synopsis implied. I neither understood it nor pretended to, and when I delved deeper into the mysteries of quantum behavior, the seemingly illogical twists and stupefying math were so complex that my brain oozed out my ears. Like Plato's allegory of the cave, I was playing at shadows.

Not content to be a genius physicist, Tarah Jacoby joined the Air Force Reserve and was solo jet qualified. Some people have plenty of spare time and a lot more smarts than I could ever muster.

But despite her academic credentials and spacefaring experience, Tarah Jacoby dressed like a normal human being. She wore a sea-foam green blouse, a subdued pearl strand necklace with matching pendant earrings, black slacks and jacket, low-heel pumps.

"Hi. Tarah Jacoby. Call me TJ."

"Mitch King."

I followed Jacoby through a maze of corridors and offices. It was like any other commercial building until I glanced through open doors and saw rows of chromatographs, spectrographs and other analytical equipment. Everyone's work area was plastered with NASA decals mixed with favored SF themes. There was the traditional *Star Trek* contingent, newer *Star Wars* fans and the more closeted *Babylon 5* groupies. If you assigned political categories, the Trekkies would probably be Republicans, *Star Wars* fans Democrats and *Babylon Fivers*? Libertarians maybe. One thing for certain, never debate the relative merits of *Star Trek* versus *Star Wars*. That could get you phasered or light-sabered.

* * *

We made our way into a section of the building where the astronauts had private offices, with name plaques like Colonel Winslow or Major DeLong. Lean agile men and women, immeasurably superior to me in every possible aspect, they smiled as we passed.

Tarah Jacoby and I grabbed some coffee in a small kitchenette, then she ushered me into her office and shut the door. We sat. I kept reminding myself to behave. Damn.

"David Meierhoff says you can help."

"What's this about?"

Dr. Jacoby pursed her lips. "Is what we say confidential?"

"Yes. If you hire me, we have the same protection as attorney-client privilege, just so you acknowledge you're hiring me."

"This will cost how much?"

"Nothing yet. We'll chat, discuss the fees and sign a standard contract. I charge hourly plus expenses, all state-approved stuff. In the meantime, what we say goes no further. Your intention to hire me is sufficient for confidentiality, even if we don't proceed."

"Okay." She nodded. "I'm being harassed, sexually. Maybe even stalked. At least I think so."

"Know who it is?"

"Yes."

"Somebody here at NASA?"

"Yes."

"Why not take it to Human Resources?"

She shook her head. "Not yet. I don't want to get anyone into trouble."

"Sexual harassment in the workplace is serious and offenders absolutely need to be in trouble with HR. And if you're being stalked, it's either a class three misdemeanor or a felony."

TJ nodded. "I know. But I have no proof. Trent thinks I'm making a mountain, you know, the molehill thing. He says it's just an innocuous office friendship."

"Trent is?"

"Trent Collins." She smiled. "He's an Air Force Major. My main squeeze."

We both smiled. "Okay. How do you want to play this?"

"I'll show you around, introduce you to everybody."

"You don't want to tell me. You want me to guess."

Another smile. "See for yourself. Tell me if I'm exaggerating or if it's real. We can take it from there."

"Deal," I told her. "I'm a friend of a friend. I'm in real estate, showing you new houses."

"Funny thing that. Trent and I have been talking about buying a place together and a lot of the staff knows. So it fits. But I'm curious. Why real estate?"

"Real estate agents are ubiquitous, like cockroaches. Only lawyers are worse."

"You're right. They're constantly underfoot." She smiled.

"And real estate agents are naturally nosy and people take that for granted. I can get extra friendly and nobody thinks anything about it."

"Sounds like a plan."

Chapter 12

TJ gave me the Cook's tour, starting with Mission Control and the VIP gallery, a great view of this nerve center of space exploration. Just now, however, not many nerves were firing their synapses, because only a few of the monitoring stations were occupied and nobody seemed to be paying much attention to anything. I could've sworn one guy was playing *Call of Duty*.

"Not a lot on the agenda?"

TJ pointed to the big wall display, the one everyone recognizes from all the space disaster movies. An orbital track was being updated as we watched. "The international space station, ISS," she said. "No significant projects ongoing, just maintenance. When there's a major mission, this place buzzes."

"The computers look like Dells. Or Toshibas maybe."

"They remodeled. Replaced all the old special-purpose computers with fast PCs. Saved a bunch. The PC brand is whatever's on sale that week."

"Everything generic now?"

"Mostly. The command consoles are special, hotshot UNIX workstations. Networked all to hell."

"When are you scheduled?"

"Launch was this month but it's been postponed. They found a glitch in the satellite we're supposed to put into orbit, so we're rescheduled in six weeks. Maybe. Right now I'm maintaining readiness, cross-training for the mission to follow, working on my communications project and helping develop a new EVA suit."

"EVA. Extra-vehicular activity, right? A real space suit."

"Yeah."

"You seem busy."

"Very."

"And in your spare time, warding off harassment."

She sighed. "That too."

"So where do we find your stalker?"

"Come on."

We left Mission Control and continued the tour. TJ introduced me to everyone. Some of the astronaut names I recognized, most I didn't. And for each of these minor celebrities there were maybe fifty ancillary technicians, electronics experts, engineers and a host of other people engaged in the business of manned spaceflight. There were chemists and physicists and every imaginable technical and scientific discipline. Most were hard at work. The remainder drank coffee, read the paper, surfed the Internet, or ran off personal stuff on the copier. Reminded me of HPD Homicide. Space folks and cops are like anybody else in the workplace, taking advantage of the office perks.

* * *

Outside, we strolled toward a couple of big metal buildings, each the size of a college basketball arena. "Training and test facility," TJ explained.

Inside the first building was the neutral buoyancy lab, essentially a huge open-top swimming pool filled with cameras, winches, cranes and several versions of the ISS grappler arm. Right now, the pool was drained, technicians cleaning up the place and switching out their equipment between experiments. What looked like airlocks were standing free in support frames, like display doors at Home Depot.

"Next best thing to zero gee," TJ said. "There's a new docking tunnel to connect between the supply modules and the ISS. We practice installing the tunnel, unhooking it, moving through it and so on. This new tunnel will be used on upcoming projects."

We climbed down a stairway to the bottom of the pool. There I met engineers, electricians, computer geeks, even some old-fashioned plumbers. Everybody was cordial but no one grabbed TJ's ass or made any other sexist gestures.

"False alarm," I told her as we walked away.

"I wanted you to get a feel for the negative before I show you the positive. Let's go next door."

Chapter 13

The second building was a lot busier than anything previous. People scurried around, checking equipment, taking notes, typing into computers.

"Building thirty-two. Space environment simulation," TJ explained. "Vacuum testing."

Tarah and I stood to the side, behind the monitors and control consoles. Between this and the test equipment was a high clear plastic wall. "A shield. Polycarbonate, right?" I asked.

"In case something goes bust."

"Bust. I dig it when you use scientific terms."

She frowned briefly. "Science is nothing special, except for the math. It's simply the study of what exists, except that we use what's called the scientific method."

"As espoused by Roger Bacon, first made essential by Newton."

She looked at me askance. "Been doing your homework?"

"You behold in me a horrible example of free thought," I said, paraphrasing Joyce. "Plus a lengthy and mostly squandered college education."

"David Meierhoff said you were a smarty."

I shrugged. "And a showoff."

"It ain't showin' off if you can do it." She grinned.

There were two steel chambers in the test area, one about the size of a double-wide trailer, the other smaller, like an SUV. All around were sensors, cameras, pipes, tubes snaking along, you name it. Each test chamber had viewports and a couple of heavy airlocks. It was chaos to me, but I knew there was purpose to each cable, pipe and fitting.

"The big one's Chamber A," TJ explained. "Where we test hatches and airlocks."

"How many astronauts does it hold?"

"Many as you can pack in," She grinned. "We bump into each other all the time."

"What's the smaller one?"

"That's Chamber B."

"Duh."

"Yeah, duh. B follows A. Funny how science works."

This reminded me of meeting Terrie Bartlett at the jail, Room Two, right between One and Three. And that made me think about Terrie herself, how I wanted to be with her. But she was safe for now, even if uncomfortable. And I had this job at hand. Digging up leads on the phantom shooter would just have to wait.

"What's different about Chamber B? Besides being smaller."

"That's for explosive decompression."

"How does that work?"

She sighted me along her arm. "Those big pipes lead over to the evacuation tanks." There were two monster steel tanks at one end of the shed. They had no windows or other instruments and just squatted there, brooding.

"Why evacuation tanks?"

"Pumps can't empty a vessel fast enough for an explosive test, so we pull a vacuum in those tanks first. They're maybe thirty times the volume of Chamber B. Then we hit the switch, high-speed valves open and cause explosive decomp in B, all the air being sucked into the receiver tanks."

"Sounds dangerous."

"For us, not really. We don't get in there ourselves."

"What's it for, then?"

"EVA suits, mostly. Instead of humans, we use test dummies. Crash and Crashina."

I laughed. "Test dummies have gender?"

"Yep. Anatomically correct."

"Malebot and femalebot created He them?"

A smile. "Not likely as well engineered. They're essentially hollow mannequins that we stuff with whatever instruments or sensors are needed for the specific tests."

"So you gonna introduce me?" I asked.

"To Crash and Crashina?"

"Depends on which of them is hitting on you."

TJ smiled again, pointed to a row of spacesuits on a rack along one side of the room. "We're evaluating a new EVA suit design. Better mobility and lighter than the old models. If the suits work out, we'll be wearing them next year at the ISS."

"You're involved in the tests yourself?"

"Yeah. We double up on our mission assignments. I work with EVA suits, then I've got my own thing, a new experiment on satellite timings."

"What's that about?"

"Einstein. Did you know that the clocks on cellphones and GPS trackers make adjustments for the time dilation effect?"

"I read something about it in Scientific American."

"Private detectives read that?"

"Also real estate agents."

"And smarties," she added.

"About the testing?" I asked. "EVA I know and I snapped to the Chamber B thing right away."

"Is that because there's a huge letter B painted on it?"

"We highly trained private detectives are duty-bound never to reveal our investigatory methods."

"But it's decomp you want to know more about?"

"Like if there was a sudden blowout in space?"

"Yeah."

"Okay," I said. "I've got to know. What would it do?"

"Like to a person?"

"Excuse the morbid fascination. Unless you mind talking."

She shook her head. "Not me. I'm pretty hardass on these things."

"So?"

"Well, you'd suffocate quickly."

"That I understand. But what else?"

"Embolism." TJ rubbed the back of her hand. "All the capillaries just beneath the skin would burst, you'd bleed out everywhere. You wouldn't lose a lot of blood but it would be pretty painful, go into shock."

I grimaced. "Not a good idea."

"Nope. Of course if you were in a suit, say, even with the helmet off, a lot of your body would be temporarily protected. You might have time to get to safety or get a helmet on."

"Like in Space Odyssey."

"That was accurate. Remember how Bowman scrunched his face and held his breath?"

"Sure."

"In truth it's a tossup. Some engineers and meds claim that holding your breath would rupture your lungs. But other say that if you don't close your mouth and hold your breath, all the air will rush out of your lungs and probably rupture your windpipe, lungs too."

"So either way you're possible toast?"

"Either way."

"Ick."

"Ick for sure. And you'd freeze."

"Space being cold."

She shook her head. "Not the whole story. Think about what happens when you depressurize a gas. Charles' law?"

From the ancient memory of freshman physics class, I dredged up vague detritus about gases and caloric content. "Hadn't thought about that," I admitted. "Like any pressurized gas. Gets cold if you spray. I saw that happen to a fume freak once."

"Those kids who inhale paint?"

"Yeah. What they do is spray it onto a rag, sniff the fumes. Or fill a balloon and inhale from that."

"But this guy did it directly?"

"Stuck the nozzle in his mouth and let loose. Froze his lungs, died when his lung tissue ruptured. Bled to death internally."

She nodded. "Same with explosive decomp."

* * *

I could hear the rattle of a large bank of vacuum pumps. Science notwithstanding, vacuum pumps make the same noise anywhere. "Are they running a test now?"

TJ consulted a nearby bulletin board. "You're in luck. They're getting ready to decomp an EVA suit in Chamber B. Crashina's the subject for today. We need to stay out of the way."

As TJ and I talked, activity around Chamber B increased, then everybody sat at their display stations behind the shield. The pumps stopped and all was ready. One guy I assumed to be the test director referred to his console displays and announced, "Ready on B." He glanced around to everyone, received nods or thumbs up, returned his concentration to the controls. There were two computer mice, one on either side of his control station, and he positioned one hand above each.

"Twenty seconds to decomp," he announced. Then he counted down just like you'd expect at NASA. At zero, he clicked both mouse buttons. There was a terrific metallic bang in the B-labeled SUV.

Naturally, even though their TV monitors displayed a perfect view of the inside, everyone got up, went around the shielding and looked in the ports. And of course TJ and I walked up and peered inside the chamber, too.

The dummy in the EVA suit was lying on a sort of recliner couch, obviously meant to simulate a launch position. There was a big rip along the left sleeve that ran from wrist to elbow where the fabric or maybe a zipper had split. Crashina appeared to take the failure with aplomb. Better her than a live person.

A couple of the technicians said, "Shit" and I concurred with their scientific assessment. Back to the design phase for the lightweight summer EVA suit.

* * *

As things were winding down, one of the engineers came over. He was a big guy, solid with weightlifter shoulders, reddish hair and trim beard, round benign face and glasses. Clark Kent on steroids. "Dr. Jacoby?"

"Hi," she said. "This is Jerry Anders. Jerry, meet Mitch."

We shook perfunctorily, but his mind was obviously on Tarah. "We need to verify your schedule. Can you go for another fitting tomorrow, say at ten?"

"Sure. I'll be around all day."

Anders nodded, marked in a notebook and went off to consult with another engineer, a short pretty blonde woman. She came over next, clipboard in hand.

"This is Pam Neely," Tarah said. "Mitch is visiting."

Neely smiled, looked to Jacoby. "I need to verify a measurement. They've got two different numbers for your shoulder size." She pulled out a tailor's tape, gestured for Tarah to turn around.

Neely ran the tape across Tarah's shoulders then down her arm to the wrist, like someone being fitted for a coat. Which was exactly what was being done. "Sixty-three centimeters," she said, writing it down. "Just like I thought, they messed up on the metric conversion. Thanks."

Business concluded, we said hello to everyone else, chatted and laughed about the bad zipper. Apparently it was an early test and the results were somewhat anticipated, so nobody was too bent out of shape. As we talked, I told people I was trying to sell Tarah a house and they should let me sell them a new place, too.

Nobody asked for my card.

Chapter 14

TJ and I made our goodbyes and walked back to her office. We grabbed more coffee and conferred. Tarah sipped. "Anyone you want to ask about?"

"It's the blonde woman who measured you," I told her. "Pam Norton—no, Neely."

"Pamela Neely, and I'm impressed. Pam's a lead test engineer, by the way. Was she that obvious?"

"No, but it's what I do for a living—check folks out." I shrugged. "I've learned how to size people up, read their body language."

"She's been on my butt, literally, for two, maybe three months now, from when she transferred to this group."

"And you asked her to stop?"

TJ nodded. "Didn't help."

"Which is why you may need me."

"Yes. If you can find a way to get her to leave me alone without making waves."

"Why do you think she chose you? Do you know each other socially?"

"Are you asking whether I'm a lesbian?" She grinned.

A blast from movie trivia past. What Rachel the Replicant said to Deckard in *Blade Runner*. But I didn't bring it up to TJ. She'd only think I was weird. Instead, "Like Seinfeld said, *not that it matters*."

She laughed. "I suppose not. But I'm straight as the next chick."

"Why you, then, and not someone else?"

She sipped more coffee. "I've been hit on by women before. Guess I look the type, never wear much makeup, into lots of guy stuff like motorcycles and sports. But that's because I'm an old-fashioned tomboy."

"Her advances. Mostly low key?"

"At work, yes. But she's stalking me. She goes wherever I do. Happy hour, lunch away from JSC, you name it. And off campus she's more forward, aggressive."

"She ever cross the line into illegal acts? Trespassing or making threats?"

"No. She's followed me home, though. I could swear I've seen her behind me in traffic. Not just once, either. And if I go anyplace public with Trent, she usually shows up."

"Major Trent Collins, right?"

"Yes. Trent and I met last year down at the Cape. Now he's assigned here, over at Ellington." Ellington is the nearby airfield, once an Air Force base where George Bush had been stationed as a Reservist, unless you happened to ask Dan Rather. Now it's decommissioned, used for light commercial planes, NASA and other government flights for the Houston area.

"And he knows about Pam Neely."

"Yes. Trent doesn't take it as seriously as I do, though. But he doesn't have to work with her all day."

"Trent will back you up on your decision, though?"

"Oh, sure. Trent's a great guy. He'll support me regardless of what I choose, ignore her or report her. Or deck her with a right hook."

We both laughed. "I hope that won't be necessary," I said. "But what should I do now?"

"See her privately, get her to back off. If she does, I'm fine with it. If she continues, I'll file with HR."

"Which will get her reprimanded."

"Fired, probably. I'm considered a high-priority asset here. But I want to avoid that if possible."

"Okay. I'll do what I can."

"You didn't mention fees."

I took a standard contract from my attaché case. "This is a boilerplate agreement that all Texas private investigators use. Hourly plus expenses. I keep receipts for everything."

TJ read it, taking ten seconds where most people would spend five minutes. "Okay. Need an advance?"

"No. And I'll call each day, provide a summary. This shouldn't take long. Two days, maybe three. I'll bill you afterward."

Tarah Jacoby nodded and signed me up. Maybe I was now a junior astronaut?

I could only hope.

Chapter 15

TJ checked her watch. "It's nearly five. Trent and I are getting together for a beer. If you have time, I want you to meet him."

"Sure. And this will be off the clock."

"Suit yourself. I'm fine either way." She frowned. "Little Miss Neely may also show up."

"How would she know? This a regularly scheduled get-together for you and Trent?"

"No. Spur of the moment. He phoned this morning. But like I said, Pam's been following me when I leave the office."

"Okay. In that case, I'll follow you, too. Where are we going?"

"Know The Outpost?"

I nodded. "Long time."

So I exited the visitor gate and doubled over to the employee exit to wait. Tarah soon drove out, flashy in her silver Porsche. And right behind, a determined set to her jaw, Pam Neely in a turquoise Nissan Sentra.

I joined the westbound caravan until they turned off about a mile from the I-45 interchange. I circled the block a couple of times to build a time gap, parked and went inside.

The Outpost has been around for ages. It's an old wooden structure that was once a barracks for Army Reserves, or so they say. Now it's a rustic tavern that serves great homemade burgers and fries, cold beer and has become one of the time-honored astronaut hangouts.

I'd been there before and liked it. Nothing fancy, nothing to write home about, except for what's on the walls. Photos and souvenirs of astronauts are hung in layers everywhere. There are shoulder patches from missions as far back as Mercury and Gemini, pictures of the original seven astronauts, all autographed.

At one corner is a special display for the lost Apollo One crew—Grissom, White and Chaffee. The adjacent wall bears two other memorials, one for Challenger, the other for Columbia. Small, framed photos commemorate other astronauts who died in training crashes and other accidents.

These somber memorials are offset by many splashy posters and photos of the successful spaceflight ventures, astronaut movies like *The Right Stuff*, autographed placards and letters from the many space travelers who had stopped by The Outpost for a brew, burger and maybe some pool. There are other astronaut bars, of course, as astronauts have always been party animals. But none of the hangouts is as authentic as The Outpost.

* * *

Tarah Jacoby was at the jukebox. I bought a longneck Bud and joined her, where she punched up some Willie Nelson. Good pick. Pam Neely sat at the bar, pretending nonchalance, and a white wine before her. But within seconds, she joined us. "Hey. Decide on that house?" As Neely spoke, she nestled close to Tarah and linked arms. TJ smiled and played the good friend, but I could sense her discomfort.

"No. There's plenty of time. Trent and I want to talk about it."

"You and Trent going to shack up?"

Tarah batted her eyes and smiled at Neely. "Shack up? Lord, I haven't heard that one since high school." *Meow*.

I stuck my face into the fray. "Hi. We met over at JSC. Mitch King, King Realty? Interest rates are lowest in years. Any thought to moving up to a nicer place?"

That caught Neely flat, as intended. "Uh, no, I rent. I prefer living in Houston anyway."

"A long commute."

"The commute I can handle. It's the lack of night life I can't."

I was about to annoy Neely some more, hoping to get her to leave, when Major Trent Collins strode in. I knew who it was because Tarah's face lit up like fireworks.

Collins was everything an Air Force flyboy could be. He was tall, trim, athletic, handsome in his blue uniform and possessed of an aura of confidence. He was also black.

I admit being surprised. Even in our supposedly enlightened age, interracial dating isn't common. And Tarah didn't mention this to me. Personally, I don't care, though it might have oblique bearing on the case. But I'm used to my clients not telling me everything. Few do.

Tarah treated Trent to a smoochy kiss. I glanced at Pamela, who was openly seething at the display of affection. Her jealousy was intense and clear for anyone to see. Emotion that strong is impossible to conceal. Neely stomped away and sat down at the bar to stare at her wine.

Trent and TJ ignored the glower. The kiss continued for a while, then they broke off and laughed, the happy couple. "This is Trent," Tarah said.

"Figured it out right away," I said. "Saw the Air Force uniform and put two and two together. I'm a trained detective, after all."

Trent smiled and we shook. "TJ told me about you. Think you can help defuse Miss Pester?"

"I'll give it a try."

"We don't want any funny stuff. Nothing out of line."

"Not from me. A friendly chat should do it. At least I hope so."

He nodded. "What about the glower in the corner tonight?"

"Tired of being stared at?" I asked.

"You betcha."

"I can fix that." So I affected a tipsy stagger, walked over to the bar and sat down beside Pam Neely.

"I'm not interested in buying a house. I told you." She stared straight ahead, refusing to make eye contact.

I leaned closer, slurred my speech. "Sweetie, I'm not always selling houses. Sometimes I like to play house."

"What?"

"Wanna go somewhere else, get a drink? Maybe come over to my place, open a bottle of wine, check out some tunes. I got a great pad, super stereo. Surround sound, if you know what I mean."

"You got to be kidding."

"No, honey. I saw you looking at me. I can tell how a hot chick like you thinks. Read your mind, y'know. Psychic about chicks. We can party."

"Fuck off."

"Took the words out of my mouth. Fuck is what I wanna do. Whadda you say?"

"Christ!" Neely slammed her glass on the bar, grabbed her handbag and stormed out. I went back to TJ and Trent, sat down.

* * *

Trent grinned. "Let me guess. You weren't chatting about real estate."

"What was your first clue? But now I understand the depth of the problem," I said.

"At first she was just friendly," Tarah told me. "Then she was in my office, we were reviewing suit alterations. And she made a pass at me."

"A pass?" I asked. "Like I just did?"

"Nope. It was an office-type lawsuit-generating sexual harassment pass."

"She got physical."

"Yep. Told me I looked tense, started rubbing my shoulders. A second later she was going for my boobs."

Trent shook his head. "That's the same ploy every lecher in every office uses. You'd think they'd come up with a new tactic."

"What did you do?" I asked.

"I'm no naïve kid and I've been through this before, hit on by men and women both. And of course we had sexual harassment seminars. If I condoned her, it would only encourage more. I was polite but firm, told her clearly to take her hands off me."

"I did exactly the same thing to TJ. Rubbing her shoulders," Trent admitted. "But she didn't tell me to stop." He grinned.

TJ took Trent's hand, kissed it. "I was wondering how long you'd wait. Any more delay and I would've jumped your bones myself."

I broke in. "You teenagers are all alike, excessive public display of affection."

TJ raised an eyebrow at me. "We are simply researching aerospace situational ethics."

"Hey, it's only the taxpayer's money," I joked. "But tell me. Does Pamela back off when you and Trent are together?"

TJ shook her head. "Hell, no. She turns up the volume, if anything. Won't take no for an answer."

"She feels rejected and that brings on jealousy," I suggested. "Makes her even more aggressive, seeing competition."

"I've never given her the slightest encouragement," TJ confessed, shaking her head.

"Doesn't matter to a stalker," I said. "Even the average office creep will eventually get the message and give up. But if she's neurotic and fixated, she imagines you're just being coy, leading her on by toying with her affections."

Trent frowned. "She going to be trouble?"

"I don't know. You may want to go ahead and file a complaint."

"No," Tarah said. "Pamela's got a good work record and she's a decent person basically. I'd prefer you have a try first."

"Okay. Let me check up on her, see whether she's got an arrest record or anything questionable in her past."

"Why?"

I smiled sarcastically. "Blackmail, pure and simple. If she's got a skeleton in her closet, it's a lever I can use to persuade her to leave you alone."

"I don't want it coming back to Tarah," Trent said. "If Pamela thinks you're threatening her, she may go to the cops and try to turn the tables on TJ."

"I have no intention of confronting her directly. There are ways and I know them. And nothing will reflect back to Tarah."

Reassured, Tarah and Trent agreed. So I told them goodbye and headed out to the parking lot. On the way to my car, I happened to glance at Tarah's Porsche. Someone had busted out both taillights and had keyed the body all around. Wonder who it could have been? B follows A. Even Nancy Drew could have solved this one. I went back inside and got TJ and Trent.

Trent knelt at TJ's car, examining the damage, angry beyond words. "Went right into the bodywork. This'll cost a thousand at least. Probably more."

"Call the cops?" I asked.

TJ shook her head. "No one saw anything."

"Damn it," Trent said. "We know who it was."

"There's no proof. I'll turn it in to my insurance."

"If you want," Trent said, reluctant. "It's your car."

Tarah looked at me. "You see what I'm up against?"

"Give me a couple of days," I told her. "That's what you're paying me for."

Driving home, it occurred to me that I may have provoked the keying by insulting Neely but after a while I put it out of my mind.

Chapter 16

I slept well and late for a change, lazy for no particular reason. I ate a grapefruit and a power bar, then called Donna Boudreaux. Terrie's arraignment was postponed until three pm because the medical examiner's lab wanted to run more forensic tests. Donna had complained but the continuance was granted.

My contacts had nothing to tell me about our Mel Gibson lookalike, and Tony Vee was not answering his phone, so I decided to proceed with the Pam Neely case for a while. I didn't intend to spend a lot of effort on it. The consequences were trivial compared to the murder, and of course there were my feelings for Terrie Bartlett. It was toward her my thoughts were directed and I'd do whatever to free her from jail. What happened afterward was anybody's guess.

Regardless, I had to address the matter involving Pam Neely. I checked my Internet sources but she had no record except a couple of parking tickets. I wanted some background info so I called a friend, Susan Kennedy, and drove down to her place to chat.

* * *

Susan Kennedy's office is in a small building right behind Borders Books at Alabama and Kirby, on the fringes of the Greenway Plaza district. I know the neighborhood because it's just down the street from Little Woodrow's, where I often drink beer, play pool and eat carryout from Mission Burritos next door. Sadly, Little Woodrow's had recently been razed to put up some swank condo. Another one bites the dust.

I parked, went upstairs to Kennedy Properties Development. The front desk was empty, but a little buzzer prompted Susan to lean out of her office door and wave me in. "Take a load off," she said, sat down and lit a cigarette.

Susan is a petite, attractive woman in her early forties, short-cropped brunette tinged with gray, kind brown eyes and a welcome, mischievous smile. She is herself a relative of *the* Kennedys, her family but a remote and church-mouse poor faction. The Kennedys are nothing if not a prolific bunch.

I first met Susan when teaching a class in firearms safety for the Pink Rangers. Most gays and lesbians are non-violent and many are outright pacifists. But night riding rednecks out for a little weekend fun of gay bashing and a predatory cycle of ordinary thugs who considered gays easy prey, and sadly so, led to a change of heart for many who grew weary of being victimized.

Since the advent of concealed handgun carry in Texas, thousands of citizens have lined up to acquire permits. Gays and lesbians are a bit behind the curve, but many finally began to arm themselves. Street crimes against homosexuals dropped precipitously and whether it is due to an increased police presence in response to gay activist complaints or from the possibility of the mugger getting blown away by a member of the Pink Rangers is moot. The gay community is a measure safer these days.

Susan Kennedy and her life partner Carrie Baker formed their own branch of the Rangers, naming it the Gunnery Gals. Most of their membership came from an informal group of similarly minded women of the *femme* persuasion.

Straight men segregate themselves into many categories, like rednecks, hard rockers, nerds and the newly defined metrosexuals and millennials. Straight women, gay men and gay women do the same, each according to individual tastes in biology or social mores. Among the self-induced separation of gay women are the *femmes*. These are women who maintain a conventional straight appearance, including makeup and clothing, their derogatory nickname being *Lipstick Lezzies*. They eschew the company of "butch" women, the stereotypical lesbians who wear masculine clothes and affect a rough attitude. Some *femme* women are also bisexual or occasionally dabble with straight men for sheer variety and fun.

I found this out at a party to celebrate several of the Gunnery Gals passing their concealed handgun carry exams. Susan and Carrie made pitchers of margaritas and kept them coming until everyone was pleasantly looped, myself included.

Knowing these women were gay didn't prevent me from looking at them through tequila goggles and assessing many as attractive. And although I remained aloof and detached, or so I told myself, I couldn't help but feel there was some mutual chemistry from a couple of the women. After weighing this in my mind, I took the easy route, excused myself and carefully meandered home.

I asked Susan about this a few days later and she laughed. "Was it Jennifer? Or maybe Cherie?"

"Jennifer. I think. I'd had a few drinks."

"A few? Both of you were fucked up. And speak of fucking, you should have gone for it. Jen pulls the old switcheroo occasionally, when she gets a wild hair up her ass. I guarantee you'd have enjoyed yourself."

"I'm not into one night stands, Suze. At least not anymore."

She grinned, shrugged. "You asked." And so went my limited introduction to social lesbianism and the vagaries of getting a wild hair up one's ass.

Chapter 17

"What brings you up here?" Suze asked. "You wanted some advice, right?"

"You said you know Pamela Neely."

Suze laughed. "Carrie calls her the Iron Bitch."

"That's pretty harsh."

"So we're supposed to be all for one, one for all? Us lezzies gotta stick together?" She stubbed out her cigarette. "Shit, Mitch. You're an old laid back Montrose type and you've got your head on straight for the most part. Gay women are like anybody else. We have the right to like or dislike anyone. Okay?"

I felt pretty small. Time after time over the past few weeks I'd been stepping in it, speaking without thinking, or as my old history professor would say, *setting my mouth into motion, then going off and leaving it running.*

"Sorry. Got me there," I admitted. "But why such a negative assessment from Carrie? And do you agree?"

"Somewhat. Pam's like some men, perpetual hard on."

"She is a bit pushy."

"That's more polite than iron bitch."

"We private detectives are always demure and modest in our criticism of others."

"Bullshit."

"Bullshit it is." We laughed. "But tell me about Pamela Neely. What sort of person is she?"

"I assume this is confidential?"

"Yep."

Susan lit another smoke. "Pam made an ass of herself about a year ago. Remember Cherie from the party? Made a move for you but you ignored her?"

"Being my demure self again. Redhead, short, a bit chunky but cute?"

"Yeah, that's Cherie." Suze nodded. "Pam had the hots for her, got into a major snit when Cherie had a fling with her, then tossed her off for a guy."

"That would put a kink into anyone's love life."

"Cherie is who she is, one of those rare and genuine bisexuals. She likes both men and women equally, sleeps around, and makes no bones about it."

"Bisexual, you say?"

"Yes. And very much at ease with her orientation."

"Pam Neely knew this?"

"She did. But she got this crush on Cherie and wouldn't let well enough alone."

"I'm not very good with hetero relationships as is," I admitted. "Gay, I'm totally in the dark."

Suze shrugged. "Who knows anything about sexuality? Everything is just a theory and all the theories are bullshit."

"That much I do know. Sometimes a cigar is just a cigar."

"You got that right," she said. "Take me, for example. I was married."

"Married?"

"Yeah. Guy I knew since junior high, then college together at San Marcos. And I thought I was straight. Or at least I'd been told this all my life and was afraid to think otherwise."

"When did you know you were gay?"

"About three years into the marriage."

"What happened? If you don't mind."

"An old college girlfriend of mine was in Houston on business. Girlfriend in the platonic sense, I mean. She'd come out of the closet herself and we got to talking, drinking. As they say, one thing led to another."

"How'd your husband take it?"

"Things hadn't gone well for us in a long time. Jim knew something was wrong. Parted as friends." She smiled. "Well, at least not enemies."

"So you found out you were gay after living the straight scene. Not an easy change in lifestyle."

"No, it's not. But relationships are difficult, straight or gay."

"And Cherie?" I asked.

"Tell the truth and just between you and me, she's a bit of a slut. Sleeps around, either doesn't want to or can't commit to anyone for any length of time."

"But you say Pamela knew this, knew what she was getting into."

"Pam's like a lot of people in love. They think they can change things."

"Never works."

"Never," Suze said. "No matter how much you like someone, want someone, no matter how much you love them, and it won't make that person love you in return. Most people can't get that through their heads."

I thought about my intense affection for Terrie Bartlett, wondered whether it influenced my decisions of late. I also wondered about her feelings for me, if any. Time for this later. "So what happened between Pam Neely and Cherie?"

"Pam kept at it, phoning Cherie, driving by her apartment and where she works. She even stuck a pair of her panties in an envelope, left them in Cherie's mailbox."

"Did Cherie lead her on?"

"The opposite. Cherie was open about it from the beginning. Everyone knows Cherie's reputation, no surprises."

"What happened eventually?"

"We'd go for happy hour, all of us. Pam would show up, usually drunk. Got everybody pissed at her. So we froze her out, asked her not to come around, to stay away."

"Did she finally get the message?"

Suze lit a third cigarette. "Pam's doing it again, isn't she?"

"Yeah. My client."

"They ever have a relationship? Pam and your client?"

"No. My client isn't even gay. Pam just made up her mind and that was that."

"Sounds like our very own Pamela Neely. Open the dictionary to *obsessive*, there's her photo."

"Any suggestions?" I asked.

"Besides dumping her body in the nearest bayou?"

"Besides."

She shook her head. "Good luck. You'll need it. It took everything short of an ass-whupping to get Pam off our backs."

"When did she give up, finally?"

Suze puffed, thought about this. "Three months ago."

I nodded. "That's about the same time she started on my client."

"Transfer of fixation."

"Sadly, yes."

"I think you're screwed, Mitch."

"It figures. My portion of woe these days is pretty substantial."

Chapter 18

On the way to my car, I checked with Donna Boudreaux again. She was offline so I left a callback. Then I drove over to Grif's Tavern in Montrose for a late lunch.

Grif's is a Houston institution, one of the original sports bars. They have a breezy front porch, patio out back for parties and a general atmosphere of friendship that's absent from most other places. Grif's has a famous hamburger, cold beer and lots of TV screens so you can check out your favorite game. The place changed hands recently but the ambiance, and more important to me right now, the hamburger, is still delightful.

I went in, sat at the bar. Helen was bartending. She's an attractive Latina with a pleasant smile and a fun sense of humor. Helen pulled a bottle of Bud from the cooler and raised her eyebrows to me.

"Nope," I shook my head. "Iced tea."

Helen poured me a big glass from the jug. "Doing business today?"

"Thought I was, but it hasn't worked out so far. Lots of wheel-spinning."

Helen grinned. "I have days like that. Join the club."

I took a long swig of tea, then, to restore my spirits, I ordered a cheeseburger with plenty of jalapenos.

A half hour later, the burger was just a spicy burn in the back of my throat and I was contemplating that beer when my phone beeped. Should be Donna calling back, so I answered without checking the number. "Hi there, sweetheart. You miss me?"

"Yeah, but don't let it get around. People will talk." The voice was deep and masculine. Joe Duggan.

"You're always teasing me," I replied. "That's why my heart sings for you, big boy."

"Jesus, Mitch. I'm glad I didn't put you on speakerphone. Wondered if you're busy? Thought you might come down to my place, say hello."

"Been there. Done that."

"Yeah, but this time I got a surprise."

"What?"

"Young lady sitting here asking for you."

"Julia Roberts?" I sipped my tea.

"Guess again."

"Julia Child? That would be my luck."

"Wrong. She's dead anyway. Try Theresa Bartlett."

My heart jumped. "What?"

"We're letting her go. All charges dropped."

"What?"

"That all you can say, *what?* So ask me why."

"Why?"

"Ballistics ID'd the slug from Trevillian. Forty-one Magnum, striations indicate it's probably from a Dan Wesson."

"And the gun she had—"

"A .357," Duggan finished my sentence. "Bullet wouldn't fit if you used a sledgehammer. And guess what the CSI boys dug out of a fence post by Trevillian's pool."

"A .357 slug."

"Right."

I realized the significance of this turnabout. "So Terrie stops being a murder suspect and becomes a murder witness."

"Right again. I always knew you were a bright kid."

"I'm on the way. Don't let her leave."

"Not to worry. Meierhoff's taken her under his wing. He's looking out for her."

I felt a twinge. Meierhoff sticking his nose in. "Be there in fifteen minutes."

I made it in ten.

Chapter 19

Duggan's office was full of people but at least Joe had tidied up somewhat, as there were chairs available. Joe was at his desk, on the phone. Terrie sat in one chair, looking tired and drained. In the chair opposite was Paul Holloway, the assistant Harris County prosecutor. Holloway brought a clerk along, who stood beside him, holding a sheaf of documents. Meierhoff was leaning against the wall, flirting with the female guard who brought Terrie down from the jail. I took a spot near Meierhoff and tried to look essential.

Terrie finally had her cigarettes. Someone had bought her a pack of Winstons. She finished one, stubbed it out, and took another from her shirt pocket. Before she lit the cigarette, she twisted off the filter and tossed it into the ashtray. You weren't supposed to smoke in the offices but nobody said anything.

Joe Duggan hung up and looked around. "Okay. Ms. Bartlett, I just spoke with your attorney, Donna Boudreaux. She regrets that she's delayed in court. But since we're releasing you with no charges, it's not necessary your attorney be present. Right, Mr. Holloway?"

Paul Holloway straightened in his chair before speaking. He is a small man, scarcely five-four, impeccably dressed in a tailored silk suit, monogrammed white shirt and handmade Italian tie. He has sculpted hair and perfectly manicured nails. His manner is also precise, but it is his education and intellect that makes Holloway so distinctive. He set academic records throughout school and his brilliant legal mind is well known throughout the state. Holloway's family could also point proudly to generations of prestigious and wealthy lawyers and jurists.

Holloway has toyed with running for Texas Attorney General, but thus far was unable to gain sufficient Republican Party backing. His problems are lack of patience and a clear disdain for everyday people, traits he makes little effort to conceal. This arrogant streak earned him the nickname *Prince Paul*, but if he could learn to temper his intelligence with some basic decency, he might well end up in the AG's office yet.

* * *

Prosecutor Holloway reached up and the clerk handed him a typed report. "Yes. Very well. I assume that Ms. Bartlett has already received her personal effects and has been formally released from detention?" He squinted at the jail guard.

She didn't answer because she was busy copying her phone number for Meierhoff.

Holloway cleared his throat in a nervous twitch, like Emil Jennings did before addressing his students in *The Blue Angel*. "Officer Quinlan? May we please have your cooperation, just for a moment? Then you may resume your more important duties."

"Excuse me, sir. Yes, the suspect has got all cleared out."

"Officer Quinlan," Prince Paul pounced on her mistake. "I must remind you that Ms. Bartlett is not a *suspect*." Quinlan gave a noncommittal nod and Holloway continued. "Yes. Very well. Ms. Bartlett, since you have 'got all cleared out,' you are free to leave without any charges whatsoever. Will you be so kind as to sign the release declaration? Thank you. And here? Thank you so much. Yes." Terrie scribbled where Holloway indicated. "Very well." He handed the papers to the clerk.

He turned back to Terrie. "Ms. Bartlett, I wish to issue my personal condolences in the death of your companion, and I also wish to apologize for the inconvenience and difficulties through which the county has inadvertently put you. Let me also assure you

98

that Lieutenant Duggan, on behalf of the Houston Police, echoes my sentiment. Is that not correct, Lieutenant?" Holloway glanced cursorily to Duggan, and having thrown him a bone, turned away without waiting.

Joe was about to speak but now clamped his mouth shut and rolled his eyes to the ceiling.

"Yes. Very well." Holloway summoned his most unctuous voice. "Ms. Bartlett, we similarly wish to assure you that the police will make every effort to apprehend the individual who perpetrated this crime, and that my office will provide a punctual and vigorous prosecution of this individual to the fullest extent of the law."

Lecture concluded, Prince Paul stood up and treated us with a smile as sincere as a politician's promise. His assistant gathered the papers and they left without another word.

I figured the Attorney General nomination would be a while coming.

Duggan stared at Holloway's disappearing back, waited a beat, and then said, "Yes. Very fucking well." Everyone laughed. Even Terrie managed a grin.

* * *

Joe smiled warmly to Terrie. "In all seriousness, Ms. Bartlett, we need to proceed. Detective Meierhoff will be taking your case. He's a top investigator and he'll get results. Detective, will you tell Ms. Bartlett what you've done so far?"

Meierhoff hunkered down in front of Terrie. "Lieutenant Duggan and I have reviewed the file. We don't have a lot to work with yet, but we'd like you to look at our photo logs. You might spot the suspect. If not, our sketch artist can make a composite drawing. Can you come in tomorrow, after you've had some rest?"

"Tomorrow? Sure." Terrie took another cigarette from the pack, broke the filter off, and tapped the loose tobacco down before sticking the end in her mouth and lighting up. She took a long drag and sighed. "Right now I'm so tired I can't think."

Meierhoff continued: "Now this may be difficult, Terrie, but it needs to be dealt with. We've talked with your business attorney, Mr. Converse. He will take care of all the arrangements concerning Mr. Trevillian. His parents live in Spokane and they've asked that the body be flown there right away. Do you have any objections?"

Terrie lowered her gaze and shook her head. "It's okay," she said quietly. "They never liked me anyway. Probably best. I couldn't handle a funeral."

"All right." Meierhoff nodded. "One more thing. It may not be safe at your house because the assailant is still at large. Do you have somewhere to stay? Friends? Relatives?"

"She can stay with me," I heard myself say.

Duggan looked sharply at me but remained quiet.

"I have plenty of room," I went on. "Terrie can use my daughter's bedroom. I'll bring her down here tomorrow for a look at the mug shots. And I think it's best she have some protection, considering that she may be in danger."

"Ms. Bartlett," Duggan asked, "will that be all right with you? Mr. King does have a valid point about your safety. But if you'd rather us assign an officer?"

"I want to stay with Mitch, er, Mr. King."

Duggan looked around the room. "Objections?"

There were none.

Meierhoff went off somewhere with the female guard, presumably to discuss an important aspect of the case. Duggan walked us downstairs. There were big *No Smoking* signs in all the halls and stairwells, so Terrie felt compelled to dart ahead of us out the main door and light up again. Before I could push the door open and join her, Joe restrained me with a gentle hand on my shoulder.

I waited, impatient.

"How's that new pistol?" he asked.

"It's fine."

"Hope you don't have to use it. Creates lots of paperwork when people get shot."

"I'll try to lessen your caseload, Lieutenant. Anything else?"

"Yeah." Joe looked out at Terrie. She was puffing away, staring through the glass doors at us, frowning. "We've been friends a long time, Mitch. You've never let your cock do your thinking for you. Don't start now."

"This is strictly business."

"Sure it is. Just tell me I didn't see that gleam in your eye."

"She's attractive, is all. I can take care of myself."

"Yeah, right." Joe squeezed my shoulder. "And I'm only talking bullshit." He dropped his hand and walked back up the stairs.

I went out to be with Terrie.

Chapter 20

I told Terrie where we were headed, up to the Heights. She was so tired she didn't seem to care and only responded in monosyllables. I said I was divorced, that my teenage daughter Chrissie sometimes came to visit from Phoenix and the bedroom was kept ready. Terrie grunted. My daughter's clothes should fit her well enough until we went to her own house tomorrow. *Grunt.* Would she like me to pick up a pizza? *Grunt.*

In the MGB, she lit another cigarette, smoke flying up and out of the open cockpit as I drove through traffic. When she flipped her first butt away, I cautioned her, redirecting her instead toward the tiny ashtray.

"Whatever."

I took advantage of the cellular superhighway, phoning ahead to Star Pizza to order a *Starburst*, arguably the finest pizza in town. Star Pizza is in a remodeled house just off Greenbriar. We sat on the sun porch of the pizzeria until the order was ready. I drank a Dos Equis and Terrie smoked three cigarettes.

Next, we drove up Shepherd, cut over to Waugh, headed north until it became Heights Boulevard. A few more blocks, a right turn and we were home.

The Houston Heights has passed through several incarnations. Originally, it held summer homes for the Houston elite, sitting above the mosquito-infested flatlands to the south—Houston proper. The Heights declined to near slum status then resurged in popularity. There are all sorts of houses and apartments, from mansions to little clapboard shacks. I live in a smallish two-story brick colonial that my wife and I picked up before real estate prices went ballistic. When the divorce came through, she moved to Phoenix to be with her father and I bought out her half of the equity with the inheritance from my grandfather.

* * *

By my front door is a modest sign, *Mitchell King, Investigations.* I'd been tempted to add a magnifying glass and maybe a machine gun logo to irritate the neighbors, but talked myself out of it.

I parked under the carport at the side of the house, next to my 4Runner and walked Terrie around the back and through the kitchen into the house. She was so tired she was wobbling. It was a chore to steer her and avoid losing the pizza, but they both made it unscathed.

I switched off the alarm, set the pizza in the kitchen, and led her upstairs. I showed her the bathroom and extra towels and gave her a brand new toothbrush, then took her to Chrissie's room.

Terrie sat unmoving on the bed while I went through the chest of drawers for some clothes. I studiously bypassed the frilly underwear and found Terrie a flannel nightgown and some T-shirts. I pulled some jeans and a bathrobe from the closet. Everything should fit, I thought, Chrissie had grown so tall.

"You might feel better after a shower."

"Too tired. Just want to sleep."

"The pizza. Want a slice?"

"Okay."

That was all the response I was going to get. I went back down and popped a slice into the microwave. When it was warm, I carried it up on a plastic plate. The bedroom door was open and Terrie lay stretched on the bed, snoring softly. She'd begun to undress before falling asleep. The work shirt was on the floor beside the bed and her T-shirt had ridden up, exposing a smooth, tanned expanse of skin that began a few inches below her navel and ran to her upper ribcage. She wore no bra and the rounded undersides of her breasts were visible, the edge of the cloth just covering her nipples. There were no tan lines.

I looked down at her for a moment, swallowed hard, then turned away, switched off the light and quietly closed the door.

* * *

I walked back down the stairs, into the kitchen and ran smack into Joe Duggan.

The slice of pizza went flying. "Jesus! You scared the shit out of me!"

"Shouldn't leave your door unlocked. Be glad it was only Unca Joe." He grinned. "The lady okay?"

"Yeah. Tired. She crashed out the second we got here." I frowned at Joe. "But why are you here?"

In reply, Joe raised his right hand, fingers up. Time for the Duggan count off.

"Three reasons," he said. "One." The first finger went down. "Paying my gambling debt. I put a six pack of Dortmunder in the fridge."

"Okay."

"Two," he said, and the middle finger was tucked away. "We got a pool game scheduled. Right?"

"Right." I had forgotten.

"And three, I owe you an apology." He broke off the count and stuck his hand out. "I was off base today, what I said about you and Terrie Bartlett. Shake?"

"No problem, Joe. No offense meant, none taken." We shook. "Want some pizza?"

"Always. First we oughta clean up that piece you dumped on the floor." Joe grinned. "Bugs."

Bugs.

* * *

Spill cleaned, new pizza microwaved, beer at the ready and friends again, we walked into the poolroom for our game. My one true passion in life is pool. I converted the garage into a billiard room, which is why my cars are parked outside. My nine-foot classic Brunswick-Balke dominates the room. The only concession to cordiality is a small wet bar in the corner.

Joe draped his jacket over a barstool, shucked out of his shoulder rig and Kevlar vest and hung his castoffs from a coat hook on the wall. The Les Baer .45 dangled in its holster like a medieval war club.

We uncovered the table and got ready. I keep several good cues for guests, and Joe selected a McDermott. The custom Richard Black is mine alone. We flipped for break and began.

A little demon came and sat on my shoulder that night. It may have come unbidden or it may have been invited by my subconscious. It came nonetheless. I'm better than Joe and he knows it, but I usually play a bit offhand to even the playing field. Tonight, though, I was relentless. We shot ten games of nine ball for ten bucks each, I savaged him in all of them, and it didn't take much more than an hour.

Later, we sat at the kitchen counter, drinking the last of the beer and picking at the leftover pizza. Joe looked at me with his crooked grin. "Sure had your shit together, Mitch. I got skunked." He dug in his pocket and counted out a hundred dollars. It was nearly all he had.

"Look," I told him. "Keep the money. Consider this square for your help on that insurance case last month."

Joe's grin disappeared. "You beat the crap outta me, that I can deal with. You make like it doesn't matter, that's bullshit. Don't patronize me. Okay?"

"Okay." I took the money and folded it into my pocket. "Thanks."

"Don't mention it. I'll get you back next time anyway." Joe drained the bottle, stood up. He threaded his broad shoulders into the straps of his holster, picked up his windbreaker and ballistic vest. "Getting late. Margaret will be worried."

I was still embarrassed for what happened. "Joe..." I was hesitant.

He cut me off with a wave. "Like I say, done is done. Give Meierhoff a call in the morning." And without so much as a *Goodbye my Love*, he walked out.

Chapter 21

The shower was running when I woke the next morning, so I went downstairs. I was into my second cup of coffee and reading the *Chronicle* when Terrie walked into the kitchen. She looked brighter and prettier than yesterday. Her face was scrubbed, hair shiny and still damp. There was a hint of eye shadow and lipstick. She wore the bathrobe and a pair of Chrissie's old bedroom slippers. They had bunny ears and looked a little silly.

"Going on an Easter Egg hunt?" I asked.

She looked down at her feet and giggled. "Saw them in the closet and couldn't resist." She turned this way and that, posing. "Stylish, huh?"

"Latest Paris fashion. They had a TV special about it."

Terrie frowned. "Huh?"

"Never mind. Just kidding. Want some coffee?"

"Love some. Got any cream?"

"Sorry, only the artificial junk."

"Have to do. Any port in a storm."

That struck a little close to home so I changed the subject. "Will it be all right, our going out to your house this morning? I mean, so soon after."

"I know what you mean!" Her voice was sharp. Then she smiled again. "Sorry. So much has happened." She looked out the kitchen window and sighed. "Sure. I can deal with it. I got to. Need my clothes and other stuff anyway."

I poured her a cup, laid out the creamer and sugar, then sat down to finish the paper. She took the chair across and ladled three spoons of sugar and two of creamer into the cup. I kept the sports and handed her the rest of the paper. She turned the pages, not really reading. She absently reached into the robe pocket and out came cigarettes and a lighter. She glanced around, snapped to the fact I didn't smoke. "Oh, I can go out back."

"That's okay. I don't mind, really," I lied. I got up, dug a plastic ashtray from a cabinet. "Hang onto this. It's the only one I've got."

"Thanks." So she lit up and saturated my kitchen, my clothes and me with fumes, which I ignored. I'd somehow manage.

Terrie was one of those people who has trouble sitting still. Her legs were crossed and her left foot bounced nervously, the bunny ears flopping up and down. I let her bounce while I read about the Astros' new and very successful season. I checked the Krazy Kat clock on the kitchen wall, its big round eyes and black tail going back and forth with the time. My daughter Chrissie had bought it for me and I loved the thing.

"Nine thirty," I said. "Time to get going. We have to be at police headquarters later so you can check the ID photos. We can grab lunch in between. I'm going to hit the shower."

"You go ahead. I'll clean up, turn off the coffee." She stood up and came around to where I sat. She put her hand on my arm and again the electric shock of desire coursed through me. "Thanks so much for your help, Mitch." She smiled. "Sorry I haven't been too nice to you. It's not intentional. I've been so tense. Give me time. Okay?"

She leaned over and kissed me lightly on the cheek. As she did, her robe gaped open and she was naked to the waist. I looked at her full breasts and brown nipples, my mind swirled with desire and I did not immediately turn away.

I stood under the shower and let the water massage my back and shoulders. I tried to set my thoughts at ease but I was enraptured with Terrie and my thoughts were not my own. Neither was my body. Seeing her on the bed last night, and again just now, created images of passionate embrace. As I dwelt on her, my body behaved as bodies will and would not be assuaged.

No time for this, I decided, and finally resorted to the approved alternative.

Chapter 22

When I got dressed, I phoned Meierhoff at the cop shop. "You have reached Homicide," he announced in a singsong tone. "If you're calling to report a murder, press one. If you've just been killed, press two."

"Aren't you worried I might be some bigwig?"

"Not. They never listen to anyone but themselves anyway. Besides, I caught your name on caller ID. What's up?"

"Joe asked me to check in. We're headed out to Terrie's—the Trevillian place. Then we'll be down your way."

"The crime boys are finished out there. They cleared the scene a while ago. You don't have to worry about messing things up. They'll be out later to take down the signs and the stay away tapes." He paused for a second. "How is she?"

"Hanging in there." I wanted to know, so I asked, "Why?"

"Just checking. She is one of my case files, after all." His voice was edged with irritation. "What time are you bringing her down for the ID session?"

"Probably after lunch."

"Okay. See you then. Gotta run."

Terrie came into the kitchen wearing her own jeans and Chrissie's *Nine Inch Nails* concert jersey. "Her jeans are too small. Shirt's okay."

As we got up to leave, Terrie noticed the pistol in its holster on my waist. "You carry that thing around with you all the time?"

"Mostly. It's like having car insurance. Never know when you'll need it."

Terrie issued a smallish grumpy complaint, shrugged and we headed out. She lived on Mission Vista Lane in the Mission Courts subdivision of Memorial. We took the 4Runner because its air conditioning would be welcome against the scorcher that was forecast today. Besides, Terrie was going to snag some clothes and the MG's trunk would be jam-packed if you put in a pair of sneakers and a comb.

As I picked up I-10 and headed west, Terrie was fidgeting, uneasy. "While you were in the shower, I called a girlfriend. Judy Hansen?"

"Yeah?"

"She lives in Dallas—Richardson actually."

"Yes?" I prompted. She seemed reluctant to be forthcoming and I had to draw her out, one sentence at a time.

"She wants me to come up and visit for a few days."

I thought about this. She'd be okay, out of harm's way, and the change would refresh her spirit. I wanted her to be here with me, but some time away would probably be best.

"Sounds good. When?"

"Later today, tonight. I need to get out of town, okay?"

"How long will you be?"

"Couple days. I'll call her and let her know but my cell needs charging. I've got the charger at the house. We can make flight reservations. I'll put it on my card."

"No problem. Whatever's fair. The police thing will probably take several hours. We'll stop back at my place so you can get online, buy your ticket, charge up your phone at the same time. Better plan for flying out about eight. That will give you leeway." I didn't want to let her go but I had to accept it. She'd be fine and I could search for our Mel Gibson lookalike in the meantime. With Terrie in Dallas, I'd have free reign.

Chapter 23

We dropped off I-10 and cut over to Terrie's neighborhood. Despite the street name, there wasn't a church in sight. Mission Vista is a quiet residential avenue set with tidy homes owned by middle executives, software engineers and dentists. The roadway curved right, then left. The asphalt pavement was clean and free from potholes. Perfect lawns ran in unbroken planes of green from perfect home to perfect street. No sidewalks. People in this neighborhood didn't use them anyway.

Illegal immigrant gardening crews fired up gasoline-powered noisemakers to clip the grass and blow the cuttings onto the neighbor's lawn. Sprinklers cast rainbow sprays onto the thirsty ground and indifferent driveways, raining on the just and unjust alike.

Two dogs drifted lazily across their turf, checking for imaginary cats to chase. A young woman energetically pushed a three hundred dollar baby stroller along the street. She wore the approved uniform of the day, white polo shirt and khaki scooter shorts. Chubby chalk-white legs pumped and shoulder length blonde hair bobbed with each purposeful stride.

We were knee-deep in the heartland of the yuppie turned millennial. This is now the focal point of American culture, a new paradigm of contentment, banner around which we are meant to rally like sparrows flocking to a crust of bread.

Regard, if you will, that primal diorama of the American Dream depicted so pristinely and devoutly by Norman Rockwell, and you behold a cheerful land, peopled wide and far with happy whiteface folk, farm and factory families all. Mom in the kitchen bustling, joyful in her destined place, mammoth turkey basted to a golden turn. Seven kids attend, apple-cheeked and scruffy. Pigtails, bare feet, childlike grins with missing teeth abound. Slingshot sags eternally from ragged overalls, mongrel dog dwells forever at the door. Meantime Dad hefts hoe or wrench or welding torch toward the future, grateful cog, prideful of his mighty labors, certain in the way he knows as right and true.

Remembrance of a Pangloss age that never was.

No Rockwell depicts the land in truth. No print displays poverty or disease. No incest, drunkenness, bigotry. No photo-painted image of the Klan perverting Christian word, no montage of the battered wife, children born unwanted and unloved, factory worker without hope for change. No *Post* cover featured black man bruised by thuggish cop, enslavement of the migrant picker, rotted lungs of miners in the dark. Yet these too are but portions of our past and aspects of our souls.

So is it now as then, our nation's tender coin possesses both an obverse and a reverse strike. The proper framework of our yearned-for lives is summed for us within the newfound Rockwells of the Magic Box and the Internet. We fret for toothpaste and for bran, for clothes and shoes and fragrances defining front of fashion and our very worth. Mom now sustains manifold roles of chef and courtesan, financial expert and social arbiter. Dad must now prevail at work, with family and with peers at golf. Added burdens fall to kids, who now are pressed to fit within the narrow mold, to know and say and do and wear the stylish thing.

TV and the Net are the source, the wellsprings from which all goodness and all wisdom flows, supplanting sage advice, tradition of religion, quest for *satori*. Thus all the homes aligned just so, the cars just so, the trendy gimmicks, clothes and food and feelings just so, the lives just so.

Yet beneath this sameness and vapid thoughtlessness, beneath the veneer of formed and ordered lives, there runs a deeper current. A darkness. Pry beneath the fancy cars, tennis courts and ballet class. Lift the rock. Still there thrives prejudice, incest, drugs and hate. Brutality and wanton ignorance, poverty of mind and dearth of spirit, with us now as ever was.

And ever shall be.

Chapter 24

Terrie's house was midway down the block. It was unassuming and modest for the neighborhood, a rambling split-level with earth-tone slate roof, vinyl siding, small curved drive in front. It looked much like the other houses on the street except for crime scene placards stuck up everywhere, so the neighbors could know everything or at least could make up stories about it.

I pulled into the drive, switched off the engine and looked at Terrie. She sat chewing her lower lip, staring at the front door as though an important message were printed there. I waited for Terrie to catch herself, asked, "Ready?"

She nodded briefly.

I got out and looked around. The air was warm, heavy with moisture, and the street quiet. The engine ticked as it cooled. No other sound or movement. I went around and opened Terrie's door.

She hesitated a bit longer, then joined me.

"Keys?" I asked. She nodded again, dug a set from her jeans, and handed them over.

The front door had yellow plastic warning tape crisscrossed like some giftwrap they'd do if you won a house on TV. But first prize here was not something you'd appreciate.

I cut the tape with my Kershaw, unlocked the door and waited for Terrie. Reluctantly at first, then with some determination to her stride, she led me in. I followed, hand on the butt of my pistol.

The lab folks had left the drapes closed and the air conditioning on, so the house was dark and cool. Terrie stood quietly in the tiled entrance hall, walked down three steps into the sunken living room and over to the big picture window. She pulled the drape cord and sunlight streamed in.

The decor was sparse Eurostyle, a big white leather sectional dominating. There were some chrome and black aluminum lamps placed artistically, a hefty glass-topped coffee table in front of the sofa. A monster stereo system and enormous flat-screen TV sat along the wall. The living room opened into a combination den and dining area, then kitchen. There was a hallway to the side that apparently led to bedrooms and bath.

The living room was spotless and neatly arranged, but something was missing. What? Then I realized there was nothing to read. No book. No magazines. No newspapers. Nothing. Terrie and her departed boyfriend must live without benefit of the written word. Maybe they were like my aunt, who once told a friend, "We don't need any books. We already have some." I half expected Montag the fireman from *Fahrenheit 451* to walk in, eating an apple and jealously guarding his secret dog-eared copy of *David Copperfield*.

I'd go nuts here in two days.

* * *

Terrie sighed, roused herself. "I can't think about what happened, don't want to." She scurried for the hallway. "I'll grab my stuff. We need to get the fuck out of here."

"Hang on. Let me check first." I eased my pistol from the holster and preceded her down the hall. I looked in the bathrooms, closets and bedrooms. The house was empty as an Episcopal Church parking lot on Super Bowl Sunday.

While Terrie packed, I went to the kitchen. Through a sort of breakfast area, a sliding glass door led to the pool. I unlatched the door and stepped out, took a break and looked around.

The entire back yard had been converted to flagstone patio. There were little tubby cacti and tall spindly fern things and other plants around the edges of the patio. Concrete frogs, too. A high redwood fence circled the yard, so Terrie could work on her allover tan.

Best not to think about that.

On the patio in front of me, a human figure outlined in blue chalk, just like the movies. The pool was smallish and kidney shaped, with a whirlpool annexed at the far end. A small gate at the back of the fence led outside. On a thick fencepost near the gate, CSI had drawn a rough blue circle, bullseye surrounding the hole where Terrie's bullet was dug out.

It made perfect sense. Trevillian chases Mel the Biker outside. Mel turns and fires. Boyfriend goes down, Terrie grabs the gun and shoots back. Everything lined up.

"Mitch!" Terrie's voice made me jump.

I ran back inside, pulling my pistol. I skidded to a stop when I saw her by the front door, puffing on yet another cigarette and pacing. There were two soft side paisley flight bags and a matching overnight case on the floor beside her. Embarrassed at my high level but uncalled for response, I quickly tucked the gun away.

"Can we get the fuck out?" Terrie said. Without waiting for an answer, she snatched up the smaller case and went outside.

I backtracked to lock the patio door, grabbed the remaining bags and joined her. She thumbed a remote control and the garage door rattled up, showing off a black BMW sedan and a spiffy red Mazda Miata.

"You sure you're going to need your car?" I told her. "I don't think it's wise, driving around by yourself."

"Hey!" She looked me in the eye and puffed angrily, making her bangs fly up. "I've been through hell." She was angry with me but I loved the gesture. "Having my car will make me feel better. And I like my independence. All right?"

I shrugged. "We're due at the cop shop. Let's drop your car by my place. You can get it later."

Terrie replied by climbing into the Miata and backing out. She thumbed the garage door back down and took off. I locked the front door, then followed her.

She put the Miata in my carport while I parked at the curb. Inside, we fired up my laptop and Terrie bought a ticket to Dallas. Then she took her bags upstairs and changed clothes. When we left, I loaned her a spare set of house keys and made sure she knew the alarm code. We grabbed Subways on our way downtown to meet Meierhoff.

I didn't get a sandwich for him.

Chapter 25

I was in Records and Information division, sitting next to Donna Boudreaux and looking at her. Donna is nice to look at. She's petite, raven-haired in her late forties, with olive skin and high Indian cheekbones on a fashion model's face. Her folks came from the bayou country of Louisiana—Cajun, or as Donna preferred, *Coonass.*

Donna wore her lawyer uniform today, a tailored gray suit with white silk blouse and a puffy bow at the neck. One slim elegant leg was crossed over the other, showing off finely patterned hose and grey pumps.

Donna and I had been friends for years. Right after my divorce, we fell into bed together but soon fell out the other side. We were definitely better as friends than lovers. Lately she'd been dating Aaron Binares, a big economy-size guy who's a research chemist at Shell and plays jazz drums evenings. She likes him a lot and so do I.

I turned to watch Terrie across the way, sitting at a computer console, scanning images of possible suspects. She wore a shortsleeve red blouse with black vest, black designer jeans and expensive flame-striped sneakers with fancy laces, the kind of shoes that gets you mugged for in the ghetto. She sat knees crossed, jiggling her foot like she had at breakfast, the huge tongue and laces of her tennies flipping and gyrating with the random flutter of a meth freak moth on a bad trip.

Terrie looked at me, smiled, then jumped up and dashed out to the smoking area to have another cigarette. She had her favorite brand now, English Ovals, those little unfiltered cigarettes with the funny shape.

"How long do you think she'll take?" Donna asked.

"Figure an hour without the cigarette breaks. Three with."

Donna grinned, then turned serious. "What's your guess? About Terrie."

I shook my head. "Don't know. She obviously didn't shoot her boyfriend, but I still can't figure a motive for why he got shot at all. The cops haven't been able to turn up anything. My hunch is that drugs are involved but that's about it."

"What next?"

"Thought I'd poke around in biker town, see if I can track down something. That's our only lead so far, unless Terrie finds a photo match."

"I can look after Terrie in the meantime, keep an eye on her."

"Not needed. When we finish here, I'm taking her to Hobby. She's flying to Dallas to spend a few days with a girlfriend."

"Let me know if you need a babysitter when she gets back— Oh! Tuesday's my birthday. Aaron and I are getting together, wondered if you'd join us at Marfreless for a drink?"

"You're celebrating a birthday and all you guys can think of is to drink with me?"

"The invitation only applies to happy hour. After that you're totally not invited."

"Marfreless sounds good. I should be able to make it."

* * *

Terrie finished her smoke and was back at the photo search when Meierhoff wandered in. He waved at us and walked over where Terrie sat and stood behind her, leaning over to check on her progress and likely sighting down the gap in her blouse, verifying she wore no bra. I didn't much care for this so I joined them to break up his little party. Meierhoff acted innocent and smiled at me. "Hi, Mitch."

I huffed a noncommittal answer and mostly ignored him. "Terrie, how's it going?"

Terrie treated me to a big smile that brightened my soul. "Okay. Boring, looking at all these jackoffs."

Meierhoff checked his watch. "After you finish this group, I'm supposed to take you to our sketch artist. She's good."

Terrie shrugged and rolled her eyes at me.

"Let's talk," I told her.

"Check with you later," I said to Meierhoff, and we left him standing at the table. We walked out to the coffee room where Terrie immediately lit another cigarette, flaunting the no smoking regs.

"At the house," she said. "Sorry I snapped at you. I was pretty tense."

"That's okay. Gone and forgotten. You're stressed out and the time out of town will do you good. And that will free me up to look for the man who shot Larry. You won't be safe until he's in jail."

"Where are you going?"

"He probably runs with bikers. Thought I'd head down to Spencer Highway and poke around."

Terrie put her hand on my arm. Again the electricity. "He's a killer. Be careful."

I said I would.

Chapter 26

I had a look at the sketch from police artist. The resemblance to Mel Gibson was missing, as was the Harley tattoo. I wondered about this but didn't want to make waves. The cops knew their business, I knew mine.

Terrie was already packed, so I drove her to Hobby Airport and saw her onto the plane. Or more correctly, up to the security gate. I didn't think the screeners would react kindly to my pistol.

"See you in a couple of days, Mitch. Thanks." As a goodbye, she treated me to a soft, lingering kiss on the cheek. It didn't leave a physical mark but it surely got my blood boiling. I carried the emotions with me the rest of the evening and into my dreams.

Terrie was there, a ghost of beauty within my sleeping mind, tenuous and tantalizing. She came to me willingly, but as I reached for her, a presence was between us, the equally vaporous Mel Gibson lookalike. In the illogic of dreams, the real actor Mel Gibson played the part of the killer yet strangely cast in his varied film roles as well. He was the disillusioned priest in *Signs*, the maverick *Lethal Weapon* cop, the loner from *Road Warrior*. At times, he was my enemy, sometimes he was my partner in a fantastic adventure and occasionally a mere bystander. Transform as he may, his entity remained a nemesis that prevented me from reaching Terrie.

After I woke, I tried to push the dream away. Its distraction would serve no good purpose. And I had the matter of Pamela Neely to deal with. I'd committed to the job and had to see it through, even though my principal interests were with Terrie.

I cleaned up, got dressed, and checked my e-mail and messages. As I headed out, the phone rang. Major Trent Collins. "TJ and I are having a party tonight, want you to come, kick back, and maybe talk a bit. I guarantee Neely won't be there. She hates me and won't deign to cross my threshold."

"Tonight?"

"Sorry for the short notice. TJ's schedule was changed and she's due at the Cape on Thursday for a final orientation before they ship her over to the Russkies for the launch. So we figured to have the party now. Can you make it?"

"Sure. I plan to see Pam Neely today and should have some news for Tarah later."

"Let's hope it's positive."

Agreed. I wanted to get the Neely case wrapped up and off my plate.

* * *

Pamela Neely lived just off Richmond in the Montrose area, a stone's throw from St. Vincent University. The neighborhood's a mix of quaint gingerbread houses and apartments with a few homes turned into offices for accountants, psychic consultants and chiropractors.

The Montrose district is well kept and ordered, people comfortable with their lives and their retro-urban environment. There are new townhomes, brash and pushy architectural encroachments upon the placid lifestyle on either side, but thankfully few of these as yet.

Neely's place was an older amenable two-story brick fourplex, two up, two down, wide porches from each apartment facing the street. With Neely at work, the Sentra was nowhere in sight, as it shouldn't be. Her apartment was number four, which meant upstairs, but which side? A glance was enough to show. On the left, the balcony cluttered with kids' toys, including a Big Wheel, bright orange toddler-size plastic chairs and tables, low rider bicycle propped against the railing, with numerous hoops and balls and other playthings.

In contrast, the other balcony was thick with hanging ferns and airplane plants, a jungle that had overgrown most of the available territory. Amid the greenery were wind chimes and stained glass hangings. A sullen gray cat perched between the vines, peering down at me with wanton slitted eyes. Pam Neely's apartment.

Today I was taking a poll on urban renewal as my cover. I wore Docker khakis and an awful plaid shirt I'd found at the Salvation Army store. Pinned to the pocket flap was a nice plastic photo ID—me smiling, bonafide of the Houston Housing Coalition research team. I even had a clipboard on which were clamped survey sheets that I'd made up one rainy afternoon. The questions were precisely what an opinion taker might ask and I wondered whether I could pick up some extra cash by sending in the results. Probably not a good idea.

I went through the motions of flipping through my clipboard paperwork and checking off some nonexistent boxes. I entered the building and took the common stairs. I knocked on Neely's door but not too loud. No answer. It took me about five seconds to slip the lock and I was inside.

Chapter 27

The cat ran to the sound of the door, then froze when it saw I was a stranger. It remained fixed in its tracks, undecided. I reached down slowly and offered the back of my hand and the cat carefully padded over to sniff. I was permitted to briefly rub its head between the ears before caution overcame conviviality and the cat scurried away to hide from the friendly but unfamiliar interloper.

I put on my disposable gloves and looked around. Pam Neely kept a clean house. The hardwood floors were brightly polished and no dust bunnies lurked beneath the furniture. The living room was decorated in sixties hippie style, rattan sofa, chairs and end tables, all with bright paisley cushions. Comfy if you're into that sort of thing. On the wall were some art prints like you buy at Pier One. A small Sony flatscreen TV and stereo sat in a corner, a CD rack featuring Tracy Chapman, k.d. lang, other pop stuff.

One wall was bookshelves, stacked and crammed floor to ceiling. About two-thirds were engineering and technical texts, associated books on space exploration and some general science. The remainder was mostly feminist and lesbian literature. I spotted a biography of Bella Abzug, one of Billie Jean King. There was a photo journal by Nancy Andrews, some poetry by Willa Cather and Marianne Moore, books by Robin Morgan and Eve Ensler.

The adjacent dining area had a big cherry heirloom Thomas Allen table and chairs, a matching sideboard, doors with those teeny panes of intentionally wobbly lead-frame glass. Handed down from the parents, I guessed, as the Colonial style didn't match the rest of the place.

The kitchen was small but clean, the walls hung with whisks, long wooden spoons, spatulas and similar artistic utensils. There was a half-bottle of Yellow Tail Shiraz in the fridge, cork forced back inside to prevent gremlin attack. No beer, damn it. I knew there was something about Neely I didn't like.

Her bedroom was uneventful. Everything in order, clothes hung carefully, chest of drawers with folded sweaters, socks, underwear neither staid nor risqué. I found a nice vibrator with several attachments, but who didn't have one of those?

The apartment was precisely what you might expect from an educated, sedate, single female NASA engineer with lesbian orientation. There was nothing I could employ as leverage to discourage Pam Neely's amorous moves on Tarah Jacoby. I also didn't find any secret plans to highjack a communications satellite, bomb the Johnson Spaceflight Center, or kill all men within a hundred kilometers.

I locked up behind me and took the back stairs.

<h1 style="text-align:center">Chapter 28</h1>

I was hoping Pam Neely didn't spend too much time roaming around after work or I'd be sitting half the night, but it was only a little after six when she parked at her apartment. I walked over, met her as she was getting out of her car.

"Ms. Neely, we need to talk."

She was of course apprehensive, a stranger approaching her on the street. I maintained my distance and stood quietly. She wrinkled her brow. "Aren't you that real estate guy?"

"Sort of."

"I'm not interested in buying a house or moving. I told you that." She paused. "How did you get my address?"

"I wasn't exactly forthright the other day. I don't sell houses for a living."

Neely stepped back until she was framed in her open car door. "And if you're thinking about asking me out, forget it. I'm not interested."

"I know you're not. But I'm not here to flirt with you, Ms. Neely. I'm here to persuade you to leave Tarah Jacoby alone."

"What? Who the hell are you?"

"My name is Mitchell King. I'm a licensed private investigator." I flipped out my ID folder to show her.

"Get away from me! Get the fuck out of here or I'm calling 911!" She dug in her purse for her cell.

"Don't," I said. "You talk to me now, or you'll be talking to NASA Human Resources tomorrow morning."

"Bullshit! You don't know anything. You've got no idea what this is about."

"I sure as hell do. Sexual harassment. Stalking. Vandalism. That's what it's about."

She stopped scrabbling for her phone. "What? I don't know—"

"Don't dissemble, Pamela. You've been making trouble for Tarah Jacoby. She tried to be polite, asked you to quit giving her grief, but you didn't listen."

"I don't know what you're talking about."

"And you keyed her Porsche at The Outpost. Broke out her taillights."

"I did not! What business is it of yours anyway?"

"As I said, I'm a private investigator."

"It's still none of your business."

"I'm not here to argue. I'm making it my business and I'm here to tell you to stop harassing Tarah Jacoby. Period."

"She's just a business associate, a friend."

"Maybe at first. But you wouldn't let it stop with friendship. You've got a thing for her and it's not reciprocal."

"What do you know about that? You know nothing."

I started to tell her that some of my best friends were gay but that would be patronizing. Instead, "Because I'm a man? Betty Friedan isn't prohibited reading, you know."

"Who are you to decide what I can or can't do? Who are you to say anything?"

"I'm your saving grace, Pamela. I'm the person who will keep you from getting fired. I'm here to rescue your job and your career. That's who I am."

"Did that fucking ni—that bastard Trent Collins hire you? Or was it those assholes in NASA?"

"I'm not at liberty to say."

"Tarah wouldn't. She—"

"She needs to be let alone."

"Did she hire you?"

"It's beside the point who hired me."

"Leave me alone! I don't give a damn who hired you or who sent you. Get the fuck away from me!"

She moved to slap me and I backed away, raising my hands to ward her off. "Okay, okay. I'll leave you alone. I'm going."

"Get away or I'll call the cops."

"I'm outta here. I tried to persuade you to leave Tarah Jacoby alone. If you choose to ignore me, so be it."

"I mean it. Go the hell away."

I started for my car. "Good-bye, Ms. Neely. Have a nice night. And a nice life."

Chapter 29

Time for Trent's party. And heaven help me, I was glad Terrie was still out of town. She was hyper enough that I didn't want to visit her upon a group of astronauts or NASA staff.

Major Trent Collins owned a spacious but conventional ranch house in an older suburb of Clear Lake, not far from JSC. Before I left home, I printed the street map off Yahoo and found my way easily despite the switchbacks and curving drives meant to emulate opulence in the midst of mediocrity. Yeah, I could've used my Garmin but I decided to rough it for a change.

Trent's neighborhood was cut from the same mold as Terrie's, downscaled by a few hundred thousand bucks per. It's all a matter of budget and standard of living.

But that is being snobby. Quiet and well-maintained suburban life is what ninety percent of the world population would give their left kidney to have, and never will. I'd disparaged Terrie's neighborhood too, and much of my attitude came from my own situation, ensconced within a nest of my own making, more urban and less placid than Terrie or Trent, more sophisticated. Nevertheless, it was the same. We all gravitate toward our chosen level of the swamp.

It was about eight and the party was going strong, cars parked along both sides of the street. By ten, people would be drifting off to home and bed. Engineers aren't creatures of the night. In my world, things didn't really get cracking until, as Eric Clapton says, after midnight.

I parked a ways down and walked to Trent's. The evening was warm, cloud cover obscuring the moon and keeping the humidity high. I could hear rock music as I neared the house, *Satisfaction* by the Stones. Most of the activity was in the back yard so I meandered up the driveway and found a bunch of folks hanging around the patio.

Many were dancing, a few with considerable vigor, a rhythmic loose-jointed funk. Most, however, affected that semi-stationary slouch that pays faint homage to the music and devotes most of the focus to conversation. Besides, it's hard to get down when you've got a hot dog in one hand, beer in the other.

Trent was poking at some chicken breasts on a gas grill. He wore a hideous chef's apron that featured a cartoon pig barbecuing what must be his own kind with gleeful morbid cannibalism. Trent saw me and waved. "Grab a beer." He pointed to a couple of big ice chests by the patio door.

So I did, grabbed a few pretzels to nibble on and checked out the crowd, mostly NASA people whom I recognized from my tour. Everyone was in good spirits and having a swell time.

Trent came over, shook hands. "Any news?" he said.

"Mostly negative, but yeah."

"Let's get TJ, find a place to talk." Trent collared Jerry Anders, the weightlifter-shape engineer I'd met. "Keep an eye on the chicken, okay?"

Anders detached himself from a couple of girls and came over. "Sure."

"Keep the chicken off to the side, otherwise it'll dry out." Trent removed his apron, held it out to Jerry. "Want this?"

"God, no."

Trent tossed the egregious garment onto a chair and we went inside to the kitchen, where we found Tarah Jacoby, chatting with friends and slicing pepperjack cheese, arranging it in an uninspired and halfhearted arc on a plastic plate. Scientists are not exactly food artists.

We picked our way through the crowd of partygoers until we found ourselves in a small study at the front of the house where Trent had a world-class computer setup. He closed the door. "What did you find out with Pam Neely?"

"I spoke with her earlier. Sadly, no progress. She denies she vandalized Tarah's Porsche, refuses to admit any harassment. She's defensive and won't budge. And I tried everything." I gave them a careful account of my conversation with Pam Neely. I however didn't mention the break-in. *Wouldn't be prudent*, as Bush Forty-one advised.

"What's next?" Tarah asked.

"You may wish to speak with her a final time, but I doubt it'll have any results. I don't think you have any choice but to report her to Human Resources and let the chips fall where they may."

She shook her head. "Hate to do that. I know she'll get fired."

I shrugged. "I don't recommend you continue as is. Your work is stressful enough without having to deal with her every day. Neely brought it on herself."

Trent hugged Tarah, smiled at me. "Last night I asked TJ to marry me. I've been asking her for six months, finally wore her down. She said yes." He leaned over and kissed her, they embraced.

"He even got down on one knee! What a rush," she said.

"Congratulations. Happy for you guys. You tell anyone else yet?"

"Just TJ's folks," he said.

"How'd it go?"

She rolled her eyes. "Talk about *Look Who's Coming to Dinner*. My mom hit the ceiling. Dad seems to like the idea, his daughter marrying an Air Force flyboy." She smiled, rubbed Trent's cheek. "My father's always been gung-ho military."

Trent noticed my skeptical glance. "I admit, it was a big obstacle, took a lot of patience from her folks, my being a Methodist."

We laughed at that. Trent sheepishly admitted, "I guess my being a brother is somewhat of a stumbling block, too."

Tarah couldn't resist teasing. "That's what I like about him the most. Wearing his dress blues all baggy, shooting his service pistol gangsta style. And all that rap music."

"Yeah. Love those rap tracks. Hip-hop too. I try to squeeze it in between the Scarlatti and Bach."

They obviously had this banter down to a practiced routine. "I hate to bring this back to an unpleasant topic, but what are you going to do about Pamela?" I asked.

They looked at each other, then Tarah spoke. "I want to meet her privately once more, tomorrow, just before I fly down to the Cape. When I get back, we'll make a final decision."

"Want me to do anything in the meantime?"

"No," Trent said. "In fact, we're firing you." They both laughed.

"I was hoping to drag this out for a few more years, rack up the hours, pad my expense account, and retire on the take."

"Sorry. You'll have to consider this your termination notice." Again, a laugh.

I nodded. "I'll mail you an invoice. But if you want me to lean on Pam Neely again, just call."

"I think you've done everything you could," Tarah said. "Or anybody could. It's up to her now. I'll let her think this over while I'm gone. But I'm not going to allow Pam to get in the way of our plans or our future."

I nodded. "Again, congratulations. Be sure to invite me to the wedding."

"Consider that a promise."

So we hugged all round and laughed some more, went back out to mingle. Several people in the living room were singing along with David Bowie's *Space Oddity*, laughing at the admonition to take their protein pills. The next track was *Rocket Man*, which prompted me to wander over to the stereo. On top was a plain plastic CD case labeled *Astronaut Songs*, a short sampler indeed. And of course everyone knew the lyrics were about getting stoned instead of actually traveling in space, but they were being deferential. Who gave a damn anyway?

I had another beer and a piece of Trent's BBQ chicken. It was tasty and moist. At least engineers are good at following instructions.

Chapter 30

I slept late again, nearly ten, and this time my dreams were free from frustrating encounters with semi-helpful actors. After a workout on my Bowflex, I had a bagel, a grapefruit, plus two big spoons of cashew butter I'd bought at Whole Foods.

I showered, caught up on my calls. Terrie's cell was offline and it asked me to leave a message. Next, I tried Meierhoff but he was out of the office. And Tony Vee didn't answer.

Nobody wanted to talk to me today.

Well, if no one was going to help, it was time to go looking for the shooter myself. I thought I'd cruise some bars by the Houston Ship Channel first, so I dressed in my used car salesman costume. This is an ill-fitting checked sports coat with plaid slacks, open collar striped shirt and cheap loafers. My leather holster would clash with the slacks, but I'd just have to endure this affront to fashion. On a lark, I took the MGB instead of the 4Runner and headed out.

* * *

The Ship Channel is directly east of downtown, so I cut through the city on Franklin Street. The full heat of the day was on the city now, and I glanced to the downtown towers that shimmered and baked in the sun, squinting as my eyes adjusted to the blaze of light.

How best to look for the killer? Except for his Harley tattoo and a resemblance to Mel Gibson, there was nothing to go on. But this lack of substantive leads was only a temporary setback. I was confident that something would turn up if only I dug for clues and followed up on my hunches.

I checked my watch. Twelve thirty. My skill as an investigator told me this was a clue. And my hunch was that La Carafe on Market Square would be open and would serve me a beer. I drove over there and was soon proven correct. My first break in the case.

I sat at the bar, savoring the cool air, sipping a Michelob from an icy mug and thinking about Mel. Where could he be? If he were a real pro he'd have flown in, done the job and been on the plane to Vegas or wherever an hour after the shooting. But, assuming Mel to be a local garage-sale hired killer, he'd still be in town making trouble for himself. So I'd try to dig up some news on him.

I got back on the road, took Franklin east past the county jail and the Astros ballpark and made it all the way through the warehouse district without running over any winos. I turned onto Navigation Boulevard and went by Ninfa's, where they serve great enchiladas and greater margaritas. The car tried to pull in of its own accord, but I held the wheel steady and continued to the ship channel.

A number of Houston ship channel restaurants and bars court the tourist trade. They have fake fishnets dangling from the ceiling with rubber fish and lobsters glued in. The waiters all pretend to be Greek and some may even be. Everyone yells *Opa!* at the slightest provocation. The most dangerous thing about these places is that you might eat the food.

I wanted authentic, so I barhopped on the back streets near the weekly rate motels and claptrap rooming houses. The Channel Lounge, Bob's and Paradise Inn were all graced by my presence. In each, I asked about a friend of a friend, a man whose name I didn't know, but resembled Mel Gibson, had a Harley tattoo and could do some work for me.

The bars were air conditioned and full of folks getting away from the afternoon heat. Still, no one had seen Mel. And I wasn't surprised. If a stranger asked around about my buddy, I wouldn't have seen him either, especially if he did the type of work that had no category listed in the Yellow Pages. I figured I was mostly wasting my time but I had nothing pressing, so it was all right. I wouldn't put this slumming on the clock anyway.

* * *

About two in the afternoon, I walked into a bar called The Parthenon. Unlike its namesake, this one still had a roof. Maybe the Turks hadn't yet decided to store explosives here.

The Parthenon wasn't too bad as bad bars go. It was a narrow place with a long counter along one wall and a row of booths opposite, separated from the bar by a wooden framework that ran to the ceiling. They'd woven some artificial grapevines into the frame and filled the empty space with wine bottles hung from wicker baskets. A row of Christmas lights twinkled along the top of the frame. 'Tis the season.

Two women sat at the end of the bar near the window, drinking and talking. One was a platinum blonde in a tight black sheath dress and a bunch of clinky bracelets. The other was a redhead in sequined jeans and a western shirt. The women glanced me over, then ignored my presence. Sitting with the women was a tall black man wearing a lavender suit and a pink silk shirt with lapels that went all the way out to his shoulders. He looked like a meth dealer from *Grand Theft Auto*.

At the other end of the bar sat an old guy, staring down into his drink as if it held his fortune. It probably did, but the fortune mustn't have been too exciting because he kept nodding off.

Two stocky men sat in a booth, drinking coffee and playing gin rummy. They were dark complexioned with jet-black hair, one of them definitely a toupee. I figured them as brothers and owners. Both wore plaid double-knits and shirts that showed off gold chains and chest hair, easily overshadowing my car salesman garb. The men ignored me, too. Maybe it was my aftershave.

I took a stool at the middle of the bar. The bartender was leaning against a wall next to the cash register, intently reading *Maxim* and chewing a plastic stirrer. He was tall and slim, with a thin pockmarked face and long blond hair braided into a thin ponytail. He wore a pullover with thin stripes and slim black peg-leg slacks. Everything about him was slim.

Slim pushed off from the stool and came over. "What can I git ya?" He had a backwoods accent.

"Wild Turkey straight up, water back." Slim thought about this a while, chewed his plastic, poured my shot and gave me some water in a glass with lipstick stains on the rim. I'd drunk a couple beers already so I left the bourbon alone and sipped the water, avoiding the lipstick.

I put a twenty on the bar. Slim took it and brought me change. I separated a ten from the bills and slid it toward him. "Maybe you could help. I'm looking for someone."

Slim blinked at me and at the ten and back at me. "Unh?" After a while, the light in his head came on. He looked toward the women. "Ya might buy one a' them a drink."

The black guy picked up on Slim's gesture and nodded to the blonde. She detached herself from the stool and made her way down the bar to me. She was a little shaky but she'd gotten her pimp's orders just fine.

She treated me to a wiggle of her hips. She was decent looking but had a lot of mileage on her, like a favorite old Buick. There were crow's feet around her eyes and wrinkles here and there but she'd covered them with several layers of makeup. Her perfume was not exactly overpowering.

"Hi." She smiled at me. "I'm Margo."

"I enjoyed your performance in Swan Lake, Miss Fonteyn," I told her.

"Huh?" Then she gave up, dumped her purse on the bar, curved her arm through mine and slid onto the barstool next. "Maybe you can buy me a drink?"

Slim stood there, watching.

I nodded to him.

"Gin and tonic?"

Margo nodded and he made her drink. The ten had vanished so I pulled another twenty from my wallet. When Margo saw all the cash Tony Vee had given me, she squeezed my arm harder. I have that effect on women.

Margo took a sip, smiled at me. "Thanks, Honey. What's your name?"

"Alexander Scriabin," I said, "But you can call me Alex."

"Alex. Haven't seen you around. New in town?"

"Live in Austin. Just here for a few days."

The black guy got up and sauntered our way. He gave me the once-over and walked on past, headed for the john.

Margo plucked the straw from her glass and downed half the drink in one swallow. She gave me a sexy little squint she must have learned from the daytime soaps. "Want to hang around? We can have a good time."

"Maybe. But I'm looking for a friend."

She pouted and pretended hurt. "Aren't we friends?"

"It's a guy I'm looking for."

Margo pulled her arm away. "Hey, you into that? I mean, everybody's got to dance, you know, but you don't seem like—"

"No, Margo, not that. I just need some work done and a friend recommended this fella to me. That's all."

"Okay, Alex. I gotta ask, y'know." Satisfied, Margo drained her drink and rattled the ice in Slim's direction. He looked at me, I nodded, and he brought her another. As Margo stirred her new drink, she noticed I hadn't touched mine. "Hey, Alex, drink up! They got happy hour till six."

I picked up my whiskey and wet my lips. She raised her glass in concert but drank most of hers. I was losing her fast. "Margo?" I said.

"Wanna play some music?" Margo spun halfway on her stool, almost falling, and waved in the general direction of the jukebox. "You like country?"

"In a minute, Margo. But this guy I'm looking for. Maybe you can help. You might've seen him around."

"Sure. What's his name?" She finished her drink and rattled for another.

"That's the problem. I don't know his name. My friend said he did good work, told me to look for him over by the ship channel. This guy looks like Mel Gibson. The actor. Seen him?"

"Mel Gibson come into th' Parth'non?" Margo enjoyed that. She leaned over and yelled to the two men in the booth. "Hey, Pete! This is Alex! He's looking for Mel Gibson! Ain't that the shits? Mel Gibson coming into a crappy bar like this!" Pete glanced up, sneered, and then went back to his card game.

Margo shrugged and slid her arm around me. "Who gives a shit anyway? Right? You staying, Alex? Let's party, you and me. Mel ain't invited."

I sat there unimpressed. Then a voice came from my right. "They got rooms next door. You thinking about a good time with the lady, or what?" It was Margo's protector, back from the john. There was still a little white powder stuck to his moustache.

"Or what," I told him. "Not staying that long." I made a move to gather up my change.

Margo hopped off the barstool and away. "He's got cash on him, Trickster." She smiled at me, a wicked twist to her lips. "Loaded."

Trickster immediately clamped my right wrist in his big hand, tilted back to get me off balance. I grabbed my shot glass from the bar and splashed the whiskey in his eyes. He flinched momentarily and slipped his grip slightly, all the help I needed. I hooked my right arm up and under his, turning the leverage back to my advantage and making him twist away. I crossed over and my left elbow caught him hard on the cheekbone. He let go completely.

I jumped back, straight into a pair of beefy arms. One of the brothers had sneaked up on me. He grappled me from behind, pinning my arms against my side. Trickster squared off and grinned.

"Now you gonna get it, motherfucker," he growled, and flipped out a long, shiny butterfly knife. Margo screeched.

I braced myself as best I could and managed a strong and very lucky *mai-geri* kick to Trickster's knife hand. The blade went clattering off and Trickster winced in pain. I snapped my head back into the nose of the man holding me. He grunted but still held on. I shifted my weight and spun sideways, drove a knuckle punch straight back into his groin. He yelled and fell away.

Trickster was coming for me again, improvising with a beer bottle since his knife was gone. I feinted to the right, stepped under his swing and came up with a *nukite* spear blow to his throat. Trickster sank to his knees and I helped him on his way with a Lou Groza kick to the jaw. I heard his teeth clack and he was out.

I turned but the other guy was crouched over, clutching his balls, toupee hanging over his ear. The guy's partner was just standing there, spectating. I scanned the rest of the bar. Margo was keeping her distance, the other woman still sat where she was and the old guy in the corner hadn't even moved.

Slim was another matter. He was coming around the end of the bar to cut me off. He had a steel pipe in his hand and he banged it on the bar to intimidate me.

I reached back under my jacket, pulled out my pistol. Unlike the pipe, it didn't make any noise, but it sure as hell got Slim's attention. He laid the pipe down without protest and went back behind the bar, keeping his hands in the air.

I looked over to the owner. "Keen place you got here," I told him, "but lousy clients." Then I was out the door.

Nobody followed.

Chapter 31

I had chickened out. Bugsy Binton, my fictional and shadow-self rough-tough PI, would have made a stand at the Parthenon and fight a gun battle with the disco-era owners and their rude patrons. Bodies would be stacked to the ceiling, laid in neat rows alongside the plastic grapevines. The cops would grill Bugsy incessantly but eventually let him go.

On second thought, bullets are expensive and it was better that I'd saved mine.

Not having any luck at the Ship Channel, I thought I'd try the true-blue biker bars. So I stopped by the house, put on some old Levis and a faded Rockets sweatshirt. I checked the loads in my pistol. Federal HydraShoks, a proven stopper. I stuck an extra full magazine in my back pocket.

My cell beeped, Tony Vee returning my call. "What's up, Tiger?" Again with the nickname.

"Any feedback on the Mel Gibson thing?"

"Nope. My guess is he's a loner, left town by now."

"Could be."

"That all you're bothering me about today?"

"If I wanted to spend time with the rougher side of biker, where would I go? Pasadena's been calm lately."

"Yep, since last year. New mayor swept out all the trash. She's on a cleanup rampage and it's making dents in the bad boy playgrounds."

"Biker bars closed down?"

"No, but they're running a tight ship. If I wanted real action, I'd head over to Mid-City."

"Mid-City? Scraping the bottom of the barrel, are we?"

"You asked."

"Any place in particular?"

"Couple bars you might try. Oasis and the Little Shack. You can't miss 'em, they're right on Spencer Highway."

"Want to come along?" I asked.

"Mebbe later. Got some stuff to do. You drivin' that little windup toy today?"

"The blue MGB? Yeah."

"Park it near the street so I can see. I'll try to catch up with you." Tony paused. "And Mitch?"

"Yeah?"

"You ain't got nearly enough balls to deal with the crowd down there. They're mostly Banditos and Satan's Slaves. Hardass folks. Watch yourself."

Good that Tony was warning me. It made me feel needed.

Chapter 32

Speaking of feeling needed, Terrie called, boosting my spirits considerably.

"I'll be back today, Southwest 842 at five-fifteen. Can you pick me up?"

"I may be stuck on assignment. I'll call Donna Boudreaux. She wanted us to get together tonight anyway. One of us will be there for sure."

"I'll see you soon, Mitch."

She hung up before I had time to tell her how much I'd missed her. So I called Donna. "Happy birthday."

"Not till tomorrow, sweet. You still on for tonight?"

"Like Polonius in Hamlet, I need to 'wring from you a favor by laboursome petition'."

"You're the only private detective I know who calls somebody up to quote Shakespeare."

"Sometimes I do feel like Polonius, often wrong but never uncertain."

"Jesus. Once a *cum laude*, always a come loudly."

"You making fun of my snooty university education?"

"Whenever possible," she said. "And the petition?"

I told her about Terrie's flight, gave her the number and time.

"Sure, we'll get her. Want us to bring her out to your place?"

"Why don't we all meet at Marfreless? Say about seven, eight?"

"Done."

* * *

Terrie's arrival arranged for, Mid City beckoned. Like all large cities, Houston has its satellite towns. Some are self-contained communities like University Place. With the prestigious Rice University at its center, this township has lovely old homes, fine shops, restaurants, and a wide assortment of specialty stores. The upscale shopping attracts high-income people from all around. Even I go there when I can afford it.

Southeast of Houston, Pasadena is a different image. It provides business zones for refineries and chemical plants that serve the nation. Mainstream commerce reigns, but interwoven with this industrial theme are thousands of homes containing solid, responsible citizenry. Pasadena may appear a cultural throwback compared to Houston, but it does point with pride to strong community values.

Then there's Mid City. Despite continuing efforts by county and state cops, Mid City flourishes. The prostitution, drug dealing and other dark trades are its lifeblood. Every big city has its toilet and I was going to visit Houston's, Mid City.

The township isn't much, really. Mid-City is stuck between the larger Pasadena on the west and Deer Park to the east. A sordid two-mile stretch of tit bars, liquor stores and taverns along Spencer Highway.

Weather forecasts called for a cold front and probable thunderstorms, and its effect was already being felt. A pleasant breeze had cooled things off, and the drive was smooth and easy. I took Texas 225 to Pasadena and booked east along Spencer.

When I crossed from Pasadena into Mid City, the change was immediate. Within a few blocks I'd passed four topless bars, two nude bars, some taverns, adult bookshops, and liquor stores. Mid City's finest recreational offerings.

I found the Oasis right away. It was a smallish concrete block bar set back from the road. There was a paved lot in front, gravel to the side. Several choppers were ranged across the front, so I gave them a pass and parked in the gravel.

An amateurish desert mural decorated the side of the building. A cluster of palm trees, now faded to mirage by the Houston sun, was contemplated by a misshapen camel that had not yet committed to seek refuge under them. Someone had used a wide blue felt-tip pen to add an enormous penis to the animal, and blue urine was streaming from the penis onto the crude figure of a man lying beneath. There was no telling who had first spawned the graffiti, because the original name of the person apparently deserving being pissed upon had been painted over. Other collaborating artists, thus challenged, had added new names, layer on layer, until the accumulation became a jumbled anagram.

Imagine the explorers who discover this artwork six thousand years from now. Shivers of delight would ripple through their ranks. They'd develop complex theories about the mores of the proud desert folk from vanished Hoo-town, waxing eloquent on the considerable significance of the phallus to such primitive peoples.

And they'd be right.

Chapter 33

I stepped into the Oasis and blinked until my eyes adjusted to the gloom. I was immediately assailed by the rancid odor of greasy hair and stink of unwashed skin. The smell rolled toward me like an incoming fog, but on little cat feet it came not.

One principal source of the fog was a big fat man standing by the door just to my right, holding a pool cue and waiting for his turn. The man was dressed in a leather vest, filthy jeans and boots run over at the heels. He wore no shirt, and every inch of his exposed skin was tattooed. Some tattoos were colorful and highly imaginative professional jobs, some bore the telltale blue-gray improvisation of the jailhouse. Beneath his fat, the man had layers of hard muscle, like a pro wrestler gone to seed. As I stepped by, he sized me up. I figured he didn't like what he saw but I didn't much care.

A row of booths ran along the left side of the room, a circular bar at the back. A half dozen people sat at the bar and I joined them in a corner seat away from the rest and ordered a Bud from the bartender. She was the female version of the guy at the door, except she was fatter and wore a T-shirt under her vest, and I was immeasurably grateful for her modesty. A reciprocating fan at the end of the bar blew me a whiff of her cologne. It smelled like overheated transformers.

I looked around the bar. People were staring at me because I was overdressed and under-tattooed, even though some of the customers were a cut above the biker by the door. Many wore first-rate leathers like Steinmark or Bates, clean riding gear and were likely stockbrokers who took the day off to slum around town.

They were tourists here, same as I. The difference was, I didn't pay token homage to the Harley flag.

I've got nothing against Harley riders, or even outlaw bikers for that matter. They go their way and I go mine. Truth be known, I hold real bikers in higher esteem than the weekend set. Bikers are at least true to their breed.

To keep harsh glances to a minimum, I turned around and minded my own business. In front of me on the grimy bar was a pert, friendly brown cockroach. In tribute to Don Marquis, I named him Archie. Archie was bent over nibbling a pretzel crumb that the previous patron had left him, and didn't notice the bartender coming with my change until it was too late. Wham! She caught him with her bar towel and flattened him, grinding him into a lump of paste that she spread evenly along the counter's surface. Poor Archie never had a chance to hop on that typewriter.

The bartender laid my change on a relatively cockroach free part of the bar. I was pleased with this and tipped her a buck. Then I handed her a business card that identified me as Charles McLaughlin, adjuster for Monarch Insurance. The address was fake and the phone number forwarded to an answering service I used for such things.

"So?" she asked.

"I'm trying to locate a witness to a traffic accident last month. The guy who got hit is insured by Monarch, and he told us there was this biker sitting at the stoplight who saw it all, wasn't involved, but the guy took off anyway."

"So?"

"So I guess the bike rider had some outstanding tickets and didn't want to hang around for the cops. This I appreciate and it's none of my concern. But if I can get him to swear out a deposition that says our guy wasn't at fault, we can settle out of court and the rider won't even need to show up."

"So?"

I sighed. "We can make it worth his time. And there's a finder's fee."

A deep rumbling voice came from my left. "How much?" It was the fat pool player, sticking his nose in.

"How much what?" I replied.

"The finder's fee. How much?"

"It's negotiable. But you don't even know what it's for."

"Don't matter." The guy grinned, displaying a wide gap in his teeth. "Anything happens here, I know about it. And what I don't know about, don't matter no way. Name's Dutch."

I gave him my best insurance adjuster smile and tried to breathe through my mouth. Even though I felt my face melting like the Nazis in *Raiders of the Lost Ark*, gagging at his stench would not be conducive to a productive relationship.

"Then, Dutch, you're the one who can help," I said cheerfully, handing him another card and repeating my fabrication.

"What's this guy look like?"

"My driver said the fella resembles Mel Gibson. You know, medium size, about forty, macho good looks. And he has a Harley tattoo here." I indicated my right forearm.

Dutch scrunched his brow in thought. "Don't ring a bell, but I could check, dependin' on the payback."

"I can pay a hundred. One-fifty if I get in touch with him by Friday."

"How much up front?"

I was being scammed and knew it. All part of the game. "Twenty."

"Make it fifty," Dutch said. "I gotta spread some around, ya know."

"Forty."

"Deal."

So I dug out two twenties and handed them to Dutch. It was a good chance that I'd never see Dutch or the money again, but I needed to grease the wheels somehow.

Business concluded, I left my beer undrunk and continued down Spencer Highway to scatter more of my special brand of bullshit in scenic Mid City. Most places, I was the Monarch adjuster. At several decent bars, I gave my real name. And presently, after working my way along the saloons and tit joints, I stood before the Little Shack.

Chapter 34

Sordid as the Oasis had been, the Little Shack was even more of a dump. It had somehow survived Santa Ana's army and several hurricanes. Maybe they took pity on it.

The Shack was a sodden, sagging wood-frame structure. Its rear wall leaned against a big oak tree that likely provided the primary structural support. The roof was a tatter of misplaced shingles sitting at random and obtuse angles, none of which seemed designed to ward off rain. The foundation had drifted into ruin and was now mainly discolored brickwork. Slatboard siding was cracked and faded, dirty with years of refinery pollution and general rot.

The place hadn't been painted since snakes walked.

There was a splintered porch running across the front of the building, concrete blocks jerry-rigged for stairs. I navigated the shaky steps, pulled open the crooked door, and went inside.

I reeled at the putrid odor of sewer backup but managed to stay on track. A string of bulbs hung from the rafters, casting spotlights and shadow across the scene. A few fire-sale tables and chairs sat along one wall, heavy, cheap-sawn picnic tables and long benches in the middle of the room. All the tabletops, chairs and even the floor were carved deeply with biker logos, initials and lewd suggestions.

Near the back of the room was a standup bar, and behind it, a mid-sized bartender with a *ZZ Top* Billy Gibbons beard. He was talking to two customers, both bikers. None of them paid me the slightest attention. If the Oasis was unfriendly, the Shack was downright rude.

I walked to the bar and stood in front of a carving on it that told me to fuck off. I didn't. Instead, I ordered a Bud and started my spiel about the accident witness.

One biker was quite tall, about six-four, scarecrow arms poking out of his shirtsleeves and long-bone shanks showing through torn jeans. His face was pockmarked with the scars of acne. He sported buckteeth and a hooknose broken several times, wore his hair in a tapered braid that came to his waist.

His pal was short, handsome and as neat as Bucktooth was dirty. He had a trimmed beard, John Lennon steel-rim glasses, clean jeans and a western-yoked shirt. The two guys and the bartender listened to my story politely enough but none knew a biker who resembled Mel Gibson.

A male voice called from the back, around the corner, "Hey Billy! You gonna play the fuck pool or you just gonna fuck around till Jesus comes?"

The small biker, Billy apparently, hollered, "Go ahead and break."

A moment later, the familiar crash of pool balls.

Billy smiled at me. "Sorry, dude. I don't know anybody who looks like that. You might ask Junior. He gets around a lot more'n I do." He pointed in the direction of the pool table then followed his own pointing.

Bucktooth shook his head. "Can't say I seen the guy neither. Know what he rides?"

"Nope. Just that it was a chopper. Can you help?" I asked the bartender.

"Nuh. Wish. Could use the money. Check with Junior, playin' pool." He tilted his head over his shoulder.

* * *

So I walked around the corner to ask Junior and found a real surprise. There, down a short hall and tucked in a sort of annex to the building, was a beautiful full-size pool table, the old type with leather web pockets. It was spotless and stood amid the ruined surroundings of The Shack like an alien artifact jettisoned by a wayward UFO. How the owner managed to keep the table clean was a complete mystery. And don't ask me to solve it, either.

Billy, the smaller guy I'd talked to, was shooting. Junior was leaning against the cigarette machine in the corner, puffing on a smoke and studying the table. He was a carbon copy of Dutch, a bit younger and smaller but cut from the same cloth. But so are lots of bikers, the unkempt and stocky guise a popular affectation.

I stood watching Billy shoot and momentarily forgot my quest for Mel Gibson. Billy was good. He was good and he was also hustling Junior. Billy controlled his English perfectly, making it appear sloppy but leaving his cue ball in a decent position for the next shot. He ran all his balls and missed the eight, deliberately.

"Damn!" Billy said. "Screwed up the money ball."

Junior grinned, pocketed his two remaining balls and then the eight. Billy paid him a five, suckering him into a game of double or nothing. Billy then won three straight and Junior had been bled enough.

"Shit! I ain't got it today. You play him."

Billy looked at me. "Five?"

Talking could wait. Meantime I could get on Junior's good side by beating his nemesis. So Billy broke and ran four balls. I also ran four, then deliberately missed, sticking the cue ball behind my six, hooking Billy on his next shot. He missed as I planned and I ran out the rack.

Four games later, I was up twenty bucks. Billy was a decent barroom hustler but he was out of his league with me. I managed to keep him in the game and also let him think he was still in command. Out-hustling a hustler is a challenge, but I was in good form today and the breaks came my way.

I won the fifth game but planned to blow the sixth and quit, just to let Billy off the hook a bit. No sense antagonizing him because he also might help find Mel for me. I was chalking up for the break when I heard a voice I certainly didn't expect. Or need.

* * *

"Who the fuck we got here? Mister Insurance Adjuster McLaughlin!" I turned to see Dutch standing in the hallway. "Except I been checkin' around. His name ain't McLaughlin and he don't do no insurance. His name is King and he's a fuckin' private cop. A goddamn cop."

I didn't answer, but stood still a moment, sidled casually to the edge of the room, keeping my back away from the other men.

Junior cut me off, moving behind me. He laughed deep in his gut. "You sayin' he's a liar?"

"Liar he be, little brother," Dutch answered. Brothers. No wonder the similarity. "And that ain't all. This nosy snoop's been asking around about a friend of ours." Dutch grinned his split-tooth grin at me. "Know what we do with nosy snoops here, Mister Private Detective?"

"Breathe on them, make 'em puke?"

Dutch gave a feral grunt and charged, head down and arms wide. If he caught me against the wall, I'd be as flat as Archie the cockroach. I spun the pool cue around in my hand and snapped the butt up into his face. It cracked him hard and he stopped in his tracks. He straightened, rubbed some blood from his nose and grinned wickedly. "I'm gonna cram that stick up your virgin ass, smart boy." He came at me again.

164

Out of the corner of my eye, I glimpsed Billy flinging a billiard ball at my head, joining the fight. I ducked under and simultaneously managed to sidestep Dutch's rush.

Luck was still with me. I aimed the cue butt for the nape of Dutch's neck, but the cue skipped over the mark and splintered across his muscular shoulders. As he rumbled by, Dutch grabbed for my shirt but missed. I reached back for my pistol and my luck ran out.

My right arm went numb from a terrific blow. I turned to see brother Junior cocking his cue for another swing at me and I barely had time to dive for cover. The cue swished across my head, boxing me on the ear with a glancing impact that made my vision spin and the world crowd in on me.

You really do see stars, you know. I fought against their dazzling image and tried to shake off the dizziness, knowing that if I went down I'd be dead or wish I were. I lurched for the corner of the room so they'd have to come at me singly. A beer bottle crashed against my head, stunning me further, anointing me with broken glass and lukewarm beer. My right arm was useless so I groped for the gun with my left, but the holster had slid around so I kept missing. My head was ringing and I had trouble standing.

Bucktooth joined in. He circled to my left and reached down into his boot, pulling out a nasty, serrated commando-style knife. Billy and Junior closed on my right, Billy with a broken bottle and Junior his trusty cue.

Dutch stood between them, blood dripping from his broken nose. He seemed to crave it, licking hungrily at the trail of blood along his lips. He held a cue in both hands, snapped it in half across his knee, tossed the shaft away, and weighed the butt with pleasure. "I'm gonna take my time with you, smartass. And I'll let the other boys help out."

I was on the verge of unconsciousness and my vision would not clear. I saw three Dutches, one, then two, all filling my foggy field of view, all coming closer. I was helpless and lost.

My brain must have been foggy as well, because a strange thing happened. Dutch seemed to lift off his feet into the air and sail cleanly across the room like an economy size Peter Pan. He landed in the corner with a crunch, with something huge and roaring filling the spot where he'd stood. My vision focused sharply and I knew what it was.

Tony Vee.

Bucktooth wasted no time and dived toward Tony, flailing his wicked blade. Tony came up with the pump shotgun from beneath his dustcoat, but instead of firing it, he shoved it muzzle first into Bucktooth's mouth, removing the teeth and somersaulting the man onto the once pristine pool table. A large smear of blood gushed from Bucktooth's mouth and spoiled the color of the felt. He lay still.

Billy and Junior decided I was no longer a threat and turned their attack on Tony. Their mistake, because Tony bought me time to regroup. Feeling returned to my arm and I struck Junior at the base of his skull with a *shuto* knifehand and he went down without a sound. Billy saw this and half turned, but I was already on him, flipped his left arm back into a chicken wing, and kneed him to the floor. I felt the arm snap as I jerked up. Billy screamed. No pool hustling for a while, I thought.

* * *

Tony looked over to me. "Ready to go, Tiger?"

I joined him without answering and we started for the door, but Dutch wasn't finished. He picked himself up from the floor and came for Tony, clutching a length of steel construction rebar that he'd found somewhere. He swooshed it around his head like an Australian aborigine with a bull-roarer.

Weary of playing games, Tony raised the shotgun and fired into the ceiling right above Dutch! In the closed space, the concussion was breathtaking. Tony jacked the slide to chamber a new round and the *tinkle* of the spent casing on the concrete floor sang out in the now silent bar.

Dutch looked at the ceiling, considered earning a similar hole in himself, backed off.

"First fucker out the front door gets blown in half," Tony said to anyone still listening.

As Tony and I walked past the bar in front, I saw a pair of boots on the floor, sticking out from behind one end of the bar, a long beard poking out from the other. Neither moved.

Outside, Tony looked me over, laughed. "Now we both got knots, Tiger. Two boneheads with matching bumps. You gonna be all right, though. Your fuckin' skull is hard as mine. Just some cuts and stuff. But you need to get cleaned up."

"Can't right now," I answered. "I'm due at Marfreless."

"Nice place. Sure you're dressed for it?"

I shrugged. "If they try to stop me, I've got my gun."

Tony laughed, waved me off. "Finding Mel Gibson has to wait, Tiger. We better get going. Those guys ain't gonna sit still forever." He opened the door of his Caddy, tossed the shotgun on the seat beside him, got in.

I jumped into the MG.

As Tony drove off, he leaned his head out the window and pointed at my car. "How often you feed the mice in that thing?"

Chapter 35

The forecast was spot on, a front sweeping in from the west. Thin cirrus clouds gave way to bulges of thick cumulus, and the temperature dropped as quickly as the Cubbies' pennant hopes. Spatters of rain flicked the windshield, causing me to pull over at a Stop 'n Rob convenience store and put up the MG's top.

This procedure was thoughtfully engineered by British automotive experts to require the services of several stevedores, a circus contortionist and two hours. I managed it myself in ten minutes but I'd had lots of practice.

I was running late, decided to forego changing clothes and reached the River Oaks area exactly at seven. I was eager to see Terrie. Parking was a challenge in this busy shopping district, but I came up behind a car that was just pulling out. Someone who thought they had first dibs on the spot honked at me but I ignored them, parked, got out and walked over to Marfreless.

Marfreless is a hidden bar, known only by word of mouth. It's slotted away toward the rear of an office building and facing a parking lot. There's no sign, no address, no notice whatever that a wonderful place exists beyond the plain, unmarked door. You just have to know where it is. I did.

* * *

First thing you notice is the music. Marfreless plays subdued classical music—piano etudes and baroque concertos. There's soft indirect lighting, a long bar with comfortable chairs, friendly bartenders, elegant waitresses and plenty of fine drinks.

Sectionals and chairs are arranged around low tables throughout the room and along the walls are racks of paintings for sale. Upstairs it's darker and there are cushy sofas where you can sit and make out with your date. Nobody minds.

I spotted Donna Boudreaux and her boyfriend Aaron Binares at a table in the corner. Terrie wasn't with them. I walked over. "Where's Terrie?"

"Hello to you, too," Donna replied. "Terrie's powdering her nose." Then she took a good look at me. "Jesus, Mitch, where you been? A dogfight?"

"Wrestling. Decided to turn pro."

Aaron reached up and we shook hands. "I recommend drums for a hobby instead. Easier on the wardrobe."

The waitress came over and stared at me. I ordered a Glenfiddich on the rocks, sat down. She walked away, shaking her head.

A moment later, Terrie returned to the table. "God! Are you okay?"

By now I'd gathered that my appearance wasn't exactly shipshape. I excused myself and went to the john to clean up. I needed it. My face was streaked with dirt and blood, my shirt stained by the beer, blood and whatever I'd rolled in at the Shack. I pulled off the shirt, shook it out, and reversed it. I washed my face as best I could in the little basin, Welsh-combed my hair to remove the broken glass and splinters. Renewed, I went back for my Scotch.

The four of us drank and talked and joked a while. Aaron was great company, telling funny stories about his experience in a jazz band. This time it was the haircut.

"Since I got that promotion at Shell I'm meeting loads of international clients and need to keep my hair short." Aaron riffled his fingers through a burrcut. "But all the other guys in my band wear their hair long—you know, musicians. For a joke, the lead guitar player gave me this hippie wig he'd bought at a costume shop, and I decided to go along with the gag and wear the wig next time we played. So we finish our first set and the club manager calls the band leader aside and tells him, 'I'm not trying to say anything bad about Aaron, but this new drummer you hired is a helluva lot better.'"

We all laughed. I felt good, Terrie beside me. She was animated, bouncing all over the chair she barely sat in, enjoying herself. Donna raised her eyebrows a couple times at Terrie's over-the-top behavior, but that was Donna's problem. My affection for Terrie was growing by the minute.

* * *

Then Donna poured cold water on the evening. When Terrie was in the bathroom again, Donna leaned over to me. "Know anyone Terrie would be angry with?"

"Why?"

"After the airport we stopped by my office. She made some phone calls from the conference room, said her cell battery was low. I couldn't hear what she was saying, but one call lasted an awfully long time, and by the end she was practically yelling into the phone. I asked her if everything was okay and she essentially told me to mind my own business."

"And?" I thought Terrie had a point.

Donna picked up on my tone of voice. "Hey, sorry I mentioned it. I just thought you might want to know."

"Fine. Thanks."

Things were chilly afterwards, so Terrie and I soon split. Donna and Aaron would want to be alone anyway, and I sure as hell didn't need more sarcasm about Terrie.

One front had passed, leaving the streets wet and gut slick. The radio said a larger storm was on its way, so Terrie and I decided to call it a night. I had a frozen Boston Market chicken we could nuke for dinner, plus a couple bottles of Cabernet.

Lightning flashed on the horizon and the rain was spitting at us by the time we got home. The photoelectric light in the carport had come on, giving me a clear view to nudge up behind Terrie's Miata and under shelter. Ever the gentleman, I got out, went around and opened Terrie's door for her.

I was bending down to take her hand when the overhead light exploded!

Chapter 36

The shot was a cannon in the still night, echoing across the neighborhood. I jerked Terrie from the car and shoved her down. "Don't move," I whispered, crouched over her prone body, covering her as best I could.

The second blast seemed louder than the first. It missed us again and shattered the windshield of my MG. Pellets of safety glass rattled around us. I didn't know where the shots were coming from because I'd had my back turned when the muzzle flashed. I rapidly scanned the whole area but saw nothing. I pulled my pistol, holding my breath and kept Terrie shielded.

Dogs all around began baying at the noise. Then I heard the scrape of shoe against concrete at the front of the house. Lightning flashed and I caught the outline of a man crouched on the driveway. Rolling to my right, I came up on my knees and fired. The bullet missed, skimming off the paving with a high-pitched *whizz* and the man darted away. I went after him but my foot slid on the wet grass and I went down on my butt. By the time I picked myself up and recovered my balance, an engine started out on the street.

A large pickup truck roared away from the curb, no lights, headed north and nerfing the neighbor's car on the way. I caught the brief flare of brake lights as he reached the corner, turned and drove away. Something was odd about the truck's silhouette but I couldn't place it.

The turmoil was over in seconds and I could hear the sirens now. I went back to Terrie, pulled her close and held her in my arms until the cops were standing around us.

Chapter 37

"Party's over," Joe Duggan said. "He knows we're here and won't be back."

It was after one in the morning. Joe stood in my kitchen, sipping coffee and dripping water onto the floor. He wore one of those cheap translucent plastic raincoats that crackle when you walk and beads of water ran down the creases and puddled at his feet. It was pouring now, the gusting wind whipping sheets of rain across the lawn.

Three cop cars and the CSI van sat askew in front of my house, mostly blocking the street, light bars still flashing blue and red, illuminating the surroundings like gaudy Christmas displays. Nevertheless, my neighbors had quit the festival and gone to bed. With the prospect of further gunfire minimal, there wasn't much purpose in staying up and braving a rain storm.

When we first came inside, I poured myself a stiff shot of Wild Turkey and chugged it, followed with another, the whiskey settling my nerves. This was only the second time I'd been fired at and the feeling was definitely not one I recommend. Terrie had a shot, too, and now she sat at the kitchen table, drinking coffee heavily laced with bourbon.

The back door opened and David Meierhoff came in. True to stylish form, he wore a snazzy tweed cap and a trench coat I'd bet was a Burberry. He took off his cap and flipped it on his arm to shake the droplets. "Nice night for ducks," he commented, poured himself a cup of coffee. We were on our second pot. Joe had already taken some outside to the uniforms.

"What's the buzz?" Duggan asked. "Find anything?"

"Under the carport," Meierhoff said. He fished a ziplock bag from his coat and dangled it. Inside was a misshapen chunk of metal. "Large caliber bullet."

"Like a forty-one Mag?" Duggan asked.

"CSI will say for sure, but yes."

"Anything else?"

Meierhoff shook his head. "Nope. Other bullets could be a half-mile from here or stuck in the shrubbery next door. We won't find anything tonight, especially in this weather."

"Doesn't matter," Duggan concluded. "Pretty good idea it was the same guy who shot Trevillian." Joe looked at me. "Sure you can't tell us more?"

"Never got a look at him. His lights were out so I couldn't ID the truck or read the tags. Just that it was a pickup."

"A black pickup," Meierhoff interjected. "Left some paint on the neighbor's car. CSI will send it to the lab for a match. Take a few days, though."

"What about patrols?" Duggan asked.

"Nothing yet. We got them looking for full-size black pickups with a dent and some green paint on the right rear, but in the rain, you can't see shi—er, can't see anything."

Terrie looked up and grinned. "If you want to say *shit*, go right ahead. Be my guest." She waved her hand in permission, voice a little slurry.

Duggan sipped more coffee. "Thing I can't figure is how he knew Ms. Bartlett was here. How he knew she was staying with you. How he knew Mitch King even exists."

"Probably my fault," I admitted. "Handing business cards out all over Mid City. Should have been more careful."

"Yeah, buddy." Joe frowned. "I'm not too happy with that little fling of yours. You got a skip trace or a cheating hubby, I'm down with that. But next time you decide to prowl around town on a murder investigation, let us do it. Okay?"

"Okay, Joe. Promise." I put Terrie in danger by my rash actions and regretted it.

"Done is done," Joe said. He finished his coffee and set the cup down. "Now. You sure you don't want us to keep a unit outside tonight?"

"No need. Got burglar bars on the windows, good locks on the doors, alarm, my guns, we'll be okay."

Meierhoff nodded. "Still, I'll have patrol do a regular drive-by, circle the block, random checkups."

"Thanks," I said. "But you guys have done all you can tonight. I'll call in the morning."

"No," Joe contradicted. "I'll stop by on my way to work, about nine. Have my coffee ready." A grin.

Done being done, Duggan and Meierhoff made their goodbyes, walked outside to the cops and CSI people, spoke with them a minute, then got into their unmarked vehicles and drove away. One by one the flashing lights cut off and they all backed out, off to another call, or more likely, a late dinner. It was soon quiet enough to hear the rain cascade onto the windows.

* * *

More lightning flashes as yet another front rode in, bringing its own thunder, a thunder far more soothing than the earlier noise from Mel's gun.

"You okay?" I asked Terrie.

"Now I am. Tired, though. If it's all right, I'm going to bed."

"Sure. I'll be upstairs, soon as I lock the house."

Terrie stood, came over to me. She put her arms around my waist and hugged. "Thanks for being here." I returned her hug and we stood there together a minute. Then she yawned, slowly detached herself, and slouched away.

I unplugged the coffee, made sure the alarm and all the locks were set, went into my pool room. I walked to the cue rack and swung it open on concealed hinges to reveal my gun safe. I'd seen this setup in an old Burt Reynolds movie and couldn't resist installing one myself. I opened the safe, took the Smith off my hip, unloaded it, wiped it with a treated cloth, put it in the safe. I'd clean it tomorrow. I reached into the recesses and retrieved my Colt Anaconda .44 Magnum. If Mel was going to come at me with big stuff, I'd up the ante. I loaded the huge revolver with 240 grain Winchester Black Talons, closed and locked the safe, went upstairs.

Light came from beneath Terrie's door so I knocked gently, keeping the gun behind me. No need reminding her of the danger we faced. Terrie opened the door a crack and peered out. I guessed she was dressing.

"Mitch..."

"Just wanted to say goodnight."

She nodded. "I was so scared."

"Me too. Everything's under control now. I'm going to hit the shower. You try to get some rest."

She nodded again and closed the door.

* * *

I was dirty and ragged from the fight at the Shack and the attack. I peeled my clothes off and tossed them into the hamper. Maybe I could salvage the jeans. I laid the big Colt atop the toilet tank and stepped into the shower.

The hot water was a delight. I used the handheld nozzle to wash the grit and bits of broken glass from my hair, rinsed off the dirt, soaped and shampooed twice. The little cuts on my scalp stung from the suds but that soon ceased.

I was rinsing off a second time when the bathroom door opened. I jerked the shower curtain aside and grabbed for the gun, but only got halfway.

Terrie was in the doorway. She wore the same old bathrobe as before, this time barefoot, minus the bunny slippers.

"Need your back scrubbed?" She untied the sash and let the robe slip from her shoulders onto the floor.

Chapter 38

Terrie was naked, her body an extravagance of sensuality. Her full tanned breasts swelled from her chest, no sag or wrinkle beneath. The breasts stood high, bearing her brown nipples erect, pointing up and out. The aureoles surrounding her nipples were dark and swollen with desire. Terrie's large breasts contrasted with her narrow waist, which in turn complemented her slender, tapering hips. The hipbones were prominent, casting highlights down her flank and into her tangled pubic curl, trimmed to a sliver that seemed to point to her inner center of desire. This was surrounded by a brief patch of white skin, the only spot on her flawless body not to have seen the sun. Her long shapely legs carried all this loveliness and sensuality to me. She looked at me with her superb deep eyes, smiling as she walked. Her breasts jiggled, making the nipples rise and fall in time with her steps.

I was transfixed, staring.

She glanced to the bathroom floor. "Think we should close the curtain? Water's going everywhere." Then she stepped into the bathtub beside me and pulled the curtain shut.

Terrie reached out and grasped my swelling penis, squeezing it lightly and making my heart race. I pulled her body against mine. She continued to stroke me as her face tilted up, her lips opened to me. A deep kiss.

Terrie's breasts rubbed against my chest, thighs pressing close. She hooked her left leg around my waist and compressed her calf against my right buttock, grinding herself into my hip. I cupped my hand beneath her right breast and began to massage it with the same rhythm she was using on me. Gently, I pinched her swelling nipple between thumb and forefinger, rolling it back and forth. I pulled the nipple out from her breast, kneaded her breast with my palm.

Terrie groaned and grasped my penis more firmly, stroking faster.

Quickly she knelt and took me fully, expertly, her fingers accenting the action.

I moaned, held back as long as I could, and spent myself, pulsing.

Terrie continued to lick me. Then she stood and threw both arms around my neck, pulling me close and kissing. I tasted myself in her. I took her hands in mine, kissing her fingers and palms, explored her breasts with my tongue, nibbling each nipple.

The water continued to spray around us as I knelt. I kissed her stomach, licked her navel, continued down and gained the sweet loveliness of her center. Terrie soon surged to a pounding climax. She shrieked with pleasure, jamming her body against mine.

She grasped my hair and pulled me up. We kissed again and once more I rubbed and massaged her breasts while she stroked me to full growth. She guided me into her, rocked against me violently. I held her in my arms as she lifted first one leg, then the other, to lock about my waist.

Terrie was against the shower wall and I pressed her firm clean flesh into mine. We kissed and thrust and ground our bodies together in a crest of passion that filled the world.

We finally left the shower when the hot water ran out. We grabbed a couple of towels and walked naked down the hall to my bedroom, me carrying the revolver, primitive and animal in my lust and in my movement.

* * *

I took Terrie in my arms, mounted her as we lay across the bed. She wrapped her legs about my waist and we coupled for an eternity. The storm bore in again, thunder crashing, bright flashes of lightning streaking through the windows. It lit us like a strobe, catching our bodies now entwined, then apart, then together. Terrie rolled over onto me and sat astride, riding and thrusting, her breasts wet with sweat and her breath coming in gasps.

Finally, we were satiated. Unable to move, we lay on the bare sheets.

Shortly after, we scooted to the head of the bed to peer out the window. A solitary patrol car glided up the street and paused before the house. Its bright searchlight parted the darkness, casting reflections over the wet lawn and pavement. Satisfied at finding nothing, the light switched off and the car faded slowly away.

Just before dawn, I woke to hear the toilet flush. Terrie came back to bed, her naked body huddling against me, leg over my thigh. "Hold me," she whispered.

Somehow, we found energy to plunge again into that ancient rhythm of desire and passion. Our bodies linked, we reached orgasm together, and lay there joined, one in flesh and one in mind, until we faded into sleep.

Chapter 39

"Can you believe these goddamn Astros? Still in first place! Who woulda figured?" Joe Duggan sat at my kitchen table, reading the sports to me. I poured myself a glass of grapefruit juice and waved the jug for Joe.

He shook his head. "Gives me gas—speaking of gas, be back in a minute." He took the paper with him into the half bath down the hall.

The phone rang, as it'd been doing all morning. Meierhoff first called to see whether there was any more trouble and how we were doing. There hadn't been and we were fine. Next, Donna Boudreaux phoned after hearing from Meierhoff. She wanted to apologize for last night and needed to know if we were all right. Apology accepted and we were fine. Now it was Tony Vee because he'd heard that something had gone down at my house, and to see if we were okay. Yes, I told him, something had gone down and yes, we were still fine.

"Need my help?" Tony asked. "I owe you."

"After you saved my tail, I'm the one who owes."

"That was yesterday. Last night I went to see Danny Angel. Remember Lou Masters and the skillet?"

Duggan was still in the john so I could talk. "Our pal Lou? How could I forget the emergence of Tiger?"

"It's because of Tiger. Lou showed at Danny's and paid every cent he owed. No argument, no hassle. Danny gave me a bonus and I figure Tiger gets half."

"The money's yours. Keep it. But you might do me a favor."

"Shoot," Tony replied, then laughed. "Does it involve that? Shooting?"

"Nope. Least it shouldn't. We found that our pal Mel Gibson drives a full-size black pickup. If you could ask around?"

"Glad to. And I take it you don't want the law involved."

Just then, Joe Duggan walked back to the kitchen, paper folded under his arm. "You're correct on that," I said, affecting a businesslike tone.

"Check with you later, Tiger." Tony hung up.

"Meierhoff again?" Joe asked.

"No. Somebody else. Client."

Joe looked up and squinted. He was an expert in human behavior and knew that I was lying. I began to fiddle around with the toaster, Joe resumed reading the sports and it was quiet in the kitchen. There was a sense of unease between us now and it made the silence all the more palpable. He stood up. "Well, time's a wasting. Gotta split."

"Okay. Need us for anything today?"

"Don't think so. Till we get the results back on those paint scrapings, we don't have much to go on. We're checking out the bikers, same as you, only we'll do a better job." Joe grinned. "And Meierhoff's going to be looking into the drug angle. That's about it."

Terrie came into the kitchen and my mood brightened immediately. She had showered and made herself up, wearing red retro stirrup pants, black boots and a blue silk blouse with designer denim jacket. She looked great.

"Hi, Ms. Bartlett," Joe said. "You sleep okay?"

Terrie gave a little stammer. "Yeah. Sure." She looked at me, turned away.

I glanced over at Joe and he had a smile in his eyes. Damn him, he knew!

Joe pointed a thick finger at me. "Watch out for big black pickups." As Joe left, he half turned as if to say something else, like Columbo. Then he changed his mind and went on. Good. I figured another lecture was forthcoming and I was glad he didn't deliver.

Terrie came to me and we kissed. Then she pulled away. "I need to do some shopping and I'm meeting a girlfriend for lunch at the Galleria. She and I talked yesterday."

"That's not a good idea, going out. He'll try again, soon as he can."

"There's a million people all around. I'll be okay. Shopping will take my mind off."

"I don't—"

"Look!" she interjected. "I'm going to The Galleria and that's that."

"Okay, okay. I'll drop you off, pick you up later."

"No, I want my car. I like driving it." She hugged me. Again we kissed.

"I'm worried about you," I said. "I don't think you're safe, running around."

"But it feels good." She abruptly reached down, squeezed me through my jeans. "Feels good like that."

I did not reply. Instead, another kiss, deeper than the first. "You follow me over there, meet me afterward, about three. I'll be okay," she said.

"I'm not—" Then Terrie slipped to her knees, unzipped me. Five minutes later and it was decided. She would drive her Miata to The Galleria.

We went out to our cars. Earlier, I'd cleaned up some of the mess but there was still broken glass around the carport and my forlorn little MGB sat there, upholstery soggy from the rain that had blown in through the missing windshield. I'd scheduled the MG for a tow to the mechanic, then a visit to Dorsey's for a new windshield and some sprucing. They'd drop it off and bill me later. Bill me a lot.

Terrie and I played musical cars until the Miata and the 4Runner were free from the carport, then we left for the Galleria.

The storm had left the city sparkling and much cooler. I ran the windows down and relished in the fresh air. Terrie drove briskly but not so fast that I couldn't keep up. The big revolver in my Uncle Mike's shoulder rig was comforting, but it was just a temporary panacea. For permanent peace of mind, I needed to find Mel and deal with him. Or maybe let the police find him, but I preferred the personal approach.

* * *

The Galleria is Houston's showplace for upscale shopping. There are three large interconnected multi-story malls surrounded by convention hotels and fine restaurants. Visitors to Houston are invariably taken to the Galleria to gawk at the Sax Fifth Avenue, Cartier and row upon row of fancy shops. Terrie dived into the center of the complex, turning into an underground garage and scooting up the ramps to score a prized parking spot near an entrance to the mall. I double-parked behind her and escorted her to the door. Hundreds of customers were going in and out and the mall was already crowded. There were local socialites, retired couples, hordes of people from all over the world, thickly packed and wholesome in their search for the ultimate Houston shopping experience. Terrie was right. I was certain we'd not been followed and she was safe here.

"Three o'clock," I reminded her.

"Three," she said. She kissed me, making my body ripple with desire. She walked rapidly through the door, lighting a cigarette as she went. I watched her disappear into the crowd, then I turned and left.

Chapter 40

With Terrie off my hands, I figured to resume my search for the elusive Mel. I turned out of The Galleria complex but got held up in traffic. There was a new hotel going up, and a big flatbed transport truck had become mired axle-deep in the grooves of mud created by the passing of dump trucks and other mammoth earth movers that carried the spoil away.

Normal size tow trucks had apparently already tried to free the stuck vehicle and barely managed to avoid getting caught themselves. Pecking order established, these vanquished drivers stood around jawing as a king-size tow truck half dragged, half hoisted the transport, saving it from the doom that befell the La Brea tar pit victims thousands of years before.

A tired and bored cop stopped me and the other cross traffic while the monster did its job. I idly watched the tow truck's heavily knobbed quad rear tires bite deeply into the sludge, spin for a second, and take hold. The tow driver expertly edged his captive prey from the pit, halted on more solid ground. The traction of the big tires and the double axles made the difference.

Suddenly I knew why Mel's truck silhouette was unusual! I thought back, then I was certain. I phoned Tony Villarreal, told him we were looking for a *dualie*.

"Those bigass trucks with twin wheels in the back, four across?"

"Yep."

"Always thought of them as training wheels for goat ropers." Tony laughed.

"You bad-mouthing those innocent cowboys again?"

"Hey, I played for the Oilers, remember? Dumping on the Irving Mookids is what I do best."

"You mean the Dallas Cowboys." I knew the script, Tony's rant on the Cowboys, how to respond.

"Naw. They play in Irving, Texas, Irving Mookids they are."

"They've moved to Arlington, y'know."

"Then they're the fuckin' Arlington Mookids." Script concluded.

"Tony, I appreciate the help."

"I haven't found anything yet. Wait till I do something that needs thanking before you start kissing ass."

* * *

I checked the time. Just past noon. There was a guy I knew, Jimmy Landon, an informant who hung with some of the biker crowd. I drove over to the old Fourth Ward, Jimmy's stomping ground, asked around. Nobody had seen him lately, My guess was that he was back in jail or maybe rehab, but I wanted to make sure. His sometime girlfriend, sometime hooker worked at the Foxy Lady, so I drove there next.

The Foxy Lady is a small topless club on Richmond near Shepherd. It's a neatly turned out two-story brick house that had been, in its time, a private home, a whorehouse, French restaurant, lesbian bookstore and florist. Now it's a tit bar and usually so empty of customers I figured it served as a tax shelter or money laundry for the mob. But girls really were there and I wanted to talk to one of them, Starshine.

I parked at the back and went inside. There were several low tables and chairs around the room, a small stage to the left and a short bar with four barstools next to a flight of stairs. The whole place was clean and well kept. At a table to my right, a couple of guys in suits talked to two of the showgirls.

Another girl hopped off a barstool and came over. She was about twenty, short and cute, lovely green eyes and blonde hair in a ponytail. She wore a silver sequined G-string, sleeveless T-shirt chopped at her midriff, high heels and nothing else. She sported a little ring in her navel circled by a well-executed floral tattoo. Her breasts bobbed under the shirt as she walked.

"Hi! I'm Tawny," she bubbled. "Want a table?"

"Sure."

She led me to a place near the stage and sat down beside me. "What to drink?"

"Draft beer. Bud if you got it."

As she went off to fill my order, the CD player clicked and Bob Seger's Silver Bullet Band began to play *Old Time Rock And Roll*. The bartender spoke into a mike. "All right, gentlemen, let's put our hands together for the lovely Candy!"

One of the girls sitting with the men stood up, took another sip of her drink and walked barefoot to the little stage. She began to gyrate to the music, swinging her hips suggestively, her eyes fixed straight ahead and focused on nothing. After a couple of choruses, she pulled off her shirt and danced wearing only a tiny G-string. Candy was nice looking, had long reddish hair, a good figure, and attractive firm breasts.

A guy at the table went to the stage and stuck a five in the front of her G-string, earning a kiss on the cheek. He swaggered back to his table as though he'd just climbed Everest.

This playlet is repeated thousands of times at dozens of topless bars in Houston, multiplied by every city throughout the country and the outcome is always the same. The girl takes your money and you go home alone. Which is a good thing because most of the men who frequent tit bars are married. Married to women who, as they would say, don't understand them. *Yeah, right.*

* * *

Tawny came back with my beer, a flat brew in a smallish glass that I paid four bucks for, five counting the tip. But beer was not the specialty at The Foxy Lady anyway. Their primary product is fantasy.

"Starshine here?"

"She's upstairs, playing pool with a customer. Should be down in a minute." Then Tawny smiled at me broadly. "You want to play a game when she's done?"

I shook my head. "No, not today. But thanks." I returned her smile and Tawny patted my shoulder, then hurried to a new customer who'd just walked in.

It was ironic. I play pool avidly and turned down a game. But at the Foxy Lady, not all the balls that got handled had numbers on them. Men would be escorted upstairs, tip the girl and she'd take her shirt off. They'd shoot pool a little and the guy would feel her boobs a lot. The occasional blowjob was also performed, assuming the client was a regular and had cash. The Foxy Lady was discreet about its services, though. They hadn't been busted in a long time. Maybe they paid off someone, but more likely the cops were simply too busy with murder and armed robbery to redirect resources to the occasional guy getting his rocks off.

Starshine came downstairs as predicted. A product of hippie parents, Starshine is her real name. She's in her late thirties, over the hill for a titty dancer. She has bleach blonde hair and long skinny legs. Once, she'd been pretty but that had gone the way of all flesh. Ribs showed under her skimpy top, her eyes were hollows and she was twenty pounds shy of slender. Addiction, like cancer, devours you from the inside, one slice at a time.

* * *

Standing with Starshine was the man I actually wanted to see, her pimp and boyfriend Jimmy Landon. He looked over the bar scene with his pinpoint eyes, recognized me, detached himself from Starshine, came over immediately.

"Mitch, my man. How's it hanging?"

"Fine, Jimmy. You?"

"Great."

He was lying through his rotten yellow teeth. Jimmy's dark hair was clumpy and greasy, woven into two braids that dangled over his ears and down the front of his stained tie-dye shirt. He was rail thin with yellowish skin and patchy blotches on his face. His eyes were even more sunken than Starshine's, and they darted to and fro with unconstrained flickering. HIV, probably. full-on AIDS, a good bet. A walking disease factory.

"Starshine and me, we're moving to California."

"Sounds good," I answered, knowing they wouldn't make it to San Antonio. "But can you help me find someone before you leave? If you have time."

"Uh, sure. We ain't leavin' till next week. Only I got to be somewhere. Can I hitch a ride while we talk?"

I agreed. I said goodbye to Starshine, tipped her a ten so she could buy some more crack and led Jimmy out to my 4Runner.

* * *

As we drove, I asked him about a biker who resembled Mel Gibson.

"Nobody I know, but I can ask some people. Turn here."

I turned. We were headed up to Jimmy's home zone, the old Fourth Ward. He soon directed me to Freedman's Town. This area sits on the edge of downtown, bisected by West Gray. It's an historic part of Houston, once home to newly freed slaves who served as domestics to the rich white folks nearby. There's a recent campaign afoot to rekindle and renew the neighborhood, turn the shacks into Afrocentric shops and restaurants, add a museum and establish a trolley shuttle to downtown. That would be a big improvement, because right now, most of the place was trash.

"Over here," Jimmy pointed.

I pulled up to a row of aging wooden shotgun houses, all alike, all sad in their squalor. Some were abandoned and boarded up. Others were occupied, mostly by the dregs of society. But this was fine with me because it was a dreg I wanted to find.

"I got to go in, ask this friend. He knows lots of bikers," Jimmy said. Then his voice took on a plaintive whine. "Uh, Mitch. Could you spot me, say, twenty?"

I pulled out the money and handed it over. "Remember," I told him, "looks like Mel Gibson."

Jimmy clambered from the truck and wandered along the row houses, turning in at the last one on the right.

* * *

I waited. And waited.

After a while, I figured Jimmy wasn't coming out, so I decided to go get him. I climbed out and walked over to the houses, reaching under my jacket to make sure the big revolver was riding free in its holster.

The sun had baked the nearby earth to broken clay, and all the moisture from the previous rain had long since evaporated. Nothing beside remained. A scrawny hissing cat scuttled from my path as I traced Jimmy's steps. I edged carefully between the little houses and saw a side door standing open, its screen torn and hanging from the broken wood frame. Voices were coming from inside, one Jimmy's.

I went up to the door, put one hand on the grip of the Colt and pushed the door open.

As soon as I stepped inside, the terrible stink of raw and rotting crap shoved at me like a pressure wave. Used to the intense sunshine, my eyes acclimated slowly to the interior gloom. I stood there trying to adjust to the stench and the dimness.

A single naked bulb hung from a frayed cord to illuminate the depravity in stark chiaroscuro. The room was piled high with trash stacked against the walls. There were empty beer cans, whiskey bottles, rotgut wine empties lying everywhere. Rivers of brown and black cockroaches slithered in and out of the rags and shredded newspapers that were cast in rotting heaps about the room.

Stuck in one corner was a large metal can, a makeshift toilet. It was full and overflowing. Piles of shit lay near the can, covered with a layer of newspaper as if that would make it all right. Hordes of flies swarmed and buzzed over the filth and the odor was choking.

Welcome to the shooting gallery.

The only furniture in the room was a stained and ripped sofa. Jimmy sat on it, wedged between two older men, one black, and one white, both wasted. All three stared vacantly at me as I walked in.

"A minute," Jimmy said.

In front of Jimmy was a cheap fold-up TV tray, and on it, cooking gear. There was a little votive candle, a spoon with blackened bowl, cigarettes and some matches, and a small foil packet of brown flake heroin. Jimmy had just finished cooking his fix in the spoon over the candle flame and was now sucking the liquefied junk into a dirty 5cc syringe, the filter from a cigarette stuck onto the tip of the needle to strain out debris. He'd already tied off his left arm with a scrap of clothesline.

Jimmy tapped at the syringe to get the air bubbles off the cylinder walls, squirted a tiny droplet from the tip of the needle, and slid the point into an already bruised and pockmarked vein. He pulled back on the plunger to suck a little blood into the syringe, ensuring that all the air was gone from the needle and also ensuring that whatever pathogens were swimming in his blood would be shared with the next user. Then he pressed the plunger home and the expression on his face transformed from hunger to ecstasy.

The needle is all. The needle is life.

"Jimmy," I said.

He looked at me with empty, uncomprehending eyes as though I were an alien creature, a wholly different species. And I was.

Human.

Chapter 41

Jimmy had been a waste of time and I'd be meeting Terrie soon, so the day was a total bust. Maybe Tony Vee would be more successful. I was thinking about heading over to the Galleria early when David Meierhoff phoned.

"What's up?"

"I was talking with Duggan. He thought drugs were still a possible factor in the Trevillian shooting and suggested I get in touch with Ken Grace. You know Ken?"

"Never met him, but I hear he's good."

"Best narc on the streets. Best since I went over to Homicide, that is." Meierhoff laughed.

"What did Grace say?"

"We ought to talk. Can you meet us for a late lunch?"

I had the time. "Sure. Where?"

"Ken's working Montrose lately. Let's do Niko Niko's."

"Now?"

"Yeah."

"Fine with me. Ten minutes."

The weather had turned around again, hot as usual, and the warmth served to create a steam-filled atmosphere. Still, a good breeze was carrying off much of the humidity and it probably wouldn't break ninety today. Mild summer day by Houston standards.

* * *

Niko Niko's is a delightful fast-order Greek restaurant on Montrose Boulevard. The food is authentic, tasty, made to order and budget priced. Much of their business is carry out, table space being limited. Regardless, they have a thriving enterprise with a continuous waiting line.

We picked the small patio to meet, partly because of the breeze, mostly because of privacy. We had it to ourselves. We sipped a beer and chatted while our gyros and falafels were put together.

Apparently the dress code in Homicide today was Edwardian. Meierhoff wore a red-flecked hound's-tooth jacket, white linen shirt with Oxford collar points, subdued tie, charcoal slacks and shiny tan Wellingtons.

"Where's your deerstalker cap?"

"Watson has it," not missing a beat. "Getting it bronzed."

I checked out Ken Grace, complete distaff of Meierhoff. Gracie is in his late forties, greying hair and grizzled beard and spoke with a carefully controlled backwoods twang for which I couldn't decide whether his accent was authentic or simply cultivated for effect. He reminded me of Jack Elam, tall and slender, and walked with a limp he'd bought when a coke dealer shot him in the hip a few years back. That didn't deter Gracie from keeping the dealer safe from early probation by drilling him in the left eye with his backup .380.

Gracie wore old blue-jeans, a fancy Levi's jacket decorated with custom silverwork, plain brown cowboy boots and a flop-brim felt hat that looked older than the three of us combined. I pointed to the hat. "You wear that in the Civil War?"

Gracie grinned with a leery snicker that made me uncomfortable, like he was laughing behind my back. "Are you referring to the Recent Unpleasantness, also known as the War of Northern Aggression?"

"Don't get Gracie started," Meierhoff warned. "He's still reenacting Pickett's Charge."

"And other encounters." Gracie offered another sideways smile.

Meierhoff took a swig of his Shiner Bock. "Okay. Here's where we are. Larry Trevillian and Terrie Bartlett, living in Memorial, together five years. Trevillian works for Steenburg Investments, top firm, has a good track record with them. His lawyer is Jeff Converse, honest guy. No flaky money deals, no funny stuff on the side we can see. But somebody walks into his house last week and blows him away. Why?"

"Insurance?" Gracie suggested.

"Half million bucks," Meierhoff replied. "Upped to a cool mill due to his death being unnatural. Never been married, no kids, his girlfriend gets it all. It's in the will. House already paid for, stocks, bonds, everything. Over two mil total."

I cringed. "Did he change his policy or coverage recently?"

Meierhoff looked at me. "We thought of that. But no, he'd signed the whole thing over to her three years ago. If she did him for the insurance, she took her slowmo time."

"But we know someone else did the shooting," I argued.

"Sure, but what if she paid the guy to do the job?"

"That's possible," I said, playing Devil's advocate. "Trouble is, even though the suspicion comes to her first, we have her shooting at the guy after her boyfriend is toast."

"Sorta makes sense," Gracie interjected. "Trying to eliminate him because he can implicate her."

"But," I countered, "If you allow that—" The counter called our order. I went inside, paid the tab, and carried the sandwiches back to our table.

* * *

A momentary silence while we ate. I thought about how I'd given in to Terrie about driving her Miata, yielding to her persuasive methods. But agreeing to drive separate cars is a long way from shooting someone. And that led me to think further. What would it take to do that, to kill someone for sex, even though the person doing the murder would insist it was done for the purity of love? Who could be led by the nose to that rancid tune? How low could someone sink for that?

I continued. "Okay, say she pays the other guy to shoot her boyfriend. What did she use for money? You looked into the bank records. No large cash withdrawals, all major transactions on credit cards, all legit."

Grace chuckled and treated us to his evil Jack Elam grin as he chewed on his pita bread. "Money ain't the only tool a woman has to get a man to do her bidding."

"Jesus, Gracie." Meierhoff shook his head. "Don't go biblical on me. There's pussy and there's pussy. But it takes a helluva lot of it to get someone to commit murder."

Which was exactly what I'd been thinking.

"Wouldn't be the first time," Gracie said, still smiling.

"Problem with their being in cahoots," I said. "She was home and therefore vulnerable to suspicion. If she wanted her boyfriend dead, she'd have chosen a time when she wasn't around and had an ironclad alibi. Duggan picked up on that from the start."

"So let's talk drugs," Meierhoff said. "What do you know about these delightful law abiding citizens, Ken?"

"I checked with my people," Gracie said. "The two of them were doing blow, but they're mostly weekend warriors, keeping it among friends, no dealing. Their buying went up recently but not a lot."

"Why weren't they busted?" I asked.

Gracie chuckled. "Hey, we start busting all the recreational users, we got to build a lot more jails, one on every corner. People like Trevillian and his girlfriend are way down our list of priorities."

"Bottom line," Meierhoff concluded. "There's no clear reason for Trevillian to get killed, except a lover's triangle. Joe and I still think Terrie's involved but we've got no evidence, nothing to take to the county attorney or grand jury."

This raised my hackles. "Does she have an arrest record?"

"No."

"Anything? Any priors?"

"The only paper on her is a speeding ticket."

"Well, shit," I said, "we can't have a wanton criminal stalking the streets. Let's pick her up and throw her in the slammer!"

"Don't get hinky with me!" Meierhoff shot back. "I wanted to discuss the case, and I'm asking for your help and input. We're leveling with you, keeping you involved. So don't start riding your fuckin' high horse, okay?"

Ken Grace laughed. "Way you two are fightin', I'd think you both got the hots for her. She that good looking?"

Meierhoff calmed a little. "Actually, yes." He raised his hands, cupped them, and I knew what he was going to say before he started. "Great gar—"

Enough! "To hell with you!" I stood up and started away.

Meierhoff quickly deterred me with a friendly hand on my arm. "Sorry, Mitch. I shouldn't have said that. Hang in here, we'll stay strictly business. All right?"

"It's okay. I'm just a little tight today. That shooting the other night." I turned, sat back down and looked over at Ken Grace. He had a bemused smile on his face, watching Meierhoff and I argue.

Meierhoff finished his beer and started again, this time in a more amenable tone. "Mitch, you need to understand. We see this all day long, year after year. We catch a homicide and we develop a feel for what went down. We're not often wrong. I talked long and hard with Joe Duggan about this case, and Duggan's *never* wrong. Checking out the drug angle with Ken was our only other lead, but that hasn't panned out so we're back to the sex thing. If you can think of a better explanation, I'm open to suggestions."

Could they be right? Did Terrie have her boyfriend killed? Were my feelings for her clouding my judgment?

No, I decided. Something would turn up, I was certain, evidence that would exonerate Terrie. The fact that I hadn't uncovered it meant nothing. I'd just overlooked some detail, some clue.

This was my case and I was going to solve it. The cops have dozens of murders to work and they couldn't give a hot damn what happened to one particular person. But it was different with me. I cared for Terrie, and that mattered. The cops could help or they could get out of my way.

"You guys in Homicide have your theories," I told Meierhoff. "But I have mine, and mine tells me that Terrie Bartlett is innocent. Maybe it's just a hunch but I'm sticking with it for now."

Meierhoff shrugged. "You could be right, Mitch. Let's hope so." Then his beeper went off. He retrieved it from his belt. "Shit! I'm half hour late to the medical examiner."

What time was it? I looked at my watch. After three and Terrie hadn't called. I stood up and made for the exit. "I'm late, too. Got to go, guys! Thanks for the talk, David. Nice meeting you, Gracie." I knew they were frowning at my abrupt departure but I didn't care.

I phoned Terrie but as usual, only got voicemail. I left a message that I was running late, please wait for me. I bullied a path through traffic, cutting people off and switching lanes, but the cars were so bunched up that it was nearly four when I made it to the

Galleria. I swung into the garage and up to the level where Terrie parked her Miata.

The car was gone.

Chapter 42

I sat staring at the white Ford Contour parked where Terrie's Miata should be. Had I picked the wrong level? No, I distinctly remembered the spot. There was a big electrical relay box on the left, the entrance to the Galleria to my right. This was it.

Someone behind me tooted. I pulled to the side and let them pass. I got out, went over to the Contour and felt the hood. Cold. She'd been gone a while. A gnawing fear tore at me. Where was she?

Once again, her cell asked me to leave a message. I phoned my house but only got the answering machine. I tried Terrie's home. Another damn answering machine. Next, I phoned Donna Boudreaux. No, she hadn't heard from Terrie. Finally, I called Homicide and asked for Joe Duggan. When he came on the line, I explained Terrie's shopping trip with her girlfriend that her car was now missing.

"When did you last see her?"

"I followed her to the Galleria about noon. She was supposed to call me at three. Now it's after four."

"She's probably still off with her girlfriend. I wouldn't worry. I'm sure she's okay."

"Easy for you to say. You weren't shot at."

"Look. If it'll make you feel better, I'll put her license number out to the patrols. You happen to know it?"

"No. Just that it's a fairly new red Miata."

"That's okay. I'll get it from online records. Go on home. She'll turn up."

"That I know. It's what condition she'll be in that worries me."

* * *

Back at my house, I put on some music. That didn't help. I had a drink. That didn't help. I paced the floor. That didn't help, either. It was nearly seven and I was going out of my mind when I heard a car drive up. That little Mazda never looked better.

Terrie got out of her car, retrieved some packages from the trunk and walked to the house. I was happy to see her and angry at her absence, both. "Where the hell have you been? Why didn't you call?"

"Shopping and spending time with my friends does not have a time limit." Terrie dumped her packages on the floor. "Lincoln freed the slaves, remember?"

"I've been spinning in circles! Christ! We almost got killed and here you go, wandering around town without protection. You're in danger, even if you don't realize it."

Terrie frowned and looked contrite. "I'm sorry. I didn't think. I was out for the first time since all the trouble, and I just, well, lost track of time."

"I went by the Galleria and your car was gone. I phoned everywhere. Where the hell were you?"

"I was only... Oh!" she interrupted herself. "Let me show you what I bought." At that, she unbuttoned her blouse and shucked it off. Her lovely breasts came free. She tossed the blouse on a chair and bent over to rummage through the packages. Her firm breasts hung down, the nipples partially erect. Desire rushed through my body.

"You ever wear a bra?"

"Nope. I have one somewhere. Why? Want me to put one on? Any objections?"

"Not now." My mouth was dry.

"Good. You like this?" She held a flowery western-style shirt up. "Pretty?"

"Yeah, but I prefer what's behind it."

Terrie fluttered her eyes and spoke with a fake Southern accent "My sakes alive! Whatever do you mean?" She let the shirt fall away and smiled at me coyly.

I didn't answer. Instead, I stepped forward and put my arms around her. We kissed, then she unzipped me. I fumbled at her jeans and soon we were naked, venting our passion on the living room floor, quick and hot.

* * *

Afterwards, I lay there panting. Terrie got up, picked her clothes off the floor and walked for the stairs, still naked.

"Shower," she said.

After some time, I finally had the energy to lift the phone and call Joe Duggan. He'd gone home, so I talked to the duty officer, Sergeant Denise Johnson. I asked her to cancel any lookouts for Terrie's car. She said she would, that she'd get in touch with Joe and pass on the message.

Another long day and I was exhausted.

I locked the house, set the alarm and went up.

Terrie had finished in the bath so I showered. When I went to the bedroom, she was waiting for me.

Chapter 43

Terrie and I were in the 4Runner, driving into the Montrose district. "We've got a side trip," I told her. "My new startup company."

"You've got a company?"

"Small one so far. I'm pretty handy with computers and being involved in security work, I put the two together and created a little technical consulting firm. We specialize in computer security and antivirus protection."

"Sounds cool."

"Cool maybe, not a lot of cash yet. So far, we're losing money but we're hoping to turn a profit next month. It's all uphill from there. Maybe."

Terrie didn't answer. Instead, she stubbed a butt into the ashtray. "My friend in Dallas, Judy? Her birthday's Sunday. She asked me to fly back up tonight. We're going to spend some time together."

"Again?"

"Yes, again. It's her birthday. I'm her friend. I'm invited. I'm going."

"Okay, fine. We'll call and make reservations. When will you be back?"

"Friday, I guess."

Nearly a week, but I knew to protest would be fruitless, so I kept quiet. I clicked on the CD player without checking to see what was in it. Pot luck. The music had scarcely begun before Terrie complained. "What is that crap?"

"That crap, my dear Ms. Bartlett, is Mozart's Piano Concerto Twenty-One."

"Why do you like that old-timey shit?" She poked console buttons at random until she managed to cut the music off and switch to FM.

"Hey!" I protested, but again, to no avail.

Terrie finally located the scan button, pushed it until some awful rap emerged, then she boosted the volume. And of course the equalizer was overbalanced so my Bose speakers rattled both the windows and my frontal lobes. "Christ!" I snapped the stereo off.

"What?"

Now it was my time for the silent treatment, so we drove along, both of us fuming, tension brimming, Terrie poking her cigarette at the window crack, my hands in a white-knuckle death grip on the wheel.

* * *

We drove south on Heights, cut over to Montrose, turned onto Fairview. I parked in the empty lot of a small red brick building with tiny windows and a sign on the front, *Leather Lads*. The sign was garnished around the edges with leather straps and buckles.

Terrie frowned at the sign. "This is your company? A fag bar?"

"I'm next door. The bar doesn't open till six."

"I can't stand fags."

"Don't tell that to Andrew. He'll scratch your eyes out." I grinned at her.

Terrie looked at me askance, still pissed. I pretended not to see the anger in her eyes.

Our destination was the side entrance of a frame house next to Leather Lads. The house was split in half and I'd rented the back. My sign said *Fairview Consultants*. Unlike Leather Lads, there wasn't any decorative artwork, not because I didn't want to add some but because I couldn't think of anything cute and having to do with computers.

It was cool inside, and quiet. A tiny waiting area had institutional chairs and tables I'd bought at a liquidation sale; clean but budget priced. As we entered, a little bell sounded. "Be with you in a second," a voice from the back, and we were soon joined by Andrew Capshaw, my staff of one. Andrew, "always Andrew, never Andy," was a handsome and thin young man with jet-black hair in a prematurely receding widow's peak offset by a neatly trimmed goatee. I thought he looked like Ming the Merciless but kept that little item to myself.

"Mitchell! You got my e-mail about the contract? And who is this lovely young lady?"

"Terrie Bartlett. A client. Terrie, meet Andrew Capshaw. He and I are partners in this little fiasco."

Andrew was his usual ebullient self. "How delightful to meet you, Ms. Bartlett. Welcome to fiasco central." He grasped Terrie's two hands with his own, a wide smile across his face.

Terrie replied with a scant grin. "Ah, hi."

"So Carson accepted our offer?" I asked Andrew.

"They did, and we can get started right away! I printed the contract. All it needs is your John Han*cock*." Flirty as always, Andrew emphasized the *cock* part. Andrew led us into the back room. Two equipment racks sat along the wall, filled with computer and communications gear. Cables in and out, color-coded coax and networking patch cables. There were flat screen monitors on various small desks about the room, a couple of HP LaserJets on adjacent tables. Andrew had printouts of Internet tracking, virus alerts and snippets of Web pages taped up everywhere.

I was proud of the enterprise and wanted to tell Terrie. "We set up our own servers to manage Websites for our clients. We put in a high-speed access line, provide an e-mail virus filter, spam filter and download sites for antivirus protection."

"Like Comcast?" she asked.

Andrew was standing behind her and he offered a little all-knowing smirk at Terrie's naiveté. Made me want to smack him.

I tried to explain further. "Comcast is mostly for home users, kids and such. And yes, they've also got a commercial branch but we provide a specialized, customized service for our clients, primarily law firms."

Andrew broke in. "Our clients are very sensitive about confidentiality. So we set up a separate hard disk drive for each customer and a clean line through our routers. We maintain individual connections for each."

Terrie shook her head. "This is all way beyond me. All I do is, like, e-mail, surf, Facebook."

I mentally shrugged. "Okay, no biggie. Let me look over the contract and we'll be on our way."

Andrew handed me the paperwork. It was a standard affair, Carson LLP being a smallish civil firm who wanted a Web presence and was concerned about spam and viruses. Andrew would set them up with a custom site and e-mail. All their incoming stuff would be filtered for spam and viruses before it reached their offices. I glanced over the contract and signed it.

"I'll have this notarized and get it over to our new clients," Andrew said. "Thank you, Mitchell."

"You're the guy I need to thank. Getting Carson was all your work."

Andrew grinned. "We got the inside track courtesy of a dear friend, Martin. He's a junior partner there."

"Didn't I meet him a couple weeks back? Shaved head, muscles?" I affected a body builder pose.

"God. He's such a hunk." Andrew sighed.

His sigh was echoed by Terrie, expiration loud as an air leak. She was bored and didn't care who knew it. "I'm gonna grab a smoke," she said, heading out.

Andrew watched her leave. "That girl has a serious chip on her shoulder about my people."

"You think?"

"Huh! I wasn't born yesterday. I can tell a mile away, Mitchell." He cocked an eyebrow at me. "She anything to you?"

"A client is all."

Andrew wagged his finger like Aunt Bea admonishing Opie. "Don't try to fib to Andrew. I could see the sparks between you and the young lady with my eyes closed." He smiled his Emperor Ming finest. "Watch your ass, Mitchell. Lord knows I can't watch it for you. You're not my type anyway."

Chapter 44

When I got to the lot, Terrie was pacing back and forth, scuffing her feet in the gravel and furiously smoking her English Oval. "Can we go now?"

We got in, I started the car, put it into gear, waited for traffic to clear.

"Who are you, anyway? Mister *Hire the Handicapped*?" Terrie's voice was snippy.

I put the car in park, looked at her. "What the hell do you mean?"

"Couldn't you find somebody else? Why'd you pick him?"

I was seething. "I chose Andrew because he's a superb computer technician and Web designer. He's smart, creative and honest. And it's none of your damn business whom I hire!"

"I told you, I don't like queers. Do you hang around them all the time, or what?"

"Andrew is gay. He's also a fine man. A friend. And I don't appreciate your comments about him." My blood pressure was up. "As soon as we get to the house, I'll call Donna. She can find you another place to stay. And we'll arrange police protection if necessary."

Terrie covered her face, was silent for a moment before she spoke. "I'm sorry. It's been tense, things so screwed up. I lashed out without thinking."

"People have feelings, you know."

"Mitch, I'm sorry, really. Can you forgive me?"

"You need to consider what you say before it comes out."

She scooted next to me. "Forgive?"

I didn't reply, just sat there. What I was waiting for I couldn't say.

"Mitch, I've been thinking. After the other night, I felt so close to you. I don't have to tell you that things weren't perfect between me and Larry. I loved him in the beginning but we were, well, splits for a long time."

"Okay."

"You have to believe me. As God is my witness, I didn't have anything to do with what happened."

"With his death."

"I didn't. That's the truth."

"I do believe you, Terrie. And my feelings for you are genuine. I don't want us to argue. I want things to work out."

"Me too. Maybe we can try again?" Terrie put her hand on my thigh, rubbing.

I became aroused, despite my anger.

She reached up and kissed me deeply. "Mitch, I'm sorry. Okay?"

Again, I didn't reply, but responded to her kisses, embraced her.

She slid lower in the seat, reached for my zipper, and tugged it down. I made no effort to stop her, looked nervously out the windows instead. It was broad daylight and we were thirty feet from a busy street. Cars zoomed past constantly but nobody seemed to notice.

Terrie reached into my pants and freed my penis, began to suck and stroke. I came quickly.

Traffic continued to pass, uncaring witness to my weak resolve.

Chapter 45

Lazy Saturdays are good for many things, mostly involving a generous and thoughtful waste of time. Since wasting time was a specialty of mine and Terrie was out of town, I figured that hanging out with David Meierhoff would be the best way to address the situation.

We were in my 4Runner, headed south on I-45. It was about ten in the morning and traffic was moderate, most folks obeying the spirit of the law if not the letter by driving a mere twenty miles per hour above the speed limit. Lots of people were on their way to Galveston and the beach because it was bright and sunny, but Meierhoff and I had planned a less aerobic, shadier, but equally fun enterprise. We were going shooting.

The Houston Police range had recently clamped down on guests and Meierhoff, not being a suck-up to the power elite, didn't have the juice for me to tag along in his wake. So when we went shooting, we'd head to a commercial range like Top Gun, Bailey's, or Frontier, where we were going today. Just outside the 610 Loop, I took the next exit and drove east a mile. Another block and we turned into Frontier's parking lot. We hauled our guns and gear out of the back of my truck and I heard muffled gunfire thumping from inside the building.

"Know what that noise is?" Meierhoff said.

"No, tell me."

"It's the sound of freedom."

"Isn't that counter to the established view? According to conventional wisdom, you cops want the populace to be gun-free, keep all the shooting fun to yourselves."

"Bullshit. That's only the top brass, guys who've been off the street so long they can't remember what it's like. Politically correct bastards. The average street cop knows different. He's glad to have ordinary folks armed and on his side."

We lugged our gun bags to the entrance. "And the concealed carry law?" I asked.

"Love it. Check the stats. Street crime has gone down in every state where it's been enacted. Soon as the perps know that John Q has his trusty sidearm, the pickings aren't so easy."

"You should run for NRA president."

"Naw. I'd have to move to DC and wouldn't be able to embarrass you at the gun range. Or take your money." He smiled. "Fifty as usual? And I spot you one out of five?"

"Fifty it is." I'd beat him eventually and maybe this would be the day.

* * *

Frontier is a well-maintained and friendly indoor 50-foot pistol range. There are about twenty booths, each with an electric target carrier, little overhead wires with pulleys like the old tenement laundry lines. You clip your target onto the holder, press a switch to send the target downrange the desired distance, then blast away. The firing area itself is separated to the rear of the building, behind a thick glass partition. Up front is a common room with chairs and sofas, tables stacked with gun magazines and the eternal Coke machine. Along one wall, the counter, a long display case filled with revolvers and automatics, holsters and other accessories. Behind the counter are shelves filled with ammo, hearing protectors and shooting goggles. Two clerks were kept busy waiting on customers today, selling them ammo, targets and advising them on shooting technique.

Decorating the opposite wall are framed John Wayne memorabilia and posters, including an autographed one from *She Wore a Yellow Ribbon*. The folks at Frontier are big fans of The Duke.

There was a fair crowd of shooters in the place today, people of every age and gender and race, checking in and out, proudly displaying targets with tightly placed holes, trying to ignore targets with scattered holes and generally chatting about guns.

Meierhoff and I had brought our own ammo and gear, so we were waved straight into the shooting area by Todd, a pal of mine working the counter. We put on our earmuffs and glasses, lugged our stuff through the range door and over to a couple of vacant stalls.

* * *

Meierhoff and I had several guns to play with today. There were our carry weapons, the new S&W 9mm compacts. I also had a Springfield 1911 .45 and my Colt Anaconda .44 Magnum. Meierhoff unpacked his pride and joy, a beautifully engineered Walther P99 in .40 caliber.

We each put up targets, ran them out to the seven-yard marker, a standard distance for close-drill self-defense practice. We loaded our magazines and started. I generally favor an isosceles stance, facing the target and holding the gun with a straightforward symmetric two-handed grip. Meierhoff uses the Weaver stance, a specialized posture where you stand three-quarters toward the target and lock your arms in a rigid push-pull triangle. It's tricky to get into but it becomes second nature after practice. Or so Meierhoff tells me. I've never had the patience to work at it enough to make it pay off. Maybe that's one reason he keeps beating me.

Meierhoff is meticulous and deadly accurate, most of his shots centered in the five ring and poking holes in the black center bull. I was wide to the left and low but soon made the necessary correction and began to match him shot for shot. For the most part, that was. I'm pretty good, but Meierhoff is the cat's pajamas. He was rapidly popping off full magazines and sending his bullets straight on top of one another. At this distance, you could cover the majority of his shots with a one-inch circle, the dead center of the black paper eaten away until only a big ragged hole remained. Myself, I was hitting the target okay, but only half my shots made the bull. Nevertheless, we were having fun, trading off pistols and admiring one another's handiwork.

My .44 Magnum is a monster, the recoil asking for two hands to control it properly. His .40 caliber Walther and my .45 were midway in power, and our 9mm autos were light enough to fire one-handed with impunity.

After playing around a while, we got serious, ran some fresh targets out and began shooting for money. Meierhoff spotting me meant that I could call a Mulligan on one shot out of five, while all his shots counted. Not that it made any difference. When you're shooting against David Meierhoff, you're at a serious disadvantage from the get-go. Nevertheless, I tried hard, managed to come in second and it only cost me fifty bucks.

* * *

Shooting at a gun range brings out the guy genes to the max. It's said that all men think they're above average in two things, driving cars and making love. You can add a third, shooting.

Next to us was this middle-aged guy who kept peeking over and trying to match our scores. Meierhoff and I noticed this, of course, just winked between ourselves but didn't let on. The better we performed, the worse the other guy fared. He was shooting an elegant Beretta 9mm but that didn't matter. His shots were all over the place, missing the target altogether at times. He was holding the gun wrong but was too stubborn to ask anyone for help. Instead, he became frustrated and that made him miss even more. He kept thumbing the carrier switch to bring his target closer and closer but nothing helped. Eventually he gave up, jammed his pistol into his gym bag and stomped out. I feared for his dog or his neighbors, except that he had zero chance of hitting them.

To the other side, a different scenario. A short chubby older guy with thinning white hair and beard was minding his own business and enjoying himself immensely, thank you. He was shooting a Glock and was damned good, carving out the center of a target at will. He then switched to a silhouette target and hit the ten-zone outlines of heart and head without apparent effort. Seemingly bored, he stenciled a near perfect smiley face on the target from about twenty feet.

While he was reloading, I interrupted him with a tap on the shoulder. "What model Glock is that?"

A gleam in his eye. "Just got it broken in. Model 30, compact, caliber .45 ACP. Ten round magazine. Wanna try?" He handed me a full magazine and the pistol, slide locked back in the proper safe manner.

Meierhoff of course kibitzed while I looked the pistol over. Like its owner, the gun was smallish and thick through the middle. And like all Glocks, it was butt-ugly, purposeful and without ornamentation or glitz. Pure business with a Teutonic determination. The grip was not as ergonomic as my Smith or Springfield, but it was okay and I acclimated after a few rounds. What amazed me was the pistol's accuracy for a smallish gun. I was driving tacks.

I dug out my own .45 ammo and ran through another full magazine. Meierhoff tried the Glock and had the same results, except of course he did even better. Which was to be expected, dammit.

When we reluctantly returned the pistol, I noticed the chunky guy's T-shirt. It read *Montrose Beer and Gun Club* and featured a dripping pilsner beer glass crossed diagonally with a cowboy-era Colt Peacemaker, a fanciful heraldic coat of arms. Below this a motto, *Beer Before Breakfast, Death Before Dishonor*.

"Beer and guns?" I asked.

"Goes together like love and divorce," the guy said cheerfully.

Meierhoff and I were driving back, headed to Grif's so we could catch part of the Astros game and he could buy me a consolation beer. I'd already paid him the fifty-buck extortion.

"Beer and guns," Meierhoff laughed. "You're a Montrose kid. Gonna join?"

"Might do. But the next gun show, I'll certainly take a look at that Glock. I'm partial to forty-fives."

"By the way, Duggan is pissed at you."

What's new, I thought. "Because I won't join the beer and gun club?"

"Because you're involved with Terrie Bartlett. Or as Duggan so colorfully puts it, *slipping her the pickle*."

I braced myself. I didn't much care for Duggan sticking his nose into my business. "What makes him say that?"

"Gimme a break, Mitch. Think anybody can put something past Duggan?"

"Oh?"

"Don't give me *oh*." Meierhoff swiveled to look at me. "It was written all over your face both times I saw you two together. You may as well have been wearing a sign around your neck."

I let that sit for a minute. Then, "I don't feel much like a beer right now. I'll drop you off at your car."

So we rode the remaining distance in silence. I'd been doing a lot of that lately.

Meierhoff disposed of, I got home and phoned Terrie in Dallas, but once more got her cell message. That happened a lot, too.

Another wasted Saturday.

Chapter 46

I was missing Terrie more than I thought possible. And it wasn't just the sex. I had genuine feelings for her. I was also certain she felt the same way about me, and I entertained the possibility that our relationship might last.

Monday, we finally connected. "Good news, Mitch."

"You're flying back early?"

"No, silly. Judy wants me to stay till Friday, like I said. Okay?"

"Has to be. I miss you."

"Miss you too. But we'll have the weekend. We'll have a fancy dinner out, go partying. And it's my treat." I could hear the excitement in her voice.

"Why?"

"What I called you about. Jeff Converse called, the lawyer, you know? The insurance company released a partial payment. Jeff got it deposited directly into Larry's, er, my account at the bank."

"That's good."

"Good? Is a hundred thousand dollars good? I've never seen that much money in my life."

"Congratulations."

"I want to ask you, Mitch."

"Anything."

"What about finding the man? Are you still looking?"

"Of course."

"He scares me."

"I'll get him. Promise."

"I trust you, Mitch."

* * *

Noon, and Major Trent Collins was on the phone. "TJ's been down at the Cape all week, checking out the Russkie launch plans. She's flying in at fourteen thirty."

"Lemme guess. That's two-thirty pm for us ordinary mortals?"

"We try to keep classified secrets from falling into the wrong hands. But yes, two-thirty. She wants us to meet her at Ellington. Can you make it?"

"Sure. What's this about?"

"TJ and I have been talking it over, about Pam Neely. Before TJ left town, she tried to get through to Pamela but drew a blank."

"Tell me about it. I got the same results."

"Yeah. TJ's fed up. She's going straight to Human Resources to file a formal complaint before the day is out. And she wants us to back up her testimony if needed."

"Why meet at Ellington and not JSC?"

"With the upcoming launch window, NASA publicity hounds are all over the place and she won't get any privacy at the office. We can grab some time right after she lands and stay out of the limelight. Then you and I can hang at JSC, see what happens."

"On the way."

* * *

Our Houston summer typically ricochets between blazing heat and heavy thunderstorms. We're beset with hot dry air from the west, coupled with moist cooler patterns swinging up from the Gulf. These two weather systems meet, and the flat terrain encourages rapid and unpredictable changes. But it sure beats snow.

Rain had fallen earlier but since let up. I drove down I-45 for the millionth time, took the Ellington exit and turned in at the gate where Trent was waiting. I parked and Trent signed me in, got me a visitor's pass. We went to the commissary to snag a Coke before TJ arrived. I sat across from him at a little table.

"Look, Trent," I said. "I'm sorry about Pamela Neely. I did everything I could to dissuade her but it was hopeless."

"That's okay. You did what you could. TJ and I both appreciate the effort."

"Least I can testify about Neely. The fact that I made a good faith effort will solidify TJ's case."

"That's something. And it will clear the air, too. We need it. TJ and I are going to formally announce our engagement right away."

"Happy for you both."

"Best day of my life when she said *yes*." Trent checked the wall clock. "We better go. TJ's due in about ten minutes."

Trent and I walked along the tarmac, stepping around recent puddles. "I checked with the tower just before you got here," Trent said. "We're due more rain later. Squalls, strong gusts. Okay for now."

"For now, yeah." I scowled at breaks in the low-hanging clouds but it mostly remained overcast. Snappy breezes whipped at our pants legs as we stood waiting, a random drop or two falling.

"TJ's flying in with two other crew, all of them in T-38s," Trent explained. "Ed Dukas is project commander, Will Fraley is communications."

"Why not hop a commercial flight? Or military transport?"

Trent laughed. "They're all solo jet qualified and putting in flight hours keeps their logs updated. Besides, you ever try to talk a pilot out of the captain's seat?"

"Like talking an evangelist out of a limo?"

"Yeah. The only complaint is that they don't get to shoot off any ordnance. T-38s are unarmed."

"Into every life some rain must fall."

Trent scanned the clouds. "Speaking of rain, I still think it'll hold off."

"Otherwise we'll get soaked."

"As you said, into every life." He glanced up and pointed. "There they are."

Typical eagle-eyed jet jock, Trent had spotted the trio of incoming planes. I looked where he indicated but saw nothing.

Then they were upon us!

Three silver darts sweeping in from the horizon, flying abreast for a little showboating. The jets flashed past faster than I could turn my head. At the far end of the field they rose gracefully, banked, swung back around and broke off in single file for their landing approach.

Another squall line was passing through and the rain pelted our clothing but not heavy enough for Trent or me to break for cover. Instead, we watched the aircraft land. They came in nearly nose to tail, an improvised Thunderbird maneuver designed to show off and impress the locals. The lead T-38 slowed, wheels down, perfectly aligned, and touched the runway without a flicker.

The second T-38 was only yards above the tarmac, tracking the first plane's path. Then it inexplicably and suddenly rose, slipped sideways, lost altitude quickly, and slammed flat onto the runway with a terrible finality.

A great and frightening fireball burst from nowhere and tumbled along the ground, rushing and billowing. The last plane tried to pull up to get clear but it was too close and was swept into the path of destruction. Fragments of metal and plastic and pieces of things I didn't want to recognize bounced into the air and scattered debris across the field everywhere with flashing and sparking and the roar of sudden flames.

Someone was yelling.

The crash trucks were already rolling and Trent was running toward the wreckage. The yelling continued until I realized that I was the one yelling.

Chapter 47

Wind shear, they said, or an undetected microburst generated by the passing squall line, or some other exculpatory jargon. Whatever, it was invisible, localized and impossible to pinpoint quickly enough to make any final flight adjustments. The gust caught TJ's plane, tossed it carelessly onto the ground like a petulant child frustrated with a new toy. The resultant explosion trapped Commander Dukas at the rear. It was determined they'd both died instantly, but who could say and how did it matter now?

The storm at large was, of course, picked up on radar and the control tower had radioed a cautionary forecast to the incoming flight. They could have landed in Louisiana and laid over until morning, since their schedules permitted.

But Tarah urged they continue because she was planning to meet Trent and another friend at the field, where they had some important business to discuss and an announcement to make. An announcement that would forever remain unspoken.

I picked up some gossip later from a reporter I knew. The three astronauts had bent the flight regulations all to hell. Low altitude flyovers were verboten, as were formation landings. And they had all come in way too fast. If not for the accident, they'd have been gigged, probably losing their solo licenses for six months. But the issue was moot and nothing would be done to the surviving Ed Fraley. A quiet memo would go out to the other astronauts, threatening dire consequences if there was any more horseplay, but that was it. Little could be gained by besmirching the memory of two dead astronauts.

* * *

In accordance with Jewish tradition, Tarah Jacoby was buried right away, as soon as the body was released from inquiry. Her parents flew in from New York City for the funeral. And there was a service at Clear Lake Baptist for Will Dukas.

I didn't attend either. I'd witnessed enough grief.

I missed Terrie, phoned her with the news. She took it in her typical offhand manner, but at least it was good talking with her. She'd be back Friday, on schedule. I wanted to drive straight down to Hobby Airport, camp out and wait for her, but decided that would be somewhat obsessive. So I remained fidgety and irritable and pissed off in general.

Nevertheless, a call from Meierhoff got me out of my doldrums temporarily, long enough for him to persuade me to join him for Tarah Jacoby's *Shiva*.

Chapter 48

"Have you ever sat *Shiva*?" Meierhoff was driving his spotless Porsche 911. We were headed to a house in University Place, just down the road from Rice University. The house belonged to physics professor Herman Berkowitz at Rice, where Tarah worked on her second PhD. I read that Berkowitz was one of her closest friends in Houston and was therefore hosting the ceremony.

"No. I don't even know what Shiva means. The etymology, that is."

"*Shevah* is the Hebrew word for seven and *Shiva* is derived from that. It lasts seven days."

"Like a Roman Catholic wake. At least that's what I understand."

"A visitation by family and friends, yes. But very serious. No frivolity, no joking around. Far more religious than a wake. It was ordained as far back as Genesis, when Joseph mourned seven days for his father Jacob."

"You sure I should even be going?"

"Tarah belonged to a Reform temple. Non-Jews are welcome to attend. And Tarah asked in her will that friends at NASA be invited. Trent specifically asked for you. And me."

"What should I do? Or not do?"

"Don't worry. You're not the only Gentile, ah, non-Jew attending."

"Still, I don't want to do anything wrong."

"Just follow my lead." We turned into the street. It was full of cars so Meierhoff parked a block away. The evening was clear and mild, the brief walk pleasant.

"Okay," Meierhoff said. "Her immediate family will be there, Tarah's mom and dad, her brother I think. They'll be sitting on low benches. That indicates a lowering of the spirit due to grief. If you need to sit down, pick a regular chair. Any food or drink that's laid out is not for visitors. Family or specific mourners only."

"Okay. What else?"

"We won't stay long, just pay our respects. Keep quiet, be decorous. Don't speak to the family unless they speak first. Respond with a few words of comfort but don't say glossy stuff like *it will all be better soon*. Shiva is for grief. The healing comes later."

We strolled to the house and stepped onto the small porch. Beside the front door was a table holding a wide porcelain bowl and a stack of small hand towels. Meierhoff nodded to it. "Orthodox Jews ritually cleanse their hands."

"Do we take off our shoes?" I pointed to a row of men's and women's shoes. Nearby was a box of disposable slippers like you get in a hospital.

"Again, mostly for Orthodox. Leather shoes are an old time display of wealth, so removing leather shoes indicates humility." He smiled. "We go in as we are."

The front door was ajar. Just inside, a thick candle was burning on a stand. "The *ner daluk* candle, means *Burning Light*. Stays lit throughout Shiva."

People were gathered throughout the house, talking quietly. I recognized the NASA chief administrator, Tarah's immediate boss and other astronauts. Quite a few attendees were in military garb, most US, some British, Russian and other countries mixed. Meierhoff and I walked around, saying hello quietly.

It was a beautiful home, full of classic furnishings and antiques, befitting of a cultured family with old-world passions.

The many decorative mirrors on the walls were each draped with a cloth, masked. I remembered reading that this was a Jewish tradition at times of mourning, the images a distraction from the more desirable inward reflection into the soul.

Meierhoff led me to the family, who were indeed seated on a low bench. Tarah's mother was a lovely woman, an older version of TJ. Her father was a surprise—tall, slender, blue eyes and blond, a reminder that not all Jews are of Semitic origin. Tarah's older brother and other family were elsewhere. I shook hands, nodded, mumbled some inane words, well meant but incoherent.

I was uncomfortable like everyone usually is at funerals or weddings or other fixed ceremonies. I wandered around, spotted Trent. He was in some low-volume chitchat with a couple of other Air Force men. We waved and that was it.

Five minutes later, Meierhoff was at my elbow. "Ready?" We made our farewell to the family, and Meierhoff said something to them in Hebrew. I asked him about this as we stepped outside.

"'May the Lord comfort you and other mourners of Zion and Jerusalem.' A phrase when you depart the Shiva house. In Hebrew it's *Ha Makom yenachem et'chem*—"

He got no further. All the cars in the driveway and on the street nearby were spray-painted with bright yellow Stars of David.

Chapter 49

Professor Berkowitz let us use the adjacent sunroom to meet the cops. It had a separate entrance and caused the least tumult. Meierhoff and I sat with a couple of University Place police and a security guy from NASA named Ken Wicks. Trent Collins leaned against the wall, sullen, staring out at the dark lawn.

People whose cars had been vandalized were interviewed, giving statements and contact information. The act was a cruel insult to everyone, Berkowitz included. Pam Neely's act had its desired effect, to convey hatred.

One of the cops, Corporal Carl Bruce, took the report. "So you and Detective Meierhoff didn't actually see Pamela Neely."

"No. She was gone by the time we got out," I said.

"Assuming it was Neely. Could have been random troublemakers, racist punks."

"You've got to take into account when she keyed Tarah Jacoby's car," I added. "Told you about that. Neely seems to have a thing for cars."

Wicks spoke up. "Neely wasn't at work today. She's been absent for the past three days, in fact. Called in sick."

"But no witnesses," Bruce said. He made another note in his log. "Anyway. We'll put out a pickup for her. And we'll canvass the neighbors. Maybe one of them saw what happened."

"I'll get you her tag number," Meierhoff said. "And HPD will also be looking."

Wicks stood up. "Anything we can do, you've got my number."

He looked over to Trent. "In retrospect, I wish astronaut Jacoby had come to us first. We'd have probably terminated Neely right away."

"Look," I said. "Tarah Jacoby was trying to do the right thing. She was hoping the situation could be defused without any formal action. And she eventually decided to report Neely. If it wasn't for..." I stopped myself. Talking further about Tarah wouldn't help.

We shook hands all round and got out of there, but it wasn't soon enough for me. The entire affair left a rotten feeling in my stomach and a continuing headache.

God, I needed Terrie.

Chapter 50

I thought things had hit bottom but it only got worse the next day. How bad? The FBI called.

"Mr. King, this is special agent Deborah Strahan. Are you acquainted with a Pamela Neely?"

"What's this about?"

"Mr. King, are you acquainted with Ms. Neely, yes or no?"

"Yes. She's involved in a case I was working on."

"When's the last time you either saw her or communicated with her?"

I thought for a second, remembering. "I spoke with her a week ago Monday. What's this about, please?"

"I'd like you to meet me at Johnson Spaceflight Center. Right away."

"Should I contact my attorney?"

"I don't think so, Mr. King. I'd like to talk. If you then decide to consult your attorney, you may. But you're not under suspicion of anything."

"Suspicion? About what?"

"There's been an incident here at JSC involving Ms. Neely."

When the FBI says *Jump,* you say *how high?*

So I promptly jumped down to JSC and was soon in the office of their security boss, a guy named Miller. Also in the office was Agent Strahan, a heavyset woman with silvery hair and a no-nonsense demeanor. We were joined by Wicks, the JSC guy I'd met at the Shiva vandalism and a sergeant from the Clear Lake cops. I figured the sergeant was here as a courtesy, since the Feds held jurisdiction for any crimes on the NASA reservation.

Strahan was clearly in charge. "Mr. King, how would you describe your involvement with Ms. Pamela Neely?"

"You said you'd explain further when I got here. An *incident,* you called it? What sort?"

"It seems that Ms. Neely has committed suicide here at JSC."

"Suicide?"

Strahan nodded. "We're certain it's suicide."

"What happened?"

There was a general glancing about the room. "It's related to some of the test equipment."

"And I'm involved how?"

"She left a note that accuses you in part for creating her situation."

I thought about what I'd said to Pam Neely. Had I pushed too far? No, I never threatened personal involvement. The worst I'd told her was that Tarah Jacoby would file a report. "In what way did the note implicate me?" I asked. "What am I supposed to have done?"

"Mr. King, this is only a preliminary inquiry. You're not suspected of anything. And we've not Mirandized you. Therefore, anything you tell us is inadmissible. We're only trying to ascertain what happened with Ms. Neely that may have influenced her." Strahan consulted a notepad. "This involved Tarah Jacoby, that much we know."

With TJ gone, there was no confidentiality. "Tarah Jacoby was being sexually harassed and stalked by Pamela Neely. Ms. Jacoby didn't want to make waves by filing charges, so she hired me to see whether I could dissuade Ms. Neely. If not, Ms. Jacoby would proceed with a formal Human Resources complaint."

"You said you met with Ms. Neely last week. What was said?"

"I warned her that she should cease her harassment of Tarah Jacoby. If she persisted, she would probably be the subject of formal proceedings. That was it."

"Did you know for certain that Ms. Jacoby was being harassed? Besides what astronaut Jacoby told you?"

"I personally witnessed one act, not on JSC property. This occurred about a week ago, just prior to my visiting Ms. Neely. Major Trent Collins was also present and can corroborate the incident."

Strahan nodded. "How else was Major Collins involved?"

"He and Tarah Jacoby were in a relationship, as you know. They both supported the idea of my attempting to put a stop to the harassment, if possible, without resorting to any official process. The objective was to prevent embarrassment for anyone."

"Besides speaking to Ms. Neely, did you engage in any oppressive or illegal act?"

That set me off. "You have the wrong idea about private investigators. We don't lurk in the shadows. I'm licensed by the state and I don't engage in illegal activities. But it seems you've already made up your mind."

"Mr. King, please," Strahan admonished.

I was angry and showed it. "No! You get me down here, sit me in a room full of officials, and ask me questions. Fine. But if I'm not a suspect, I think I'm due some consideration. What happened?"

Agent Strahan looked to the others. "We want to set things straight, Mr. King. And we're being honest with you. You are not a suspect nor are we contemplating any charges. We've spoken with Lieutenant Duggan in HPD Homicide and he vouches for you. We don't believe you've done anything irregular."

"Why the push, then?"

Miller, the JSC security guy, cleared his throat. "Ever hear of *bad cop, good cop?*"

I threw up my hands. "Are we on TV? Is this *Law and Order*? Christ!"

"Mr. King," Miller said. "We needed to stir up some dust. Call it a feint. Anything to see how you reacted."

"Well, you got your reaction!" I stood up to leave. "If you want anything else, you can contact my attorney, Donna Boudreaux, Cohen and Boudreaux. I'll give you their number."

"Mr. King," Agent Strahan waved me down. "We said we were being frank with you, and we are."

"So don't insinuate, okay?"

She nodded, glanced over to Wilson. "Maybe we should show you what we've been talking about."

Chapter 51

They led me through the offices, out the back door and over to the pressure test building. An FBI medical examiner van was parked in the adjacent driveway with several police vehicles nearby. Some cops were hanging out, smoking.

Inside the building were more police and medicals, generally in the way and not doing much of anything. A security guard was posted at the entrance but she let us through.

Everybody was clustered around Chamber B. Someone was taking photos through the viewport.

"What happened?" I asked. But I already knew the answer, even though I didn't want to acknowledge it.

Miller surveyed the scene. "Best we can tell, she bypassed the safety mechanisms. It's not supposed to be possible, but she knew the system, front and back."

"She killed herself in the decompression chamber?"

"Yes. We put a couple of our technical people on the analysis and they deciphered her programming. She wrote a new set of override routines. She also physically jumpered across the alarms and jammed a couple of the blowout safety valves. It was tricky."

"The safeties didn't work?" I asked.

"They're designed to prevent accidents, not deliberate sabotage, especially by someone who knows precisely how they function. She came in here about three this morning when there was no other activity, told security people she had some paperwork. They didn't think anything was wrong. She apparently had everything planned, because it only took her a few minutes to set up the procedure."

"You mentioned a note."

"She taped it up by the door. You're welcome to read it. I don't recommend you look inside the chamber. And be sure not to touch anything."

I walked to the chamber door, excused my way past the other people. Just outside the airlock was a small stack of clothing, jeans and a pullover neatly folded, atop it a pair of sneakers, white cotton panties, and a bra. Where Pam Neely changed into a pressure suit, I assumed. A sheet of plain paper was taped next to the window. It was computer printed but signed at the bottom. The note was sad, her angry desperation and grief was gut-wrenching.

> *I loved Tarah but everyone was against us. They didn't even give us a chance to be together. If we had time, Tarah would have loved me back, I'm certain of it. But the NASA bastards decided that she should fuck that nigger instead. They forced her like they forced me. The NASA assholes could not allow love between two women. NASA hired that asshole Mitchell King to undermine my love for Tarah and probably kill me. Now they have killed Tarah instead of me. I don't have a reason to live now, but I don't want that bastard detective Mitchell King to kill me first. But I have made my own decision and will do it my way. I will prove all the assholes and bastards wrong and fuck all the niggers and the kikes and everyone else. Tarah Jacoby I love you! — Pamela*

I tried to digest the diatribe. I knew she was a bit unbalanced, but I hadn't understood the depth of it. Even so, tragic. Could I have done more to prevent it? Who knows? But I couldn't do everything for everybody. Nobody appointed me the universal arbiter of the world's social problems and maintenance supervisor for unrequited romance.

Finally, against Miller's recommendation, I looked inside Chamber B.

I thought that Pamela Neely would be in a pressure suit, but she was naked. She'd laid her frail human body on the recliner where she apparently meant to be discovered in repose, but the trauma of explosive decompression had changed her intended composure to torment.

Her body was covered with blood. Surface embolisms had bloomed everywhere on her skin, creating a mottled pink and red pattern like some perverse tattoo. Rivulets of crimson ran down from the ruptured larger veins and arteries to pool in the recesses of the couch, drizzle on the floor.

Somewhere I'd read a description of this scene, or thought I had. Then I remembered Kafka's *In The Penal Colony*. Pamela Neely's scarlet body was a perfect example of the teaching machine's diabolic embroidery, except that a litany of her sins did not decorate her skin. Instead, only blood, any specific sin of small import now.

Neely's legs were constricted beneath her as the muscles had tightened in rictus. Her hands clawed around her mouth where she'd tried to prevent the outrush of gas from her lungs, but failed. Webbed between her fingers was a frothy sagging mass, lung tissue that burst from her open mouth, sagging onto her face in a parodic red balloon. There was no telling how long she endured the pain but it must have been incredible while it lasted. Her fingernails had scrabbled at her face, leaving long furrows that signified the agony.

I stumbled away from the blood inside Chamber B and made my way to a nearby chair. Dizziness overcame me and I put my head between my knees, wrapped my hands around my throbbing mind.

"You okay?" Agent Strahan said.

"In a minute."

"Mr. King, don't take the note seriously. It's obvious she was ill and in need of help. You're not to blame." She put her hand on my shoulder, a gesture of comfort.

I looked up at her from between my fingers. "Blame? You don't know blame. You have no idea." I staggered away, found the nearest restroom. I ducked into the stall and stooped over the toilet, retching.

An empty stomach and an empty soul. Unclean.

After a while, I could navigate. I washed up, tracked down Agent Strahan, begged off further interviews for today and made a hasty exit.

Chapter 52

Little sleep that night and I was exhausted on Friday. But I forced myself into a Bowflex workout, expending what spare energy I had left, if only to lessen my tension.

Normally I took care of the cleaning myself but today I brought in the rent-a-maid, preparatory to Terrie's return. She did a lousy job but I tipped her anyway. I was focused on Terrie and cared for little else, wanting only to smooth over her return tonight.

Later in the afternoon, I puttered around the house, straightening up stuff that the maid had gotten wrong.

Meierhoff phoned. "About Neely. A mess. I heard about it."

"Yeah."

"I want to reassure you about the other thing, the shooter dude. You know how we work a murder, repo man never sleep, neither do we. An okay guy like Trevillian gets offed, we keep working it, following it up no matter what. We'll find him. And the report on the paint scrapings should be ready any time. I'll let you know when it comes."

"Thanks," I said. "Whatever will help."

I knew what he told me was a formulaic response, designed to calm the nerves of the bereaved family. Everything was therefore peachy keen except for one small detail. The murderer was still out there gunning for Terrie, and no one knew his name or whereabouts. The FBI report would tell us the make of Mel's truck, but it still wouldn't tell us who he was. I suppose I should have told Meierhoff that the truck was a dualie, but I needed to keep a few things confidential.

Myself, I'd racked my brains for a way to locate Mel but ran out of leads. Houston's a big city and there are lots of pickup trucks. With Mel's probable connection in the biker underground, he'd have some shady shop fix his dent and never let on. Or he may have simply left town for good and we'd never find him. Way I figured, if Mel was still here, I'd have to lure him out of hiding by traipsing around Mid-City again and placing my thick neck on the chopping block for him to swing at. Another tour of Mid-City was all I had to go on.

* * *

All I had, that was, until Tony Vee phoned. "You home?" he asked.

"If I was out, would I be answering?"

"I'm calling your fucking cell, duh! You could be in goddamn China."

"I'm goddamn home, okay?"

"You'd be nicer to me if you knew what I got you for Christmas."

"Christmas in June?"

"I hear ole Santa's sleigh right now, and I'm driving it straight to your house. The cops ain't there, are they? Or that chick, what's her name, Terrie?"

"She's in Dallas, visiting. Nobody here but us little old private eyes."

"Good. I'll be there in a few. You better have some cold beer."

Dorsey's had delivered my MG, all cleaned up and complete with a new windshield and inspection sticker. I was outside checking it over when Tony pulled his Caddy under my carport. He was wearing his trademark clothes—black jeans, black pullover, boots. The jeans were scuffed and stained, the shirt torn in a couple of places. Tony was a neat dresser so I knew the disarray was recent. From what, I couldn't say.

I handed him a Bud longneck as he walked over to me. "Thanks," he said, and drank half the bottle in one gulp. "Long drive from Mid-City."

"Why were you swimming in that cesspool?"

Tony shook his head. "Jeez, Mitch. First you ask for help, then I come through for you and all I get is denial. And they call us football players dumb." He turned the bottle up and killed the beer. He reached out and took my full one, handing me the empty in trade. "Cold beer's good on a hot day."

He leaned back and squinted up at the sun. "How hot you think it is?"

"Ninety-three, last I heard."

Tony walked back to his Caddy and thumped on the trunk lid with the bottom of the bottle. "How hot you think it gets in there?"

I knew something was up. And with Tony, I was glad neither Terrie nor the cops were here to see what it was. "Inside the trunk? Pretty hot, I guess." I could see the waves of heated air quivering off the metal.

"Let's not guess," Tony said, "let's ask." He thumbed his remote to pop the trunk lid. Dutch was inside. He was hogtied, wrists bound to ankles, his body arched backwards in a tight arc. Dutch was naked save for a pair of dingy briefs, and he had cuts and bruises all over his body. One of his eyes was puffed and red, his right ear torn and bleeding. He was covered with a sheen of sweat and the stink of him was enough to make a sewer rat turn green. Anger mixed with raw terror was visible in his eyes.

I looked around quickly to check whether the neighbors had a view into the trunk. No, Tony parked so my house blocked the line of sight. We were the only ones who beheld Dutch's predicament.

"Hey, Dutch," Tony said affably. "Hot in there?"

Dutch didn't answer because there was a big strip of duct tape wound around his mouth and head. He moaned and strained against his bonds. But the way he was trussed up, he could pull all day and there'd be no effect except to tighten the knots.

"Know what, Dutch?" Tony told him. "Think I'll park in the sun, play some golf, a nice easy eighteen holes, and couple of drinks in the clubhouse after, dinner maybe."

I pulled Tony aside. "What the hell are you doing?"

"Playing twenty questions with Dutch, only there's just one question and I haven't asked it yet." Tony finished the second beer. "But I see that our contestant is ready."

Tony leaned over Dutch and spoke gently into his bleeding ear. "Now, Dutch, we need some help. My pal and I are looking for this guy. He drives a black dualie pickup and looks like Mel Gibson. He's got a Harley tattoo on his right arm and he likes .41 Magnums. You know who he is and you're going to tell me. Agreed?"

Dutch didn't move, and in response, Tony shattered the beer bottle against Dutch's head! Dutch thrashed around in the trunk from the force of the blow. Fresh blood ran from his scalp and dripped into his eyes.

"Agreed?" Tony asked again. This time Dutch nodded. "Now Dutch," Tony explained, "I'm gonna take this tape off your mouth. If you tell me what I want, I'll see that you're cleaned up and set on your way." Tony lectured Dutch the same way he'd done Lou Masters over his gambling debt. "You holler, cuss, say anything else, I'm putting this tape back on and I'm going for a long drive in the sun. Understand?" Another nod.

Tony reached down and flicked the end of the tape loose, then unwound it, none too gently. As soon as the tape came off, Dutch yelled, "Fuck you!"

Tony seized a handful of Dutch's hair, lifted his head off the trunk floor, and pasted him with a huge right. *Bam!* The entire car shook from the impact. "Name?" Tony demanded. Again, Bam! "Name?" Dutch didn't speak. A third time, *Bam!* Still no reply.

"Okay, Dutch," Tony said, "You're forcing my hand." He reached down beside Dutch and grabbed a tire iron. He took Dutch by the shoulder and rolled him onto his back so that his groin was exposed. Tony aimed for Dutch's balls, raising the tire iron for a blow.

Dutch growled something inaudible.

"What? What did you say?" Tony asked, a wide smile on his face.

"Allison," Dutch mumbled. "His name's Allison, Victor Allison, Vic. That's his real name. Don't know exactly where Vic lives. Trailer park down by Reliant and the old Astrodome, I think. Owns a Silverado. That's all I know. Honest."

Tony waved the tire iron. "You lying to me, Dutch, I'm gonna play a tune on you." To emphasize the point, he let the tire iron drop of its own weight onto Dutch's balls. Dutch yelped.

"Tellin' the truth. But Allison, he's a stone killer. He finds out I said somethin', he'll kill me soon as spit."

"He ain't gonna find out," Tony reassured Dutch. "Nobody will know. And since you've been such a cooperative guy, I'm even gonna pay you a couple hundred." Tony leaned up close to Dutch. "But you drop a dime on us, let him know we're coming, I'm gonna find you, beat you like a fucking rented mule on a Saturday night."

Dutch was quiet.

Tony turned to me. "Got that name? Victor Allison. Silverado. Trailer park near Reliant Stadium."

I was openmouthed at Tony. I'd known him capable of violence, but not to this extent. Nevertheless, I welcomed the information. "Guess I should thank you."

"That you should, pal." Tony picked up a roll of duct tape from the trunk and stripped off a piece. "Don't worry, Dutch," he said, and began to wrap the tape around Dutch's head, covering his mouth again. "This is just to make the ride home quiet. I'm not gonna whack you anymore. Unless you get outta line, that is."

Tony closed the trunk and looked over to me. "Snag me a couple brews for the road, Tiger."

* * *

After Tony left with his trophy, I phoned my contact in the Texas Department of Public Safety. I couldn't trust Dutch to keep his mouth shut for long, no matter what the threat. I had to act fast or I'd lose Victor Allison for good. It took ten seconds for my informant to come up with the address of Victor Allison, owner of a 2002 Chevy Silverado. He lived at 430 Concord Circle, number sixteen.

I checked online. Concord Circle was a dead-end street just off South Main, down near the stadium complex. I didn't know whether the address was a trailer park, but I'd bet on it. I phoned Terrie and for a change she answered right away.

"You're flying in tonight?"

"Yeah. I'll be there, don't worry."

"Problem is, I won't be there myself, or I may not."

"Donna Boudreaux picking me up again?"

"Can you take a cab to my place? I'll pay you back."

"Yes, sure. But why?"

"I've got a lead on our boy Mel Gibson. I might be busy."

"What? The police catch him?"

"No, just me. I think I found him. Maybe. If so, I'll be looking for him tonight, so you're on your own at the airport. I'll be home as soon as things work out. You've still got a key and you're okay with the cab thing, right?"

"Yeah, I've got plenty of cash. But be careful. The guy scares me, Mitch."

"I know. I'll watch out. And Terrie?"

"Yes?"

"I love you."

"I know," she said, like Harrison Ford in *Star Wars*, and clicked off.

I didn't know what to make of that but I didn't have time to speculate. I had a job to do.

* * *

Before I went to see Vic Allison, formerly Mel Gibson, I paid a visit to my gun locker and put the Smith into a holster as a backup piece. I unloaded the Black Talons from the Anaconda .44 Magnum and replaced them with something very special, Glaser Bluetips. These are high velocity pre-fragmented rounds, dozens of little microspheres inside a plastic casing. Glasers are among the most lethal of any ammunition, equivalent to a small shotgun shell at pointblank range. Dinosaur loads.

Chapter 53

I decided to take the MG instead of the 4Runner because it was smaller and I could maneuver easier. I changed into dark clothes, just like Tony Vee, then headed to Vic's house to have a little chat.

Soon I was sitting near the intersection of South Main and Concord Circle, checking out the Redbird trailer park. I'd driven past it twice to get the layout. The Redbird was not a well-organized place, just a sprawl of scrubland fronted by a crude wooden sign over the entrance, advertising monthly leases and sales. Several smallish, broken-down trailers sat tightly parked at the front, each bearing a price scribbled on cardboard stuck in a window. To the rear of the property were the residential trailers. They were widely scattered among the pine trees and shrubbery, making the Redbird a fairly private and isolated place to live. Or hide.

I left the car in a nearby strip shopping center and strolled along the roadway, keeping a sharp lookout for black Chevy dualies. There was a thick stand of trees at one side of the trailer park. I stepped into the woods, carefully making my way until I found a small clearing that offered a reasonable view of Vic's trailer.

Number sixteen was at the extreme rear of the park, some distance from the other trailers. It was a modest structure, probably one bedroom. There was a flat parking area in front, a tiny flowerbed where nothing grew and flip-down metal steps leading to the trailer door. A motorcycle was chained next to the trailer, covered by a tarpaulin. With my binoculars I confirmed a Harley Sportster, its rear wheel missing.

Next, I went back to my MG, drove to a Long John Silver, grabbed takeout fish and chips, a large Sprite. Nothing had changed when I returned.

I drove along South Main and found a perfect spot, an unused dirt driveway that led down to an old reservoir pump house. I parked the car unseen from the road, wolfed down the food, took the Sprite, my binoculars and pocket Maglite, an empty plastic trash bag and returned to the little clearing in the woods that overlooked Vic's trailer.

* * *

I opened the bag flat to sit on, my back against a tree. Vic had few neighbors. Good. The trailer nearest Vic's was unoccupied, *for rent* sign in its window. Better still. I sipped the Sprite, sucked on the ice, waited. One hour. Two. I got up, stretched, walked deeper into the brush and pissed. I returned, sat again. Three hours. The sun began to slant sideways through the trees and things cooled off. In Houston, cool is a relative term because it was still about eighty. The shade made it tolerable.

A little brown chameleon crawled along a nearby branch. He paused every few inches, bobbed his head, puffed out his red throat sac. He was on the prowl for love, and his rotating bug-eyes looked everywhere for the object of his desire. I don't know whether he found it because he soon passed around the bole of the tree and out of view. I wished him luck anyway, envious of his one-track brain, single purposed and fixed upon its unique goal.

Would that I could focus my mind similarly, shut down the higher functions, concentrate reptilian upon the one task ahead, the target. I needed that singular direction tonight.

* * *

It was about six when Victor Allison turned up. The Silverado pulled into the trailer park and dusted along the rough hard pack lot until it stopped in front of his place. There was still a dent in the doublewide right rear fender.

Vic got out, carrying a bag of groceries. He unlocked his trailer door and went in. The screen banged behind him but he left the solid door open. A minute later he came out with a toolbox and a can of Coors, and I had my first good look at him. Vic was about my size but heavier, with muscular chest and arms. I could clearly see the Harley tattoo on his forearm. He had mid-length sandy hair, even features and did indeed resemble a youngish Mel Gibson. He retrieved a carton of Marlboros from the truck and walked over to his Harley. He seemed in no hurry.

While he smoked, Vic fiddled with the bike for about an hour, covered it again and went inside, the main door still open. Lights came on. Vic walked around, moving past the kitchen window, apparently fixing dinner.

I waited five minutes and then it was time. I stood up, covered the binoculars with a few leaves, quietly picked through the branches until I reached the windowless end of Vic's trailer. As I slowly edged around the structure, keeping close to the wall, I heard Waylon Jennings playing from the open door. Vic passed once more and I leaned back into shadow until he'd gone by. I pulled the Colt from my shoulder holster and cocked it. I stepped up to the screen, opened it and quickly went in, closing the solid door behind me.

* * *

Vic stood over a fry pan, stirring some link sausages with a fork. The sausages sizzled and popped. When he heard the door, he turned and looked at me.

"Who?" he began, then saw the gun in my hand and went quiet.

I raised the gun halfway. "Don't move. Don't do a thing."

Vic stood there as ordered. I rapidly checked the surroundings. The living room was at one end of the trailer, to my back. I was standing in a tiny breakfast nook next to a foldout table. An overhead fan above me gave a steady breeze, carrying the sausage smell. Vic was in the compact kitchen, midway along its length. Behind him would be the bath and bedroom, a typical trailer.

"Why did you shoot Larry Trevillian?"

"Shoot who?" Vic's voice was calm.

"Larry Trevillian. Don't play games."

"I don't know what you're talking about." He smiled an easy smile. I looked beneath this facile grin, peered into his eyes, and knew that this man would kill without a moment's consideration. One of us would not survive the night.

"You shot Larry Trevillian then you tried to kill Terrie Bartlett and me. Why?"

"I don't—" he began, and flipped the pan of hot grease at me!

* * *

I fired but missed as I dived away, landing hard on the floor. Flash of bright pain as grease spattered my face and hair, but the bulk of it missed and splashed against the wall. As I tried to regain my balance, Vic reached beneath a towel on the counter, came up with a big revolver and fired.

A jolt rang my head like I'd been hammered by The Hulk. Everything seemed to slow down. My hands wouldn't work properly and I couldn't get my feet beneath me.

Vic laughed and stepped over where I squatted. I made an effort to bring the muzzle of my gun to bear, but Vic got there first. He slapped the side of my head with his gun barrel and my vision pinched in. Vic laughed again and pulled his gun back for another blow.

No! I wouldn't let him beat me!

260

I summoned a fraction of clarity from somewhere, forced myself to concentrate. As Vic swung the gun down, I grappled his wrist and rolled back, sticking my foot in his gut and flinging him overhead to the end of the trailer. His gun went spinning away.

I got to my knees as Vic pulled himself up from the living room floor, frantically searching for his gun. The Colt was still in my hand but I was groggy and couldn't get my muscles to function. Vic appeared as through a narrow tunnel, his face contained and ringed in a circle of haze.

He had to quickly decide whether to find his gun or come for me without it and, in one second, he made the choice. Vic pounced across the room toward me, grinning widely with the joy of my imminent death.

My second round took him square in the mouth.

Chapter 54

I managed to roll to my left as Vic dropped beside me. I hopped away from him, gun cocked, ready to fire again. It wasn't needed.

I looked fixedly at Victor Allison, my mind clearing until I finally resolved the image. Much of Vic's mouth and upper jaw was blown away by the blast of the .44 Magnum Glaser, a jagged hole where his lips and teeth had been. His left eye hung from its socket and there was a red blotch where the other should be. Most of the back of his head was gone, as were his brains. There was blood and bone and tissue everywhere on the ceiling and walls. I felt a gentle spray on my face and looked up to see the overhead fan broadcasting remnants of Victor Allison throughout the trailer. I barely made it to the john to lose what remained of my dinner.

Outside, it was quiet. No flashing red lights, no sirens, no curious neighbors. Gunfire at night is common in semi-rural Houston, and those who'd heard our shots must have chalked them up to random potshooters.

I took a look at myself in the bathroom mirror. There were burns on my face where the grease hit. There was an oozing red strip along the left side of my head, token of Vic's near miss. And what looked like some of Vic's brains stuck in my hair. I cleaned up, tried to do it without looking in the mirror again. I began a quick but methodical search of the trailer. I put a couple of small plastic storage bags over my hands so as not to leave prints.

First, I checked Vic's pockets. Set of keys, pack of cigarettes, and a lighter. I stepped carefully over the pools of blood and found Vic's gun in a corner of the living room, under the TV stand. I stuck my ballpoint pen into the trigger guard and lifted it. A Dan Wesson .41 Magnum. Cops don't like loose ends so I carried the gun over to Vic and laid it near him, just out of the blood. The rest of the living room had nothing to show.

Vic was a neat person with few possessions and his bedroom was orderly. He had some decent clothes—Harley cold weather riding gear, several pairs of jeans, T-shirts. On a shelf in the closet, I found a little metal tackle box and inside, three bags of grass and some white powder I guessed was coke.

A packing box on the shelf was labeled *Personal* and the papers inside capsulated Victor Allison's life. Birth certificate. High school diploma. Automotive repair trade school. Marriage and divorce papers. Army records with good conduct discharge. A set of California parole documents, then something that perplexed me. It was a stack of Army awards and ribbons for marksmanship. Expert with rifle and pistol. This continued in civilian life: medals from a gun club in Riverside, California, for rapid-fire open sight competition. The name on these was Victor Slade but I knew it was our recently departed Vic. Ex-cons can't legally have guns in California. Or Texas, for that matter.

If he was such a good shot, why had he missed us twice that night at my house? I wrote it off to the rainy weather and continued my search, still looking for some clue as to why he'd killed Larry Trevillian.

The nightstand by the bed was all that remained. On the table, a brimming ashtray and a Dean Koontz novel. His wallet contained some cash, his Texas driver's license, assorted ID cards. The shelf beneath the table held a Stephen King paperback and two skin mags. In the drawer were two tightly rolled joints, a small tube of KY jelly, an open pack of Marlboros and a couple of Trojans. Sum and content of the swinging bachelor life.

As I poked through the drawer, I flipped over the pack of cigarettes and saw one of my regular business cards slid in under the clear wrapping. That confirmed how he'd found my house. In addition to the bogus cards, I'd scattered quite a few of my real ones that day in Mid City and he'd evidently picked up my address from this. Not smart to have the cops find it. Too many questions. So I carefully teased the card from the pack with the tip of my car key. After taking the card out, I casually turned it over.

On the back was the number *173-5257*.

* * *

My breath stopped instantly and I sat down stock still on the unmade bed. I recognized the handwriting on the card because it was mine and I knew where I'd been when I wrote it: in the jail, sitting across from Terrie Bartlett. This was the card I'd given her.

A piece of my world ended then, the earth opened to swallow me and I was sent spinning into anguish, a black pit with no bottom. I may have briefly gone insane. *Terrie.* I cried fiercely, harder than I'd cried in memory. Tears poured from me and sobs came in ragged, childlike gasps. *Terrie.*

I could have sat there all night, locked in a fugue of despair and self-pity, but I realized I had to work quickly. If I delayed contacting the cops much longer, the deteriorating condition of Vic's body would make them suspicious.

Running on vapor alone, still sobbing, I began. First, the ashtray. I found a roll of foil in the kitchen, pulled off a sheet, dumped the ashtray contents on it. There they were, brownish English Oval butts. I put them aside and scoured through the remainder, picking out any telltale filterless Marlboros and their companion unused filters. Three each. I poured the regular ashes back into the ashtray and stuck some of the normal Marlboro butts into the mess to make it look reasonable.

Carefully I shredded the evidence, including my business card, flushed it down the toilet. The foil I wadded up and tossed into the woods behind the trailer. I also checked the garbage, but thankfully the kitchen bag was new, only holding a couple of beer cans and Vic's sausage wrappers. I checked through his papers for Terrie's phone number or some other link, but found nothing. I could only hope that Vic hadn't squirreled away some incriminating bit of information in a dark recess of his trailer. An oddity these days, he had no cellphone, at least not one I could find. Whenever he'd called Terrie it must have been from a pay booth.

Next, I went out, retrieved my binoculars with the help of the Maglite, walked to my car, drove back inside the Redbird trailer court and parked by Vic's truck. I stowed my binoculars and 9mm Smith in the trunk, gave the trailer a final look-see and called Donna Boudreaux at home.

"There's been trouble. Bad." I briefly explained the situation to Donna, omitting the incrimination of Terrie.

"Jesus, Mitch."

"Yeah. I'm going to phone Joe Duggan now. If they arrest me, I'll get back to you."

"Get back regardless."

Next, I phoned Terrie. She didn't let me talk. "Mitch! I just got to your house. You sound worried. What is it?"

"Terrie, this is very important. I need you to listen carefully. I'm only going to say this once."

"Okay, what?"

"Victor Allison is dead. I shot him."

"God! Are you okay?"

"I'm fine. But I want you to know. I took care of everything. Cleaned it up. Anything you had at his trailer is gone. Nothing left to connect you. You're safe."

"Mitch, I—"

"I did it for you, Terrie. I love you."

"Yes," she said.

Finally, I called Joe Duggan.

Chapter 55

"You stupid fuck!"

I sat in the back of Joe's unmarked cruiser. He was in the passenger seat, Meierhoff behind the wheel. Both of them looked out the windshield at the medical examiner staff and various cops finishing at Vic's trailer. It was dark inside Joe's car and I felt alone. Joe swiveled around, elbow over the seat back. "Did you hear me? I said you were a stupid fuck."

I was quiet.

Joe shook his head in frustration and turned away. The coroner's van pulled out. Two marked cop cars and one unmarked still sat by the trailer. A gaggle of the Redbird tenants stood on the fringes, waiting for something more to happen. It probably wouldn't, and soon they'd begin to turn back to their own abodes.

Joe suddenly exploded. He pounded the dashboard with his big fists, and Meierhoff and I both jumped. "Stupid fuck! Stupid fuck!" he shouted, pounding.

Then his voice went soft. "Detective Meierhoff, what possible charges do we have against the aforementioned stupid fuck?"

"Homicide in the second degree, criminal trespass, interfering with a police investigation, illegal discharge of a firearm in the city limits and being a stupid fuck. I can come up with a few more if you like."

There was silence.

"Well?" Duggan finally asked.

"Well what?" I said.

"Well, are you going to tell us what happened?"

"I already did. I got Victor Allison's address from a biker in Mid City. I came here. He attacked me. We fought. I shot him."

"Don't give me that bullshit!" Joe roared. He turned to face me again. "You lied to us! We trusted you, helped you, but the second you got a break, you worked it alone! We could have taken him alive, you idiot! But you had to play it like some cheap movie asswipe, go in there, blazing away. You stupid fuck!" He sat squarely again and glared out the windshield.

I was silent and not a little afraid. They hadn't handcuffed or charged me yet, but they could do it anytime.

* * *

A uniform cop came over to the passenger side and bent down. "Lieutenant?" he said.

"Yes?" Duggan replied, restrained.

"We're finished. The lab boys will come back tomorrow to clean up. Anything else?"

"This is Detective Meierhoff's call. I'm just here to bear witness," Duggan answered.

"Sir?" The cop seemed confused.

"Never mind," Meierhoff told the cop. "You guys can go. Make sure you put the crime tape over the door."

"Already done. Have a nice night."

"Same to you," Meierhoff replied, and the cop walked away.

Soon the cars pulled out and we were by ourselves.

"Detective Meierhoff," Duggan said. "Would you take a stroll? I want to be alone with the stupid fuck."

Meierhoff got out, leaned back inside and looked at me. "We're cutting you loose, King. But you be in my office at ten tomorrow morning and you bring your goddamn lawyer." He turned to go, then came back. "You're a total cocksucker, you know that?" He shut the door and walked away.

Duggan lifted a hand, silhouetted against the dim light. "One," he said, pulling a finger down, "Vic Allison's gun will match in ballistics. Trevillian case closed." Joe's temperament was steady and I felt a little relieved.

"Two," and another finger followed, "Allison shot at you tonight and technically you were defending yourself. Allison case closed."

He added the ring finger. "Three. There's nothing to tie Theresa Bartlett with either killing. Bartlett case closed. And four," the little finger completed the fist, "you think you got it all wrapped up and you probably do. So you're gonna walk."

Duggan suddenly spun around, facing me, and reached back with both hands. He grabbed my jacket, jerked me upright from the seat as if I were a rag doll.

"You listen to me, Mitchell King." His voice was slow ice and, despite the darkness, I could see the steel glitter in his grey eyes. "I know you planned this and I know why. If there was a shred of evidence, I'd have your license in one hand and your balls in the other." Duggan pulled me closer until his face was an inch from mine. "Do you realize what you did? Do you? You poor miserable weak fucking bastard, you killed a man for a piece of ass!"

Duggan let me go and I fell back against the seat.

He got out of the car, opened the rear door for me, pointed to my MG. "Now you take off before I change my mind and haul you down into those woods to beat your sorry self to a bloody fucking pulp."

I started for my car.

Duggan called to Meierhoff. "Done is done, David. Let's blow this fucker." They turned away from me, got in their car and drove out.

I needed to be with Terrie. That was all I had now and thankfully she'd be waiting. I'd gone through hell, crossed my friends, squandered all my good will with Duggan and Meierhoff, but at last Terrie and I could be together. I sped up and let the night air carry me home.

When I got there, both the Mazda and Terrie were gone.

Chapter 56

I panicked and tore through the house like a madman, running up and down the stairs, calling her name. All of Terrie's things were missing from Chrissie's bedroom, her makeup no longer in the bathroom. After frantically searching along the street for her car, I headed back inside and felt a crunch under the doormat. My spare keys.

There was only one place she could be. Her house. I phoned but got the damned answering machine, direct to voicemail for her cell. Was it possible Vic Allison had a partner? Dutch or someone else, maybe? If so, she was still in danger. The fact that she'd taken all her things only meant that she'd gone home voluntarily. After she got there, trouble may have been waiting.

I didn't dare call the cops. There were too many problems for them to become involved all over again. No, I had to take care of this myself, same as I had done with Victor Allison. They'd taken my .44 Mag for evidence, so I retrieved the Smith from the MG trunk and stuck it onto my belt. I streaked out I-10 to Terrie's house.

It was late and there was only sparse traffic. I may have broken a couple of land speed records getting there and it was lucky I wasn't clocked by radar, because I wouldn't have stopped.

There were several cars parked in Terrie's driveway, two more on the lawn, none that I recognized. As I neared the house, I heard the thumping of her stereo, pounding out some cruddy bass tracks at top volume. I drew my pistol, held it down by my side, and tried the front door. Unlocked.

* * *

I stepped into the living room and saw some people I'd never met, all in swimsuits. A nice looking young man and woman were sat on the sofa, another woman knelt beside them. The man wore a green-striped French cut, the woman beside him a red mono. The woman on the floor wore only the bottom of a yellow bikini, displaying her small but lovely breasts.

The man looked up and waved me over. "Hey, come on, dude. Plenty for everybody." Before them on the coffee table was a mirror and on the mirror, several lines of coke. An upscale version of Jimmy Landon's chemical playtime. The bare-breasted woman leaned over to snort the white powder through a little metal straw. On the table was a screw top bottle holding about two ounces more. Beside that was a bottle of Korbel champagne and some tulip-shaped glasses. I concluded that Terrie Bartlett was not in danger and put my pistol away.

I left the trio to their indulgence and quickly checked the bedrooms. Clothes were piled on a bed but no people were in them. I walked back through the living room where the man again waved at me, but I went straight to the back of the house, into the kitchen.

On the counter sat a store-bought deli tray and a big platter of peeled shrimp, a row of liquor bottles and mix nearby. There were two picnic coolers on the floor, one filled with bottles of champagne, one with cans of beer. The kitchen floor and counter were wet and littered with bits of food, and there were empty bottles and cans in the trash. Evidently, they'd partied for some time. If I guessed, the fun began right after I phoned Terrie to tell her she was scot free.

The patio door that led to the pool was open, letting the air conditioning fight against the muggy night. There was music from patio speakers and some splashing in the whirlpool at the far end.

It was too dark to see clearly, but I made out several people in the water.

Presently a slender figure detached itself from the group, heaved from the pool, and strolled toward the house. A masculine voice from the pool: "Bring me a beer."

The figure resolved itself into Terrie Bartlett. She padded along the tiles, dripping water, a smoldering English Oval dangling from her fingers. Terrie wore only a microscopic white thong bikini bottom that didn't completely hide the soft black tendrils of pubic hair. Her full bare breasts were even lovelier than I remembered. They stood high and firm, nipples erect from the night air.

Terrie came into the kitchen and was halfway to the champagne cooler when she saw me. She stopped, took a drag from her cigarette, grinned. "Well, if it isn't the boy detective. I thought you'd be in jail."

"Justifiable shooting. They let me go."

"So what brings you out here to suburbia?"

"Came to party."

"I don't remember sending you an invitation." Terrie smiled, unconcerned about her nudity.

Regardless of what she'd done, regardless of what happened, I wanted her. Lord, I still wanted her. I pushed that feeling aside. "What's the story? Who was Vic Allison to you?"

"None of your business, Mitch. Now fuck off."

In answer, I picked up a bottle of Scotch from the counter and flung it over my shoulder without looking. The bottle crashed onto the tiled hallway and the pungent odor of whisky quickly filled the room.

The man's voice, again from the pool: "Terrie? You okay? Got my beer?"

I picked up a second bottle of booze to throw it but Terrie stopped me, her hand on my arm. "I'm fine," she called out. "Just dropped a glass." Then she looked at me. "What do you want?"

"The whole truth and nothing but, like they say."

"Okay, fine." She shrugged, making her breasts bounce. "Come on. We can talk in here." She turned, picked up a pack of cigarettes and a lighter from the counter, walked nonchalantly down the rear hallway to the garage. As I followed, I admired her naked backside, her tanned smooth shoulders, her long and beautiful legs, only the thin strap of the bikini marring the cleavage of her taut brown buttocks. The perfect body, so inviting. God in heaven, I wanted her even now.

* * *

Terrie led me to a small room off the garage that was remodeled into a mini gym. She parked herself on the seat of a stationary bike, lit up, and motioned me to sit on the weight bench.

"Why did you have Larry Trevillian killed?"

She puffed on her cigarette. "I did everything I could but it was hopeless. He was doing more and more coke all the time, morning, night, whenever. He even started smoking crack. He was hooked badly."

"And?"

"His work was going downhill, he was missing days at the office, and people were starting to talk. I tried to get him to cut down, get him into therapy, but it was no use." Terrie took another drag, blew the smoke out, and looked me straight in the eye. "I cared about him but I wasn't going to let him drag me down."

She lifted her hands to indicate resignation. "I've been on my own since I was fourteen, left home after my gym teacher raped me, nobody took my side. I bounced around the country, scraping things together, turning tricks just for a place to crash, doing whatever to keep alive. Then I pulled myself out of the gutter, learned how to act nice, read a lot of books, made a new life. I met Larry. He treated me fine, gave me all this." Terrie gestured, sweeping her arm to show me the house.

"But Larry was losing it."

"Right. I invested too much in Larry, came too far to start over again. So I asked around with some people from the old days and they connected me to Vic."

"You used him to get rid of Larry. What did you promise?"

"Fifty thousand from the insurance. In the meantime I kept him interested."

"Sex."

"Yeah, sex. I work hard to keep my body in shape because it can get me things." Terrie stubbed out her cigarette on the handle of the cycle, tossed the butt on the floor, smiled at me. She put her hands beneath her breasts and lifted them. "These have brought me a lot, haven't they, Mitch?"

"Including me?"

"Including you." She let her breasts fall and crooked her little finger at me, forming a hook. "I had you like this." Smiling wickedly.

"Did you plan to shoot Vic Allison from the beginning?"

She nodded. "A guy like that, impossible to trust."

"But you missed."

Terrie nodded again. "I'd been practicing but I got excited."

"And with you in jail and Vic out there waiting, you needed help. So you picked me."

"You picked yourself, Mitch. The second we met, you were all over me."

"I was that obvious?"

"Not really. But like I said, I've been around and I know men."

"What if I said no? What if I played it straight?"

"There was that Jew cop, Meyer… whatever."

"Meierhoff."

"Whatever, like I said. He had it for me, too. And if not him, there'd be somebody else who'd come along. There always is."

"So why did Vic shoot at us that night if you and he were partners?"

"I called him, told him where I was, that everything would be okay. He wanted to see me right away but that was impossible. I told him I shot at him out by the pool to make the story look good, but I don't think he believed me. He was pissed and I guess he wanted to make a point."

I remembered her extended Galleria trip. "So you met him the next day."

She nodded. "When I got to the Galleria, I picked up some things, went over to his place. But after we screwed, I was so tired I fell asleep. That's why I was late getting back."

I thought about how she'd deflected my questions that night, the method she used. And later, when I was ready to break off with her, another treat thrown to me, keeping me in line. "You never felt anything for me?" I had to know.

"Don't get me wrong. I like to fuck. And you're good in bed, I'll give you that. I must have come a dozen times that first night. But you're too old for me. I need younger men. Besides, your price is too high."

"Meaning I'd eventually get fed up, go to the cops."

"Yep."

"What if I go to them now?"

"Chance I have to take. But what are you going to tell them? You're home free, same as me. You talk to them, you'll go to jail too. And there's no proof anyway. You said you got rid of it, right?"

"I did it for you, Terrie."

"Yes, and I gave you a good time in return, didn't I? But the way I see it, our business is finished."

I stood up. "You know what you are? You're a cold hearted psychopath."

"And you," she replied, still smiling, "are a fucking fool."

"Terrie," a voice from the hallway. "Where you been?" A well-muscled young bleach blond man walked into the room. He was wearing a blue Speedo and holding a can of Miller Lite in one hand. "Who the fuck is this?"

"Just a guy I know, Brad. He stopped by but he's leaving." Terrie hopped off the bicycle seat and went over to join her newest lover.

"Let me guess," I said. "He's the girlfriend you were visiting in Dallas."

"She's real. I know her from when I lived there. She was my cover so I could meet Brad. He drove down here yesterday."

"Hey," Brad said. "What the fuck, calling me a girlfriend?"

Not the brightest bulb in the chandelier was Brad. "Don't worry your pretty blond curls about it," I told him.

Brad stiffened, clenched his fists.

"Don't mind him, Brad," Terrie said. "He's outa here."

"I may decide to stay."

Terrie backed up until she was leaning firmly against Brad. She reached behind herself and began to massage his groin. "I already said," she told me. "You're not invited. I got all I need right here." She smiled her deep, seductive, well-practiced predatory smile.

"You heard her," Brad said. "Beat it, dickhead."

"Watch her close, Brad. She'll stick a knife in your ass for a fucking quarter."

Brad took Terrie by the shoulder, moved her aside and came swinging for me. Like most bodybuilders, he relied on his bulk and didn't know about fighting. He telegraphed his punch by dropping his right shoulder and I simply nodded out of the way. I feinted a right hook, and when he dodged, I kicked him in the balls. As he was going to his knees, I pulled my pistol and slammed it flat against his temple. He was down like a sack of wet dirt and I was suddenly giddy with cheerfulness.

Terrie pointed. "You. Get the fuck out. Now!"

I stepped around Brad. He was beginning to stir and would soon be back in the whirlpool, getting his sore rocks off. More power to him.

I walked back through the house, Terrie following. As I passed the kitchen, I grabbed an open bottle of Jack Daniels from the counter and guzzled, fighting against choking and keeping it down. Still holding the bottle, I went over to the three people partying in the living room. "Hi," I said. "Ever try Jack and coke?" And I poured the whiskey into the open bottle of cocaine. It overfilled and sent the mixture spilling out onto the table and floor.

"Hey!" said the guy. He stood up and grabbed my arm.

I answered by sticking the barrel of my pistol up his powdery nose. "You talkin' to me?" I asked, a lame Travis Bickle impression.

The man quickly pulled back. I dropped the empty bottle onto the living room carpet, went out and drove away before I started shooting people.

Chapter 57

I found the nearest convenience store, picked up a six pack of beer and a foam can holder to put between my legs. Then I drove randomly through residential streets, chugging the beer, tossing the empties straight into the air to let them fall rattling on the street behind me. When the beer was gone, I picked up another six, went through most of that, too.

I stopped by the Richmond Arms but Julia wouldn't serve me because I was drunk, or so she insisted despite my pleas to the contrary. But there's more than one bar on Richmond, so I began to try each of them, progressively moving east toward home.

A long time later, I was sitting in some unknown and unnamed tavern near Kirby. I'd been knocking back shots of Wild Turkey followed by draft beer, boilermakers potent and simple. My head was buzzy but I could still remember what had happened, so I kept the drinks coming. The bartender was cooperative and I tipped him accordingly. Several places had refused me service, but I was determined to tie one on and my perseverance was finally paying off.

I overdid it, though. When I came back from the john, I sat down in the air next to the barstool. My tail landed on the floor and my drinking was cut off in one fell swoop. Amazing how my well-being tonight was dependent on the vagaries of the friendly bartender. The guy stuck all the remaining change in my jacket pocket, despite my efforts to tip him the odd fifty. Then he tried to get me out the door. Not being successful, he asked me if I wanted a cab.

"No. Can't trust a cab. Gotta drive myself."

The bartender made a valiant effort to keep me from driving but I would not be dissuaded and I showed him my pistol to make the point. He relented to my brilliant logic without further ado and let me stagger off into the warm night.

* * *

This is silly, I thought. Why don't I go home? I had set out to get drunk and accomplished my goal, so what remained? Problem was, I couldn't get my car to steer north. Somehow, I found myself headed east on Alabama instead. "Hey," I said, talking to myself as I drove. "Good idea. The house is too far. Stop by Grif's, leave the car there, get some coffee and a cab home." At least I thought I'd spoken this aloud. The concept was valid anyway.

I drove carefully but not so slow as to attract attention, keeping one eye closed so the double images of passing cars would not confuse me. I crept along Alabama, stopping religiously at each traffic light and I was pretty sure they were mostly red when I stopped. The litany of cross streets rolled on—Greenbriar, Shepherd, Woodhead, Dunlavy, Mandell, and then finally Yoakum. Just one more light, Montrose, and I was a block from Grif's.

The Yoakum light turned red as I approached, so I stopped at the intersection, obeying all traffic laws like a good responsible drunk. The red light was blurry but still visible. I closed my eyes for a moment to rest and when I opened them, the light was still red. Damn long light, I thought. So I closed my eyes again and when I opened them the second time, I found that the light had changed from solid red to flashing red and blue. Interesting, but what could it mean?

It was about then I noticed someone standing by my driver's door looking down at me. I didn't know if there was any connection between the flashing lights and his standing there, but soon I surmised that he was a cop and that I'd been busted.

"Sir," the cop was saying, "how much have you had to drink tonight?"

"Not enough," I replied, smiling pleasantly, hoping to lessen the tension with a little joke.

But it fell on deaf ears. "Sir, please step from the car."

I wanted to, I really did, but my legs just wouldn't obey. I made some offhand gesture that caused him to reach down and snatch my keys from the ignition, killing the engine. "Hey," I protested, "I was going to Grif's!"

"I don't think they would serve you in your condition, sir. Now will you please get out?"

Finally, I managed to comply. I opened the door, swung my legs out and pulled myself from the low-slung seat. I wobbled quite a bit and reached out to steady myself on the cop's arm. Instead, he turned me around and leaned me up against the fender of the MG.

I reached back to show him my gun, thinking I should let him know I was armed, and that was when I instantly found myself sprawled on the pavement, the cop's knee in my neck, my face pressed into the roadway.

He jerked my pistol from the holster. "Hands behind your back!"

I did, and was tightly handcuffed.

He frisked me while I lay there, pulled me to my feet, leaned me over the trunk of his cruiser and began to look through my pockets, finding my PI folder right away.

"Christ, Mister King, you might have a PI permit but it don't give you the right to drink like a fuckin' fish then try to drive. You oughta know that."

"Need help, Harry?" someone said, and the voice was familiar.

"Under control, Phil. He's carrying a piece but turns out he's a private eye. Drunk on his ass though."

"Lemme see," the other voice, nearer now. A moment later and, "Hoo, boy! Lookit who we got here!" It was Phil Jenks, my favorite Nazi-flavored cop.

I was seized roughly and jerked up, spun around. Jenks towered over me, grinning with rare amusement. "I know this cocksucker," he said.

"Drunk and disordered," the other cop laughed.

Jenks took me by the shoulder and held me upright. "Now, Mister Hotshot Private Detective, I want to hear you say your ABCs."

"He don't need to," the other cop interjected. "He's so drunk he can hardly stand up. We can skip the other tests."

Jenks turned to glare at his partner. "I want to hear some ABCs and I want to hear them right fucking now." He looked back to me. "Come on, hot shit, lemme hear 'em. A... B...C..."

I decided not to humor him and stayed quiet. Whap! He jabbed me in the stomach with the knob of his baton. An intense blister of pain burst in my gut, I bent over and every drop I'd drunk that night came gushing out. Jenks stepped back but not fast enough. The hot vomit shot out my mouth and up my nose and I spouted onto Jenks' trouser legs and shoes.

"You son of a bitch!" he yelled. He bashed me on the head and I went down. Jenks rained baton hits on my arms and shoulders, and with each blow, the pain rocketed through my body. I tried to keep quiet but I couldn't, and cried out. The assault continued and things began to go black.

Then through the haze of drunkenness I heard, "You hit him again, fuck face, you deal with me."

I opened my eyes and saw a pair of shiny polished brown loafers.

Meierhoff.

Chapter 58

Jenks' partner Harry helped me up. My arms were throbbing and they took the handcuffs off so I could regain some feeling. Jenks had gone to sit in his cruiser and sulk that he hadn't been allowed to flail away on me till next October. My head still throbbed from the booze and baton blows, and it would be doing so for some time to come, but I was otherwise okay. A few bruises. My leather jacket had absorbed most of the direct impact.

"You're fucking lucky, you know that?" Meierhoff's voice was taut, angry. "I just happened to be driving down Alabama and recognized your car."

"Thanks."

"Don't bother with the thank yous. I'm not hanging around. Got better things to do than babysit a fuckin' loser. And they're still going to take you in. Drunk driving is drunk driving and you're goddamn wasted."

"Make sure my car gets towed by somebody who cares. That's all I want."

"That's all you're likely to get, Mitch. You've run out your string, both with me and with Duggan. He doesn't want to see your smartass face again for a long time."

"Tell him I'm sorry, honest. I know that's not much, but it's a start. And you too, David."

"I hope that's not just the booze talking." He walked to his Porsche where his date was patiently waiting and they drove off.

* * *

Because of Jenks' behavior, they had another cop car drive me downtown to the Hotel Riesner. A big black cop whose badge said *P. Brown* took charge.

"Got to cuff you again, pal," he said. "Regulations."

I was wobbling from the alcohol but I managed to turn around and let him put them on.

"I left 'em loose, dude," Brown said as he ushered me to the backseat of his cruiser. "I locked 'em but don't lean back or they might tighten up anyway."

I sat sideways and Brown got in and drove. I didn't catch his partner's name. On the way, they talked baseball. They had gone to a bunch of Astros games and were planning to go Sunday. I faded in and out of the conversation, trying to rest, and by the time we arrived at the Hotel, I was reasonably stable, although a headache was quickly growing behind my eyes.

We went into the cop shop through the back, via a door off the parking garage. They frisked me again, took off my cuffs, sat me in a holding cell with a dozen other drunks and assorted miscreants while the paperwork was sorted out. They walked me through booking, photographed and printed me, gave me a docket sheet with my case number. They asked me to blow in the Breathalyzer and I thought, "What the hell," and did.

I blew a point two three, nearly three times the legal limit. Apparently, there was a betting pool going with the intake staff on these tests and I made one cop happy by winning it for him. I had therefore accomplished one positive thing tonight.

Next, they checked me over in the small infirmary and determined that I'd live at least until the dawn. This was a big disappointment because I didn't want to face myself when I sobered up.

I got to make a call. Unlike the movies, you can actually call as many people as you wish, but I needed only one, Donna Boudreaux.

"Mmmh?" came a sleepy male voice. Aaron Binares.

"Sorry to disturb, Aaron. This is Mitch King and it's urgent. I need to talk to Donna."

"Minute," he grumbled.

"Mitch," Donna said, sleep in her voice. "What?"

"I'm in jail. Hotel Riesner. DWI."

"Jesus, Mitch."

"Yeah. Come get me out tomorrow?"

"Sure. You okay?"

"Fine. Sorry for being such trouble."

"Hey, what are lawyers for?"

* * *

I rode up in the express elevator to seven, the men's jail. The elevator is steel clad and there's a metal lattice door across the back half where they put the rowdies. One guy they locked in there, while the rest of us intakes just stood beside the cops like we were regular passengers. Which of course would change the moment we arrived at our floor.

We were frisked a third time and escorted politely into our cells. They separate the violent inmates from the others and I was put into an eight-man holding cell for non-aggressive prisoners, most of us drunk drivers.

Being nonviolent didn't make the cell a joke. It was steel, and thick steel at that. The floor was plate steel, the walls were bars of steel and the top was steel bars, too. We were essentially in a steel cage that sat alongside other similar cages, all in a larger room. They often build jail cells freestanding that way, then install the lights, heating and air conditioning outside the cells to prevent vandalism.

Between our numerous trips to the urinal and the little water faucet in our cell, and trying to distract ourselves from the simultaneous attacks of drunkenness and hangover, we temporary jailbirds passed the time by sharing our predicaments. My cellmates were a mixed lot. Four of us were routine traffic stops, three with drunk driving, and one weed possession. A fifth guy made the top of my sympathy list. He was just in from Scotland, a petroleum engineer who'd flown from Aberdeen to Houston to close a big deal for his oil company. Only he'd missed the meeting, getting plastered beforehand and rear-ending a cop car stopped for a red light. Whether he'd still have his job was open to conjecture.

The sixth guy wasn't drunk or stoned. He simply decided to spin donuts through his ex-wife's prize rose beds. Tried to spell his name in them but the cops arrived too soon for that burst of creativity to be realized.

The last two men we couldn't make out at all. They were dark-skinned guys who happily conversed between themselves in a language none of us could understand. Among us we had a working knowledge of English, Spanish, French, German, Greek, Gaelic and a little Portuguese, but nothing cracked the code. After a while, we gave up and let them talk.

* * *

There's constant noise in jail. Everywhere the metal doors clang, cages rattle, people holler and babble. The hard surfaces of the enclosed space reflect the sound back upon you, making it even more intense. So we could not sleep and instead we just froze, thanks to the vaunted chilled air we breathed. We let our hangovers ride, hoping that the next minute of throbbing would be less than the previous one.

Sometimes it was.

Chapter 59

I sat on the edge of my bunk, head in my hands, and thought. Thought clearly for the first time in a great while.

What had I done? Dear God, by my own hand and with malice aforethought, what had I done?

I'd been in part responsible for Pam Neely's suicide and indirectly the death of Tarah Jacoby, which in turn wrecked Trent Collins' life. But that screw-up was only the beginning.

I'd shot a man, killed him. I'd done so willingly even though Terrie had manipulated me toward that goal. The realization of it rolled across me in waves and, with each wave, I reeled from the enormity of my misdeeds.

I had betrayed everything and everyone. First, I turned my back on my friends, then on my principles, and finally on myself. And there was no health in me.

Here I was in jail, company with and party to those deeds I had ridiculed only days before. And here in jail I belonged. Soon I'd be out, of course. The drunk driving charges would wend their way through court, and with a clean driving record and a good lawyer, land me on simple probation and let me keep my license. An expensive inconvenience. It would cause me to rethink my alcohol consumption, yes. To modify my driving and drinking habits, yes. And its burden would pass, yes.

But that misdeed was not the source of my pain. My true transgression was one for which no probation, no fine, no court judgment would suffice. And prisoner to this crime I would always remain.

The crime was murder.

294

About the Author

Sam Waas

Sam Waas has been a writer throughout his adult life. He began by editing an underground newsletter while at the University of Kansas, and has freelanced ever since. He's written book reviews for major dailies, strung for newspapers with sports car racing coverage, and has written articles for gun magazines and local newspapers, varied pieces for slick monthlies, and short stories, screenplays and essays. He's also written numerous book reviews for the online mystery website *Over My Dead Body*.

Recently, Sam's concentrating on his Mitch King private detective novels, based in Houston and the surrounding Gulf Coast region. There are three novels thus far: *Blood Spiral*, *Blood Storm* and *Blood Vengeance*, and he's now writing his fourth Mitch King novel.

Sam worked in science, technology, and research for many years. He was involved in polymer physics, programmed for structural engineering firms, worked with high tech computer ventures, and has also edited petroleum exploration and production specifications as a tech writer. Sam believes that his science and engineering background augments his fiction, in that it provides insight into meticulous details which lend texture and flavor to his mystery novels.

Sam is a longtime fan of classical music and opera, and as a classically trained baritone, sang in opera, chorales, and Episcopal Church choirs. He also enjoys classic rock and progressive jazz. A voracious reader, Sam's favorite book is James Joyce's *Ulysses*, which he's read several times and of which he's made a personal study. He also enjoys books on Imperial Roman history, quantum physics and cosmology, science fiction, biographies and of course, mysteries. Besides Joyce, his favorite modern mainstream authors are Cormac McCarthy, James Dickey and Joseph Heller. His favored mystery writers are Bill Pronzini, Robert Crais and John Sandford.

Sam enjoys attending opera and classical concerts, pistol shooting, playing chess and pool, and just hanging out at the local pub. He makes his home in Houston where he lives with his boon companion and girlfriend.

Chapter 1

It was nearly midnight when I stepped off the splintery wooden porch of the tavern and headed toward my car. I'd finished my tedious business with the bar owner and only wanted to get my weary self home before Houston dumped yet another rain squall on my head.

The earlier shower had let up, but water still pooled throughout the poorly lit and uneven gravel of the parking lot. I was negotiating a large puddle near a Silverado when I smelled cigarette smoke and heard a muffled cough. This small distraction put me on edge because muggers often target drunks leaving taverns as easy prey. I was sober but the robbers wouldn't care. I didn't see anyone, but I reached beneath my jacket anyway, hand on the .45's grip, loosening the pistol partway from its holster.

A sudden movement in the shadows, a metallic click. Something bad was going down.

I stepped back but put my foot into a chuckhole and slipped, falling square on my butt. Before I had time to cuss, fire erupted where my head had been a moment before and I was partially dazed from the muzzle flash and noise. I quickly scooted behind the truck's big rear tire, pulled out my pistol, clicked off the safety, and stayed quiet.

My ears rang from the blast but the cycling of the pump shotgun was still unmistakable. I even heard the little *ching* from the empty shell casing hitting the gravel. Who it was I didn't know, but he wasn't as much a mugger as murderer. I had about two seconds before the attacker got around the tailgate for another shot.

I peered under the truck frame and saw cowboy boots creeping along on the other side, silhouetted by a distant streetlight. I aimed, fired, and got lucky. There was a grunt of pain and a man's body landed with a whump. He was wriggling around on his back, trying to point the shotgun toward me beneath the truck. I fired at his bearded face three times, and then rolled away to seek better shelter, putting more vehicles between the shooter and me.

No further movement from the man and nothing else immediately threatened. I hit the release and the nearly empty magazine dropped free. I grabbed a full mag from my shoulder rig and slammed it into the pistol.

I cautiously rose to my feet, peeking around the far side of a rusty pickup. As people began yelling from the doorway of the bar, I eased from behind the truck, aiming my pistol at the man lying on the ground, ready to fire again.

It wasn't necessary. One of my hollowpoints got him straight through the neck and tore a gaping hole. There was plenty of blood and he wasn't getting up again, ever. I took a closer look and recognized an old nemesis. He and I had a scuffle last spring and he'd sworn to get even. But typical for him, things just hadn't worked out his way. A half-smoked gore-splattered cigarette lay beside his head. Should have known that smoking was bad for his health.

After making sure nobody else was trying to kill me, I clicked my .45 on safe and walked toward the bar. Everyone was calling and gesturing but I paid no attention. Things were fine until the excitement and emotional surge caught up with me, and all the steam and piss and vinegar inside went swirling away. I sagged to grab at the porch railing and plunked down on the top step, pistol dangling idly from my fingers. I gasped and choked back tears.

Tell-Tale Publishing would like to thank you for your purchase. If you enjoyed this novel and would like to read more from this or some of our other fine authors, please visit our website.

http://www.tell-talepublishing.com